STARRY SKIES OVER PRIMROSE HALL

JILL STEEPLES

Boldwood

First published in Great Britain in 2023 by Boldwood Books Ltd.

Copyright © Jill Steeples, 2023

Cover Design by Head Design Ltd

Cover Illustration: Shutterstock

The moral right of Jill Steeples to be identified as the author of this work has been asserted in accordance with the Copyright, Designs and Patents Act 1988.

All rights reserved. No part of this book may be reproduced in any form or by any electronic or mechanical means, including information storage and retrieval systems, without written permission from the author, except for the use of brief quotations in a book review.

This book is a work of fiction and, except in the case of historical fact, any resemblance to actual persons, living or dead, is purely coincidental.

Every effort has been made to obtain the necessary permissions with reference to copyright material, both illustrative and quoted. We apologise for any omissions in this respect and will be pleased to make the appropriate acknowledgements in any future edition.

A CIP catalogue record for this book is available from the British Library.

Paperback ISBN 978-1-80280-723-3

Large Print ISBN 978-1-80280-722-6

Hardback ISBN 978-1-80280-721-9

Ebook ISBN 978-1-80280-725-7

Kindle ISBN 978-1-80280-724-0

Audio CD ISBN 978-1-80280-716-5

MP3 CD ISBN 978-1-80280-717-2

Digital audio download ISBN 978-1-80280-720-2

Boldwood Books Ltd
23 Bowerdean Street
London SW6 3TN
www.boldwoodbooks.com

To Nick, Tom and Ellie
With Love

1

The old barn in the grounds of Primrose Hall had never looked prettier than on that late summer afternoon. Recent renovations had seen the brickwork repointed, the structural beams restored to their former glory and a new rosewood floor fitted. With the double doors opened out onto the gardens, allowing the scent of meadows and summer blooms to waft inside, the light and airy building had been transformed into a romantic oasis. Along with spiralling foliage, intertwined with fairy lights, swathes of gold ribbons hung from the rafters, complementing the dark cream of the walls, the light oak beams and the soft hue of the red bricks. Long trestle tables were adorned with gold-flecked linen runners, and jam jars were filled with white roses and gypsophila, creating a rustic and charming ambience.

Pia sat back in her seat, took a sip from the champagne flute in her hand and allowed herself a smile of satisfaction. All the hard work had paid off and she was delighted for her best friend, Abbey, and Sam, whose special day it was. Pia shuffled her chair up nearer to Jackson, who rested a casual arm around her shoulder, and leant down to whisper in her ear.

'Have I told you, you look absolutely beautiful today?'

Pia laughed and shrugged away a shiver at the sensation of his breath upon her neck. He had. Several times, in fact. Not that she would ever grow tired of hearing him telling her those words. She cast a glance over his relaxed body, reclined on the seat, thinking he looked pretty good himself, in a French blue silk suit that accentuated his natural masculine grace.

Dragging her gaze away from Jackson, her attention was distracted by a flurry of activity further along the main table where Sam Finnegan got to his feet, a bemused smile on his face. He looked suitably dashing and handsome too in a soft grey three-piece suit, his pristine white shirt open at the collar, shirtsleeves rolled up, his tie long-since abandoned. He paused a few moments, soaking up the warm ripple of goodwill and laughter that radiated in his direction from the gathering of guests in the room.

'Well, hey, look, I'm as surprised as anyone that I'm actually standing here today.' A smile played on his lips and his eyes sparkled in amusement. 'Anyone who knows me, and I'm including all you good people in front of me, will know that I'm not the marrying type. And yet, somehow, here I am. Honestly, I couldn't be any happier.'

Sam reached out a hand to thread his fingers through his bride's. 'Meeting Abbey was the best thing to ever happen to me. It was something I never expected. When I first set eyes on her, sitting on the bench, not too far away from here, actually, over in Primrose Woods, I knew I simply had to go and talk to her.'

Abbey looked up at Sam, her love for her new husband evident to see in her expression.

'Although I have to say, Abbey seemed much more enamoured with my dog, Lady, than she was with me on that first meeting, and to this day, I still believe that if my new wife were to have favourites in our household, then I wouldn't be at the top of the list.'

'It's not true!' Abbey threw back her head and laughed, before looking over her shoulder at the assembled audience with a grimace, as though it might actually be true. For a moment everyone's attention was diverted towards one of the guests' tables where Sam's work colleagues, fellow park rangers from Primrose Woods Country Park, were seated. They had the responsibility of looking after Lady, the springer spaniel who in fairness must have realised the auspiciousness of the occasion because she'd been on her best behaviour throughout the wedding ceremony and was now sitting contentedly by the table, alert to any titbits that might be in the offing. For once, her liver and white coat was gleaming clean with no sign of the usual muddy paws and grey tinge to her fur that came from spending the best part of her day outside in the elements, scrabbling around in the undergrowth. A white bandana printed with red hearts was tied around her collar, which made her look even more adorable than usual, even if no one would have believed that was possible.

'Don't worry, I'm not one for long speeches,' Sam went on, 'so I will keep this short, but I do have to say a few heartfelt thank-yous. Firstly, and most importantly, to my wonderful bride for agreeing to be my wife in the first place.' A collective sigh of sentiment wafted around the room, along with a few whoops from the rangers' table. 'I am so lucky and grateful that I get to share the rest of my life with you.' He shook his head as though he still couldn't quite believe it.

'To Bill, thank you for entrusting me with your daughter. I know that my feelings for Abbey are only matched by your own and I promise I will do everything within my power to make her happy. What I could never have anticipated when I got together with Abbey was finding a real and genuine friendship with you. We clicked from the start.'

Bill pressed his lips together and nodded his agreement.

'You're my walking buddy, my drinking pal, fellow member of the Primrose Woods quiz team, a wise counsel, as well now as my father-in-law, and I have to say how grateful I am on all those counts.'

Abbey dropped her head on her dad's shoulder and if you were to get close enough, you might have noticed the emotion brimming in both their eyes.

'Lizzie, what can I possibly say?'

Lizzie Baker, wearing a fetching floaty chiffon dress in shades of lilac, was sitting on the other side to Bill, their hands gently interlocked beneath the table.

'I simply don't have the time here to express my gratitude for your friendship and support from the moment I first arrived at Primrose Woods. Walking into the Treetops Café on my first day, you greeted me with that gorgeous sunny smile of yours, urged me to try one of your bacon butties, handed me a cappuccino, insisted it was on the house, and you've been looking out for me ever since.'

Lizzie smiled and blushed. She'd recognised a kindred spirit in Sam. They had both been emotionally vulnerable and out of sorts at the time. Lizzie because she'd recently lost her beloved husband, David. Then her only daughter, Katy, had moved to the other side of the world shortly afterwards and Lizzie had been left to work through her feelings of grief and isolation alone. Sam had gone through a similarly dark period as his best friend and girlfriend had fallen in love and run off together, just before his beloved mum had died, far too prematurely, from cancer.

Arriving at Primrose Woods, Sam had been determined to

make a new start, and Lizzie's constant and friendly presence in his new daily routine had been a big help in making the transition.

'Lizzie won't mind me telling you that she always showed...' He paused over his choice of word. '...what you might call a zealous interest in my love life and was hopeful of marrying me off to someone.'

'Anyone,' said Lizzie with a shrug, which was met with much laughter from the guests.

'It was just my luck that Abbey and Bill were having lunch at Lizzie's place when I was replacing some fence panels in the garden. I recognised Abbey as the woman I'd chatted to in Primrose Woods and when Lizzie invited me to join them for lunch, well, I wasn't going to let that opportunity pass.' A wide smile spread across his face at the memory. 'It must have been fate, because the rest, as they say, is history. Abbey, Bill and Lizzie, together with Luke and Rhi...' He gestured towards a good looking young couple on a nearby table. 'You became the family that I'd always been looking for. I found my tribe with you guys.' He took a breath, the emotion of the occasion clearly threatening to overwhelm him. 'Anyway, thanks to you all, from the both of us, for coming and joining us in this celebration and for making our wedding day even more special than we could ever have imagined it to be. Finally,' he said, just stopping the guests as they were about to break into a round of applause. 'I have to give a huge thanks to Jackson Moody, owner of the wonderful Primrose Hall and to his hugely efficient assistant, Pia, Abbey's great friend from school, for stepping in when our original venue, the village hall, was closed. They very generously invited us to hold our wedding here in this amazing barn, and honestly, there could be no more fitting venue. Primrose Woods is our happy place. The beautiful backdrop to where we first met, so it will always hold a special place in our hearts. To be able to have our reception here really is the icing on the cake. Thank you, Jackson and Pia, and to all of you for sharing this wonderful day with us. Now come on,' he said, holding up his champagne glass to the room, 'let's get this party really started!'

With the speeches over, the guests started scattering, mooching around to stretch their legs and chat to fellow guests, while music began playing through the sound system.

Jackson turned to Pia and took her face in his hands, tidying the escaping strands of hair from her French plait.

'Hey, let me see you. You've not been crying, have you?' Jackson's brow furrowed.

'No!' Pia batted his hands away playfully. 'Well, maybe,' she said, with half a smile as she widened her eyes to hold back her emotion. Jackson reached for the pink silk pocket square from his suit jacket.

'See. I knew this would come in handy today,' he said, handing it over gallantly.

'Thank you. It almost seems too luxurious to use.' Pia ran the silky fabric through her fingers.

'No, you go right ahead.'

'It was a lovely speech from Sam, wasn't it?' Pia dabbed at her eyes with the cloth. 'I'm so happy for them both. After everything that Abbey went through with her ex, she deserves her happiness; they both do. They're so lucky to have found each other. A match made in the stars, don't you think?'

'If you say so,' said Jackson, with his customary touch of cynicism. He leant across to kiss her and Pia's eyes fluttered close in anticipation, as she awaited the touch of his mouth upon hers.

'What are you two lovebirds up to? Looks like the romance of the occasion's got to you. I can understand why.' Pia and Jackson's moment of intimacy was interrupted before it had even started by the arrival of Declan Ashby, one of Sam's fellow rangers from Primrose Woods, who rested a hand on each of their shoulders. He had a big grin on his face as he spoke. 'It'll be you two next, tying the knot, I don't doubt. Well, remember me when you draw up the invitation list, won't you?'

Pia laughed awkwardly, while Jackson rolled his eyes exaggeratedly and gave a firm shake of his head.

'Hey!' Pia elbowed Jackson in the ribs in mock outrage, feeling the slight all the same.

'Don't worry, love,' Declan said, laughing. 'He's only joking.'

Jackson's lip curled involuntarily, the shake of the head even more emphatic this time.

'Why spoil a decent relationship by getting married? Although perhaps best to keep that to ourselves on a day like today.' Jackson held a finger to his mouth, before that familiar seductive half smile returned to his lips while Pia's grin grew ever-more fixed, determined as she was not to give away her true feelings.

Declan had been right about one thing. Pia had lapped up every bit of the emotional intensity of the day. Who wouldn't? Well, apart from Jackson, that is. It wasn't the first time he'd made clear his views on marriage, although she hoped he might have come up with a better way to describe their relationship other than 'decent'. Pia and Jackson were happy together; wasn't that the most important thing of all? Even if she was beginning to realise that their individual long-term plans, their hopes and dreams for the future might be very different indeed.

2

After the celebrations of the previous day, which went on into the early hours, when Jackson and Pia had danced their legs off and drunk far too many glasses of champagne, Sunday morning rolled in at a leisurely place at Primrose Hall. After a reviving mug of coffee first thing, Jackson had hopped on his motorbike on the pretext of collecting the papers from the village shop, although Pia knew it was the perfect excuse for him to take the scenic route around the country lanes, enjoying the freedom and exhilaration that came from navigating the twists and bends of the open road. She couldn't help worrying, especially when it had been a motorbike accident as a teenager that had been the catalyst for him leaving the village and not returning until several years later.

To take her mind off what Jackson might be doing, Pia gave in to the insistent demands of Bertie the Dalmatian and headed outdoors for a walk around the grounds of Primrose Hall, a favourite part of the day for both of them. It was the last weekend in August and the gloriously sunny weather of the past few weeks showed no sign of lifting, the sun warm and caressive on her bare arms. The gardens, filled with the scents of the vast array of blooms, expertly tended by Mateo, were at their finest, their colours painting the landscape with their beauty.

There wasn't a day that went past when she didn't pinch herself that she got to call this place home.

Although it was only six months since Pia had arrived at Primrose Hall, employed as a personal assistant to Jackson, in some ways it seemed much longer. They'd had such a busy summer overseeing the hall's busy social calendar. There'd been the monthly craft days at the stables, the inaugural and very successful classic car show in the grounds, and a couple of weddings too, one for Abbey and Sam, and the other for Pia's brother, Connor, earlier in the summer. The weeks had simply flown by.

To think that she'd almost turned down Jackson's job offer, not wanting to work for the man who had broken her heart when she was still a teenager. Back then she'd believed Jackson was as madly in love with her as she had been with him, so she was left devastated when he simply upped and left the village, without so much as an explanation. He didn't even say goodbye. When he returned ten years later, as the new owner of the recently restored and renovated Primrose Hall, Pia experienced a rush of emotions: excitement, curiosity and anger, but mostly anger. How dare he turn up after all that time without making any mention of their previous relationship or giving any apology? Instead, he'd had the audacity to offer her a job when she attended an interview held at the Treetops Café in Primrose Woods. She'd barely been able to make sense of Jackson's sudden reappearance in the village and was adamant that she would have nothing further to do with him, but her good intentions didn't last long. She'd quickly had to put her principles to one side. With the sale of her late parents' home going through and facing a future without anywhere to live or a job on the horizon, Pia couldn't sensibly turn down Jackson's offer of a well-paid job with live-in accommodation. She'd decided it would work as a temporary solution until something better came along.

Now she didn't have any regrets about making the decision to come and live at Primrose Hall. She'd quickly settled into her new role and been made to feel very welcome by the whole team. Not only Jackson, but Mateo the gardener, Ivy the housekeeper and Frank the maintenance man, who all worked together towards the upkeep of the house and in the running of the events at the hall. The fact that she and Jackson had resolved their differences and rekindled their teenage romance had only added to the appeal of life at the hall. Even if it had made life a tad more complicated.

'Come on, Bertie,' she called, hearing the familiar and reassuring rumble of Jackson's motorbike returning. 'We should get back. Time for breakfast.'

As she approached the back door to the kitchen, she heard chatter coming from inside. She smiled, recognising Jackson's mum, Ronnie's, distinctive and engaging voice ringing out.

'So how did it go, Jackson? I saw you all lining up in front of the barn for the photos. It looked wonderful.' Ronnie had been desperate to hear all about the wedding, and with her impeccable sense of timing seemed to know precisely when breakfast was in the offing.

Pia slipped off her trainers in the boot room, still listening in on Jackson and Ronnie's conversation.

'Yep. It was a great day. It all went off without any hitches,' he said, opening the Aga door and popping a tray of sausages inside. 'Everyone seemed to have a great time and we had some good feedback about the barn.'

'I bet Pia was pleased. I know that she really wanted to make it special for her friend.'

'Oh, Pia was in her element. She loved every moment of it. She's such a romantic. There were a few tears shed, although none from me, I hasten to add.' Jackson gave a low chuckle.

'Aw, I bet. She wears her heart on her sleeve, that one. You know, you need to be careful not to break that girl's heart. I don't think any of us would every forgive you if you did.'

'What do you take me for?' Jackson gave Ronnie a sharp glance, while there was a bemused smile from Pia, still craning an ear from the boot room. She would have to go inside soon or else she might hear something she'd really rather not. Although there was no need for Ronnie to worry on her behalf. Pia had had her heart broken once before by Jackson. There was absolutely no chance she would let it happen for a second time.

'I thought I heard voices,' said Pia, pushing through the kitchen door, with Bertie barging her out of the way so that he could get through first to say hello.

Jackson had made a start on cooking breakfast, which had become a regular part of their Sunday routine ever since their relationship had changed from purely professional into something more intimate. Pia would always offer to help, but Jackson would wave a hand and tell her to sit back and relax, which she didn't need telling twice. She loved to watch him move around the large country kitchen so effortlessly, clearly relaxed and happy in his role as head chef. The aromas of coffee and cooking bacon wafted in the air, greeting her nostrils. Pia fetched some orange juice from the fridge and sat down at the kitchen table opposite Ronnie.

'Jackson was just telling me all about the wedding. I hear it was a good day.'

'It was simply perfect. Everything about it. The service, the food, the weather. Abbey looked beautiful in her dress, didn't she, Jackson?' Pia went on, not waiting for Jackson's reply. 'It was a very simple shift design in cream satin, but the effect was stunning. I've got so many photos I need to show you.'

Pia sighed, as the memories of the day assaulted her. Memories that would stay with her forever.

'Pia was a hot mess all day long,' Jackson teased.

'I was not,' she said indignantly.

'You were. Every time I looked at you there were tears in your eyes and a big soppy grin on your face.'

Pia shrugged and helped herself to a piece of fruit from the wicker basket. She peeled back the skin of the banana and took a decisive bite. 'I couldn't help it. It was a very emotional occasion. Weddings always affect me that way.' She fanned a hand in front of her face.

Ronnie smiled and took a sip from her mug of coffee, enjoying hearing her son and Pia's differing accounts of the big day.

'So does this mean we'll be seeing more weddings at the hall?' Ronnie asked, with half a smile on her lips, as she exchanged a glance with Pia, suspecting she already knew the answer to her question. 'I should imagine it could be a real money spinner.'

'It's not about the money.' Jackson gave Ronnie a withering glance. 'Besides, we've got so many other plans for the hall. We want to run events that will benefit the whole community, similar to the classic car show we held in the summer.'

'I must admit, that was good fun,' Ronnie said.

'Pia's book festival is coming up next month, then it will be our first bonfire extravaganza night, and before we know it, it will be Christmas carols in the courtyard. Plus there's the regular craft fairs over in the stables. We simply don't have the time or the resources to make this a dedicated wedding venue. Besides, I don't want this place overrun by drunk revellers every weekend. Primarily, this is my home... our home,' he corrected himself, laying a hand on Pia's shoulder as he served the plates filled with sausages, bacon, mushrooms, hash browns, tomatoes, fried eggs and beans, 'and we all need to be happy in what we're doing here. I don't want the running of the hall to become a chore, and I think it might if we had a succession of wedding parties.'

Pia looked up into Jackson's face, appreciating his effort to make her feel that this was as much her home as it was his, but despite their closeness and the fact that she'd moved from her own self-contained apartment within the hall into the grandeur of the master bedroom in recent weeks, she was aware that she had no real security to speak of. After all, only a few months before Pia had arrived at Primrose Hall, Jackson had been in another relationship with an impossibly glamorous interior designer called Tara. That relationship had faltered and Tara had vacated the hall, nursing a broken heart. Would her own relationship with Jackson become just as dispensable one day?

'Fair enough.' Ronnie helped herself to a slice of granary toast from the basket on the table, breaking into Pia's thoughts. 'As long as I'll still be allowed to have my wedding here one day, then that's all that matters to me,' she said airily.

Jackson shook his head indulgently. 'And which poor chump do you have in mind for the role as leading man? Just so we know and are suitably prepared.'

Ronnie pressed her lips together and lifted her chin, sweeping her head to one side in a show of defiance. 'I'm not sure yet, but I remain hopeful. Once you give up on the idea of love, you might as well give up on life itself.'

'Well, I certainly admire your optimism,' said Jackson.

'What was your wedding to Rex like?' asked Pia. 'Was it a big do?'

Seeing Ronnie roll her eyes and hearing the accompanying snort of derision, Pia wondered what had possessed her to ask such a question when she knew just how tempestuous Jackson's parents' relationship had been.

'Well, of course, we didn't have any money so it was all done on a shoestring. And it was a bit last-minute. There were only about fifteen of us, our families and a few friends. It was at the registry office in town, and we didn't book a reception, we couldn't afford to, so we just went on a pub crawl afterwards, ending up at the Three Feathers in Wishwell. I think there might have been some sandwiches and cakes, but that was about it. Of course, Rex was absolutely rat-assed, and that was before he'd even got to the ceremony. I suppose you could say that it set the entire tone for our marriage. Mind you, I think we were probably as bad as each other.' She paused a moment, her fork in the air, lost in her thoughts. 'It all seems like such a long time ago now.'

'That's because it was a long time ago,' Jackson said gruffly, displaying his customary lack of sentimentality.

'And that's why you've always been so anti-marriage, no doubt.' Ronnie gave a small chuckle. 'You didn't have a very good example in me and your father.'

Jackson tilted his head to one side and scrunched his mouth in thought. 'I'm not anti-marriage at all. I think it's a great institution. For other people. If they think they can make it work, then great. It's just not for me.' He shrugged his shoulders in that infuriating way of his that brooked no argument.

Pia was receiving the message loud and clear. That was twice in two days Jackson had mentioned, in no uncertain terms, where he stood on that particular subject. He obviously didn't want her getting any funny ideas on that front.

Now she focused on her breakfast. It was delicious, but the turn in the conversation had taken the edge off her appetite. She might have agreed with Jackson's point of view a while ago. She hadn't given marriage a second thought then. There'd been no reason to when her whole focus during her twenties had been caring for her parents. Boyfriends, marriage and babies were something to consider much further into the future. There'd been the occasional date, but nothing that had materialised into anything more. It was only when her mum passed away, and she and Connor had to sell the family home, that Pia was forced to contemplate what she wanted from her future. The job at Primrose Hall had been a lifeline but was only ever intended as a stopgap. She hadn't anticipated settling in so easily, forging close relationships with the rest of the team and finding so much more than just a place to live and work. Primrose Hall had become home to Pia and Bertie. More than that, though, Jackson Moody had got beneath her skin and, despite her best intentions, she'd fallen for his charms again, just as she had when she was a teenager. Now she couldn't imagine any kind of future without him in it.

She cast a glance at him as he tucked into his breakfast with gusto. Her thoughts had strayed towards all those big milestones in life only because her brother and her best friend had recently married. It was only natural to compare yourself with those around you. Pia felt she had a lot of catching up to do, in life and in love, making up for all those lost years, but she was in no hurry to take those next steps. Not yet, but definitely one day. It wasn't as if her biological clock was clanging in her ear; rather, it was whispering gently sometimes when she was least expecting it.

'Talk of the devil.' Jackson glanced at his phone on the table beside him. 'Dad's on his way down. I wish he wouldn't get a taxi. I've told him before that I'm more than happy to go and collect him on the bike.'

'I wonder what he wants, and on a Sunday morning too,' Ronnie grumbled. 'I knew this would happen as soon as he arrived back in the village, making a nuisance of himself, turning up whenever the fancy takes him.'

'He's not making a nuisance of himself. He's always welcome here,' said Jackson firmly. 'At any time. As you are,' he said, softening his words with a smile.

'But I live here,' Ronnie protested.

'You live in a clapped-out old van in the grounds of the house. Why, when there's your pick of several bedrooms in this house, I will never know, but I'm happy to tolerate your whims, and you coming and going whenever you like. It's only natural, though, that I would extend the same courtesy to Dad.'

'Huh!' Ronnie pushed her finished plate away, then crossed her arms in front of her chest.

'Anyway, I thought you and Dad were good these days. The pair of you seemed to be getting on like a house on fire the last time he was here.' Jackson glanced at Pia, who bit on her lip, trying not to smile. It was obvious that Ronnie still had feelings for Rex by the way she acted around him, becoming all giggly and flirtatious in his presence. Pia had joked with Jackson that she could see the pair of them getting back together. The very idea had horrified Jackson. He couldn't deal with the drama that came with Rex and Ronnie being in the same room together for any length of time.

'Well, obviously I try to rub along with Rex, for your benefit mainly, my darling,' Ronnie said disingenuously as she reached across and touched her son's arm. 'But honestly, your father is as flaky as he ever was.' She exhaled a sigh. 'I'm not sure why I expected he might have changed in the intervening years, but he hasn't. We'd planned to take a day trip to the coast this week. It was even Rex's idea, but he called off at the last moment. Just like the good old days,' she said with a humourless laugh.

'Well, he'll be here shortly. You can ask him about it. I'm sure there must be a reasonable explanation.'

'There always is and there always was,' said Ronnie wearily. 'He has all the answers, but I'm not sure I'm interested in hearing them these days,' she said, feigning nonchalance. 'I won't be jumping through hoops for that man any more, that's for sure. Right, well, I ought to go and get myself ready for the day,' she said, running a hand through her silvery hair and forcing a smile. 'Thanks for breakfast.' She pushed back her chair and stood up. 'It was delicious.'

'See you later,' Pia called, feeling a pang of sympathy for Ronnie as she watched her leave the room. Despite Ronnie's assertion that Rex was of little importance to her these days, Pia knew her better than that. Ronnie had once confided that Rex, despite all his shortcomings, had been the love of her life, even if their relationship had been brief and tumultuous. His reappearance in the village after several years' absence living in Spain had stirred up a whole pot of emotions. Jackson's shock had quickly been replaced by gratitude that he'd been given the chance to rebuild a relationship with his father, who had been mainly missing during his childhood years. For Ronnie, though, it had brought up a whole raft of different feelings, guilt and regret over what might have been. Pia recognised Ronnie's vulnerability and sensitivity where Rex was concerned. She recognised it because it was the exact same way that she felt towards Jackson.

3

Rhi and Luke took their drinks and sat down at the table in the bay window of the Three Feathers, the sun's rays warming their backs. Rhi rested her arm along the edge of the seat and exhaled a sigh of contentment.

'Hasn't this been the best weekend ever?'

'It's been great,' said Luke, picking up his glass of lime and soda and taking a hearty glug.

Rhi's gaze drifted around the bar as she soaked up the atmosphere of the popular village pub. It was busy with afternoon revellers, enjoying a pint of beer or a glass of wine before returning home for their Sunday dinner. The chatter and laughter of those customers making the most of the glorious weather wafted in from the beer garden. 'It's so good to be back.'

Rhi and Luke had travelled down on Friday night, staying with their respective families, ahead of Abbey and Sam's wedding on the Saturday. They'd managed to cram so much into the weekend, catching up with friends and old work colleagues, and relishing yesterday's celebrations. Rhi was still riding high on a wave of adrenalin. This morning they'd visited

Primrose Woods, the location of many of their meet-ups before they'd become a couple. They'd walked along the Woodpecker Trail, hand in hand, revisiting their favourite spots – the bench beside the lake, and the rickety bridge over the stream – stopping to take some selfies as the late summer sunshine cast a golden glow through the trees. Then they'd stopped for a latte and a frangipane traybake in the Treetops Café. It was just like old times.

Now, before they started on the journey back to Dashford-Upon-Avon, Rhi had insisted on making a flying visit to the pub to see her old bosses, Malc and Jan. From the moment Rhi had walked through the front door it was like being wrapped in a warm hug.

'Hello, sweetheart.' Gerry, one of the pub's regulars, had been standing at his usual spot, propping up the bar, and it was as if Rhi had never been away. He'd turned to embrace her in a bear hug. 'Are we going to see you back behind the bar here soon? We've all missed you, you know.'

'I'm afraid not,' Rhi had said with a frown. 'We're only down for the weekend, but I couldn't pass up the chance to pop in to see how everyone's doing.'

'I've already told her,' Jan had said as she poured a glass of wine for Rhi and a soft drink for Luke, which Gerry insisted on paying for, 'there'll always be a job here for Rhi if she wants one.'

Rhi had beamed, happy to be back amongst her old friends. This place was special to her because it had been a safe and welcoming environment at a time when she was at her lowest point. When she'd discovered the man she was in love with, a senior manager at her place of work, was already engaged to someone else, she'd walked out on him and her job in one fell swoop. With no idea what to do next, she'd been grateful and relieved to find a job at the Three Feathers to tide her over. Jan had taken her under her wing, and offered her as many shifts as she wanted, plus a good helping of moral support too. Now, being back in the convivial atmosphere of the pub, it was as though she'd never been away. It occurred to Rhi that coming to work here was the start of her turning her life around. She'd been just beginning to get to know Luke better then, and together they'd joined the Primrose Fancies pub quiz team, along with Abbey, Sam, Lizzie and Bill. Their unlikely friendship group had opened up a whole new social scene for them all. Happy times indeed.

'You miss this place, don't you?'

Luke's question jolted her out of her reverie.

'The pub?' She looked across into his intense blue eyes, which always held the power to enthral her. 'Yes, I suppose I do. It's so lovely seeing everyone again.'

'But more than just the pub. I mean living here. Having your support network of your friends and your mum around you. Being able to pop over to Primrose Woods whenever you want to.'

Rhi gazed at Luke across the table, wondering what he was getting at.

'Of course, but that's what makes it all the more special when we do get to come home. We'll be back for Christmas and that's really not that far away. I was talking to Pia and she was saying that this year's Christmas carols event at the hall is going to be so much bigger this time around, with a traditional festive market and a full-on winter illuminations display.' Rhi's voice took on a dreamy quality. 'I can't wait to see it because it was such a special evening last year, although Pia has said she can't guarantee the snow.' Rhi laughed at the memory. It had been so romantic standing hand in hand with Luke in front of the hall, which had been lit up in a golden glow against the dark night sky, listening to the carollers' tuneful renditions fill the air. With the unexpected flurry of snow falling in soft swirling flakes around them, it had been a magical moment that was now etched on Rhi's brain.

Now, Luke raised his eyebrows at her, tilting his head to one side as though inviting her to elaborate.

'Well... I mean, Dashford is lovely too...'

It was true. It was a beautiful town set on the river with a popular and thriving arts centre, a wide range of eclectic shops and a huge choice of bars and restaurants, but it was none of those things that had made the decision to move there such a simple one. Last Christmas when Luke announced his plans to leave, to take up a new job a hundred miles away from her, Rhi was devastated. She couldn't tell Luke that, though. Their relationship had only recently turned into something more romantic and she hadn't wanted to put any demands on him or appear needy. Rhi was resigned to the fact that theirs was destined to be only a sweet holiday romance that they would both look back on with fondness.

So when Luke had suggested that she go with him, and they moved into the riverside flat together, she couldn't have been more delighted. She realised what a special person Luke was and hadn't wanted to risk losing him. She wanted to give their relationship a proper chance. Upping sticks and going with him was absolutely the right decision and she hadn't regretted it for a moment.

'Yes, but would you want to move back here if you could?'

'What?' She paused, deciding to let her response slide, not wanting to dwell on it. 'Why are you even asking that?'

'It's been good to see you looking so happy this weekend, that's all. And when you talk about this place being home, I can hear the excitement in your voice and see the light in your eyes.'

'Yes, but I'm just as happy being with you in Dashford.'

'Sometimes I feel guilty for having dragged you away from here. It's okay for me; I get to go into the office a few times a week, while you're stuck in the flat, looking at the four walls of the spare bedroom all day.' Rhi had been working hard to get her virtual assistant business off the ground and had a good base of clients now. She might be a little isolated, but it was worth it, knowing Luke would be coming home to her at the end of the day.

'Ha.' Rhi snorted a laugh. 'You hardly dragged me. I came very willingly. Besides, I can always get outside and take a walk along the riverbank when I get stir-crazy.'

Their apartment on the river was in a beautiful spot, but the charms of the cutesy Cotswold village were very different to those of Primrose Woods. Dashford was pretty as a picture; the postcards of the meandering river and stone cottages sold in all the gift shops were testament to that fact. It was a buzzing, vibrant town and often at the weekends it would be overrun with visitors.

The beauty of Primrose Woods was something else entirely. The natural, rugged landscape covered several hundreds of acres and you only had to walk a short distance along one of the myriad tracks to be alone amongst the stunning countryside, the only noises coming from the resident wildlife. Rhi always found walking amongst the towering trees nurturing and energising, helping to get her thoughts in order and providing a clearer perspective on anything that might be troubling her.

She missed those regular visits to the woods with Abbey where they would put the world to rights, gossiping and laughing, before joining Lizzie in the café for one of her special daily sweet treats. Admittedly, her life had completely altered since moving to Dashford, but she'd been happy to embrace the change to be with Luke. They were happy together and life had to move on; it couldn't stay the same forever.

'You could always come back if you wanted to?'

'What?' Alarm rose in Rhi's chest as she jumped on Luke's words. 'And leave you in Dashford? No, that would never work. I'd miss you too much and who knows how it would impact on our relationship. I can't believe you're even suggesting it.'

Luke laughed and reached a hand across the table, interlocking his fingers with hers. 'I meant us both coming back. We could find somewhere to live around here.'

'But what about your job?' Rhi's forehead creased as she appraised Luke's expression, looking for hidden meaning, ignoring the bubble of excitement rising in her chest.

'Well, I could work from home a couple of days a week. How long does the journey take? An hour and a half tops. That's not so bad if I was only doing it a few times a week.'

'What about the flat?'

'Short-term let until the end of the year. So if we want to make a move, then now would be a good time to start looking.'

Rhi's gaze drifted around the bar, the swell of conversation and laughter enveloping her, making her feel a part of something much bigger. It wasn't often Rhi was lost for words, but now was one of those times. She hadn't even considered moving back here, but now that Luke had put the idea into her head, she realised there was nothing she wanted more.

'It's only an idea,' Luke said, releasing his hand and picking up his glass, fixing her with those lovely blue eyes, a half-smile at the corner of his lips. 'Have a think and see what you reckon.'

4

'Are you okay?'

Pia had cleared the table and was loading the dishwasher, before putting the pans into a sink of steaming hot water, when Jackson came up behind her, placing his hands on her waist, his breath warm on her cheek. She turned, their lips meeting, his arms wrapping her in a strong embrace. When she came up for air, she smiled.

'I'm fine,' she sighed.

'Are you sure? It's just that over breakfast you seemed a bit quiet. And thoughtful. You're not upset about me teasing you over the wedding?'

'No,' she said airily, wholly distracted by Jackson's proximity, the hardness of his body up against hers. 'I knew you were only joking.'

'Good, and don't let Ronnie get to you either. I know she can be a bit full-on at times when she gets a bee in her bonnet. You just need to let it all go over your head. That's what I do.'

Pia had never been any good at hiding her feelings, but that seemed to be especially the case as far as Jackson was concerned. She would have to try harder at keeping her emotions under wraps so that he couldn't easily decipher her every thought. It was most unnerving how he had the ability to do that. As for Ronnie, Pia had grown close to her since arriving at the hall. She admired Ronnie's outgoing and flamboyant personality, but she could see through the façade and knew that Ronnie was a sweet and kind soul underneath, and not nearly as confident as she pretended to be. Sometimes she felt sorry for Ronnie because of the way Jackson spoke to her.

'You know, you should cut your mum a bit more slack.'

'What? Are you kidding me?' He held Pia at arm's length, his gaze roaming her features. 'I give her far too much slack as it is. She does exactly what she wants whenever she wants and the rest of us have to fit in around her. Besides, she might grumble, but really she's living her best life, treating this place like it's a hotel, taking off in her van whenever the fancy takes her.'

'You say that, but she hasn't done it since I've been here. I think she's mellowed over the years from what you've told me. She enjoys her creature comforts these days and being here, a part of the Primrose Hall family. I know she has her funny ways, but I think it's sweet how she's always trying to please you, Jackson. She's so proud of her boy and rightly so.'

Jackson gave an almost imperceptible snort of derision. Although he insisted that he didn't hold grudges and had long since forgiven Ronnie for her many absences during his childhood years, Pia suspected that sometimes, deep inside, Jackson reverted to being that young boy. The one who had struggled to understand why his mum would disappear for months on end, following her dreams, while he was left to live with his aunt in the village. Now, she looked into his dark brown eyes, her heart expanding with love for him. How could she ever understand the nuances of Jackson and

Ronnie's relationship when it was so different to her own childhood?

'I'll see Dad, he might want to go out for a ride on the bike or a lunchtime pint at the Three Feathers, and then I'll get started on the dinner. Roast beef with all the trimmings. How does that sound?'

It sounded wonderful, another one of the traditions they'd recently adopted at Primrose Hall. Sometimes it might be just the two of them, but anyone who happened to be around, Mateo, Frank or Ivy, had an open invitation.

'Ronnie's already booked her place at the table. Maybe I should invite Rex to join us too. Do you think the pair of them can get through dinner without it turning into a slanging match?'

'They're always on their best behaviour when I've seen them together. Well, almost,' said Pia, smiling, remembering a few hurled insults, but she was certain there wasn't any real malice behind them.

'That's one of the things I appreciate about us.' Jackson tenderly stroked Pia's cheek. 'That we don't have that kind of drama in our relationship.'

'Well, I would hope not. After what, only a couple of months together? It might be a bad omen if we did.'

Pia was very aware that their relationship was still at the honeymoon stage, riding on an all-consuming wave of romance. That was certainly how it was for Pia, although she couldn't talk for Jackson. As much as she was enjoying the ride, she was very definitely her mother's daughter and a cautious voice rang at the back of her head, warning her to be sensible and not to get too carried away. Putting her entire faith into Jackson had landed her in trouble in the past and she knew how Jackson was able to turn his back on a situation once it no longer served his purposes.

'No bad omens around here. Only good ones. Besides, it might be only a couple of months but it feels much longer,' he said with a wink.

Pia laughed in mock outrage, and Jackson was quick to reassure her, pulling her closer, his lips hovering enticingly over hers. She knew exactly what he meant. Sometimes it felt as if all those years since they were teenagers had fallen away and they had been together forever, but really they were still in the very early stages of their relationship. Still finding things out about each other. Still discovering if their hopes and dreams for the future aligned with each other's.

One thing she was certain of was that she would never grow tired of the distinctive earthy scent of Jackson, nor the intensity of his eyes when they landed on her face, or the way her body reacted to his touch.

Now, Jackson's strong embrace and passionate kisses chased away her worries and her body melted into his arms. She was completely lost in the moment until a loud rapping at the back door interrupted them both.

'That's Dad,' said Jackson with a smile, reaching out a hand to Pia's face as he reluctantly pulled away.

'I'll go,' said Pia, laughing and fanning herself with her hand to cool the heat soaring around her body. She made her way across to the back door, pulling it open with a flourish. 'Rex! How lovely to see you. Come on inside.'

Immediately, her smile wavered and she knew something was amiss just by looking at Rex's expression. Usually, he would bowl in with a big grin on his face, his mood upbeat with a chirpy greeting rolling off his tongue, but there was no sign of his sunny personality today.

'Forgive me for just turning up like this, but I needed to

speak to you, Jackson. Something's come up.' He shook his head as he wandered into the kitchen, looking from Jackson to Pia, as though whatever it was he was about to divulge wasn't going to be good news.

Pia's stomach tumbled and a sense of dread rose in her chest as she caught Rex's expression. He looked pale and his face was drawn with concern. *Please, God, don't let him be ill.* Not when he'd only just come back into Jackson's life.

'Look, there's some stuff I need to be getting on with. I'll leave you two to talk. I'll come and say goodbye before you leave,' said Pia, thinking she ought to make herself scarce. She squeezed Rex's arm and he locked his hand firmly onto hers.

'Don't go, love. I'd like you to stay if you're not too busy?'

'Of course I'm not. I just thought you might want some time alone with Jackson. Let me put the kettle on, then. I'll make us some coffees.'

'Come on, then, Dad. Spit it out. Whatever it is, it can't be that bad.'

Rex grimaced as he reluctantly sat down on the kitchen chair offered by Jackson. He perched on the edge of the seat as though he might leap up at any moment and rush out of the door.

Pia busied herself with making the drinks, glad of the distraction, aware of Rex's tension permeating the room. Every time she turned around, he was glancing at her as though waiting for her to sit down. She took the hint, picked up the mugs and placed them on the kitchen table, pulling out a chair to join them.

'Well, I've had some news. And it's been a bit of a shock.'

'You're not ill, are you?' Pia couldn't help herself. She reached across and grabbed hold of Rex's arm.

'No,' he said, his forehead crumpling in confusion, and Pia

saw the flicker of relief that washed across Jackson's face. 'It's nothing like that.' Rex took a deep breath, steeling himself. 'Where do I start? I had a message come through on Wednesday night. From someone called Tom Mellings?'

Pia and Jackson exchanged a glance and shrugged. The name wasn't familiar.

'He asked if he could call me as he wanted to chat about something. Well, of course I was curious so I agreed. When he rang, he asked if I'd known his mum, Diane Mathis, and after racking my brain, it came back to me. We're talking over thirty years ago now, so is it any wonder my memory was a little hazy, but when nudged, I certainly remembered her. She was lovely. Blonde and bubbly with a very distinctive laugh. I can hear her laughing now.' He fell quiet, his gaze drifting out of the window. 'Anyway, Tom told me that she'd died a couple of years ago, but there was something he needed to talk to me about. He wouldn't tell me over the phone and asked if we could meet for coffee. I went to meet him in town on Thursday.'

Pia nodded, hanging on Rex's every word. It might explain why Rex hadn't turned up for his planned day out with Ronnie in the week. 'What was it he wanted to tell you?'

'Well, he just came out with it. Sat on the opposite side of the table, sipped on his coffee, looked me straight in the eye and said... "Well, this is a bit awkward, but I think you're my dad." Just like that.'

Pia audibly gasped, her gaze immediately turning to Jackson, gauging his reaction.

'What?' Jackson ran a hand through his hair, his features twisting in confusion.

'I know, I know, that was exactly my reaction too.' Rex dropped his gaze, his hand smoothing over the table in front of him. 'I couldn't make any sense of what he was telling me.'

'So this woman, Diane, you two were *together*?'

'Yes, we were, but it was only a short-lived thing. Six weeks tops, I reckon. It was such a long time ago, I can't really remember the details. We went on a few dates together, had some fun. Then it must have fizzled out. I know that I met Ronnie shortly afterwards.'

'So why has this guy suddenly turned up now, claiming to be your son? What does he want from you?'

'To find out who his real dad is, I suppose. He told me that the man he always thought was his dad left when he was about six years old. He only saw him occasionally over the years after that.' Rex raised an eyebrow at Jackson and pursed his lips together, looking contrite. It wasn't lost on any of them that it sounded uncannily like Jackson's own upbringing. 'They had a difficult relationship, but Tom was never sure why. He wasn't close to his dad, but he put that down to them not spending much time together. His dad remarried and started a new family and Tom rarely had any contact with him after that. There was the occasional birthday and Christmas card, but they hadn't seen each other in a few years and then Tom received the news that his dad had died, about three months ago now.'

'That's so sad.' Pia was struggling to take in everything Rex was saying and what it might mean for him, and, more importantly, for Jackson too.

'At the funeral, his aunt, who he hadn't seen in years, took him to one side and told him that his dad wasn't his biological father. Apparently he met Diane when she was six months pregnant and they decided to quickly get married. The baby took his name and he was brought up as their child. And that was that. It was a well-kept secret and there were only a few family members and friends who actually knew the truth. They decided, Diane and her husband, for whatever reason, not to tell Tom either.'

'Blimey, that seems strange,' said Pia, more to fill the silence than anything else. She glanced across at Jackson, who had fallen quiet, his gaze wandering out of the window. 'Why wouldn't they have told him? It seems a cruel thing to do. Everyone has the right to know who their real parents are.'

'I don't suppose for one moment that it was their intention to be cruel. I'm sure they only had Tom's best interests at heart. They probably wanted to put the past behind them and start afresh as a family. They wouldn't be the first people to do that. It just so happened that Tom was one of those to discover the truth.'

'But it doesn't seem fair that their decision, made all those years ago, has prevented you from having a relationship with your son.' Pia felt outraged on Rex's behalf, on his long-lost son's behalf and on Jackson's behalf too. 'You do realise what this means, don't you, Jackson? You have a brother out there.'

Jackson's eyes widened and there was a nonchalant shrug of his shoulders, as though the news was of little consequence to him.

'How do you know that it's true, though?' Jackson turned to Rex. 'He's claiming that you're his father, but how can either of you be sure? I'm not casting aspersions on his mother, Diane, but who's to say that there weren't other men on the scene at the time?'

'I hear what you're saying, and I have to admit the same thought crossed my mind. But only for the briefest moment. When I looked into Tom's eyes as he was talking to me, I knew, instinctively, deep down inside' – he tapped his chest with his closed fist – 'that he was my son. I had no doubt about that.' Rex gave a wry laugh. 'You'll only need to look at him to see it for yourself. He looks just like you, Jackson, just like me.'

Jackson nodded, his silence filled with tension and suppressed emotion. Pia wanted to leap up from her chair and wrap her arms around him, to tell him it was okay, but she didn't want to interrupt Rex when he was in the middle of telling his story. It clearly wasn't easy for him. His voice quivered as he spoke and he shifted uncomfortably in his seat, wringing his hands together. There would be time enough later for Jackson and Pia to discuss the ramifications together.

Rex took a sharp inhalation of breath. 'I'm sorry, Jackson. So very sorry.'

Jackson gave his father a quizzical look. 'Why should you be sorry? There's nothing to apologise for.' Despite his placatory words, there was a brusqueness to Jackson's tone.

'Oh, but there is.' Rex shook his head. 'I messed up as a father big time. There's no disputing that. I let you down, son. I wasn't there when I should have been and I regret that. If I could go back and do things differently then I would. These last few months, coming back to the village, getting to know you, and Pia of course, feeling part of your family, well, it's meant the world to me. I'd never had that before and it feels good. Now, well, it seems that not only have I been a shit father to you, but it turns out that there's another kid out there who's missed out on having me as a father figure in his life. Some might say that was his good fortune.'

'Yes, but if you had no idea of Tom's existence, then you can hardly be blamed for not being there for him.'

'Thanks, Pia. I keep trying to tell myself that, but I can't help feeling bad. Not so much for me, but for the pair of you boys.' He glanced at Jackson, who was barely able to make eye contact with his dad. 'This isn't a problem, is it, Jackson? This won't come between us?'

'Why should it come between us?' Jackson forced a smile, but Pia could tell by the way he held his body and from the set of his features that he was battling with all sorts of inner turmoil. 'I guess it will take a bit of getting used to, that's all.'

'Yeah, for everyone.' Rex's eyes were awash with emotion. 'I mean, it's different for you and Tom. I've always known you and loved you. You've been in my heart and thoughts since the day you were born, even when I wasn't around.' He gave a wry smile. 'Although I know that doesn't make up for not being here. Tom, well, I shall have to start from the beginning with him and see where it takes us.'

Jackson leapt off his chair, his sudden action startling both Pia and Rex. They watched as he snatched up his empty mug before striding across to the sink. He pulled open the dishwasher door with force, his back now to Rex. 'Look, Dad. It's fine. Honestly.'

Pia caught her breath. Jackson sounded anything but fine.

'Is it, though? Come and sit down, son, please.' There was a plaintive tone to Rex's request. Pia gave the subtlest of nods to Jackson to encourage him to do as Rex asked. Knowing Jackson, he probably wanted nothing more than to be done with this conversation, to turn his back on the uncomfortable situation and head outside. Some conversations shouldn't be avoided, though, and this was one of them.

Reluctantly, Jackson re-joined Rex at the table.

'Look, I've come to realise, probably a bit late on in my life, that there's nothing more important than having your family around you. Who knows what will come of this? It could be a really a positive thing. You might decide you'd like to meet your brother one day.' There was a hopeful edge to Rex's voice. 'I think there's only about eighteen months between you.'

'Really? Well, don't bank on it!' Jackson's response was quick and emphatic.

'Jackson!' Pia's brow furrowed as she chastised him.

'What?' Jackson threw his arms in the air. 'I appreciate you have to do what you need to do, Dad, but this guy... my brother...' Jackson faltered, making the distinction clear. 'My half-brother. I'm not sure I'm interested in meeting him, to be perfectly honest with you.'

Pia couldn't bear seeing the hurt in Rex's eyes as he bit on his lip, nodding his understanding.

'Don't say that. I appreciate all this is a bit of shock, but once you've had time...' she began.

'Pia, please don't. This is really nothing to do with you.'

Suitably chastised, Pia sat back in her seat, crossing her arms, a heavy silence filling the void, until they all startled and looked at each other at the sound of footsteps approaching.

'Oh, jeez, that's all we bloody need. You do realise this will go down a treat with Ronnie?' said Jackson.

'Did I hear my name mentioned?' Ronnie swanned into the kitchen, her head held high, a coat of red lipstick freshly applied. Pia couldn't help noticing that she had loosened her hair from its tie since breakfast too so that it now fell loosely on her shoulders. A scent of orange blossom and spices heralded her arrival. She pulled out a chair next to Rex and granted him the widest smile, tapping his knee fondly. 'It's hardly surprising you'd be talking about me,' she said with a jaunty expression, 'but now I'm here, you can fill me in on all the juicy details. What exactly have you been saying?'

5

'Good grief! Has someone died?' Ronnie cast her gaze from Rex across to Jackson and then Pia, as she caught the awkward atmosphere in the room. 'What on earth have you been talking about? It can't be that bad, surely?' she joshed, but quickly realised the others were in no joking mood.

'It's nothing,' said Jackson. 'Not everything has to be about you, Ronnie.'

Rex let out a heartfelt sigh, looking defeated. 'I should tell her. She's bound to find out sooner or later.'

'Tell me what, exactly? What's going on? Ahh, I know, you're leaving again, is that it?' Ronnie pointed a red manicured fingernail in Rex's direction, searching his expression for answers. 'Well, don't say I didn't warn you, Jackson. I knew your father would hang around for a few months at the most and then he'd disappear off into the sunset again. I can't see why you're all so surprised.'

'No, it's not that, love,' said Rex quietly, dropping his gaze to his clasped hands on the table.

Alarm flittered over Ronnie's features, her eyes widening,

and in the exact same way as Pia had done, she grabbed hold of Rex's arm. 'You're not ill, are you?'

'No, I'm not ill. Why does everyone keep asking me that?' He shook his head and gently batted her hand away, sighing. 'Something's cropped up, that's all. Something unexpected.'

'Well, tell me, then,' said Ronnie, growing impatient now. She shuffled her chair up closer to Rex, who seemed to shrink smaller under the intensity of Ronnie's scrutiny.

'The thing is...' Rex lifted his head to look Ronnie directly in the eye. 'I've discovered I have a son. Another one. One that I had no idea about until this week. His name's Tom.'

Ronnie's face, always expressive, displayed the whole gamut of emotions from confusion to disbelief to surprise within a matter of moments before finally landing on one final and overriding emotion. Her nostrils flared.

'A son? What do you mean? How can you possibly have another son? That's ridiculous.' She laughed, looking around at the others, hoping to see her own fleeting amusement reflected in their faces, but she found no merriment in their features. Only the dreaded confirmation of what Rex was telling her.

'Oh God! Please tell me it isn't true. How old is this lad?' Ronnie looked stricken, her face folding in on itself, the tears in her eyes clearly visible.

'Let me pop the kettle on,' said Pia, jumping up and giving Ronnie's shoulder a squeeze as she walked past. 'I'll make us another coffee.'

'Scrap the coffee. I don't know about you lot, but I could do with something much stronger.'

* * *

'You've got it all wrong.' Rex tried to placate Ronnie, but with the help of a large sherry, she'd filled in the missing gaps in Rex's story and made up a whole new scenario of her own. 'This happened long before you and I even got together so I don't see why you've got the hump with me.'

'Well, it's nothing less than I would have expected from you. How could you let this happen?' Pia couldn't help feeling sympathy for Rex, hearing Ronnie's admonishment and Jackson's simmering disapproval. 'Did you really expect that we would be pleased? That we would throw our arms in the air and welcome this stranger into our lives?'

'I didn't expect anything from you,' Rex said sadly. 'Perhaps a little understanding, that's all. It's as much a shock to me as it is to everyone else.'

'Oh, Rex! But this could only ever happen to you. Don't you see that it makes a mockery of what we had together. All those years when I thought we had something special, with Jackson being an only child for us both and of course it was all a complete façade.' Ronnie waved her arms in front of her dramatically. 'It turns out that there's always been another woman, another child. God forgive me, but how many more could there be out there?'

'Ronnie!' Pia and Jackson chided her at the same time.

'Well, I think it's a perfectly reasonable question in the circumstances,' she huffed. 'I can't believe you didn't have an inkling about all of this.'

'None whatsoever. How could I be expected to know when I was kept in the dark?' Rex dropped his head into his hands.

Jackson had withdrawn into himself, his attention taken by something indefinable through the kitchen window, and Ronnie was bristling with energy and high emotion. Pia held herself still, listening attentively, hoping to be the calm and reassuring presence in the room. Ronnie sighed heavily.

'I'm not sure why you're feeling so hard done by.' Jackson turned to confront his mum. 'This isn't about you; it's about Dad and... Tom.' Jackson took a breath before uttering his newly found brother's name, as if the very act of saying his name aloud made his existence a reality for them all.

'But where does that leave the rest of us, Rex? We were just getting to know each other again. We had plans. You said you were going to take me to the seaside on Thursday.' Pia heard the plaintive tone in Ronnie's voice.

'I'm sorry about that, love. And I'll make it up to you, I promise, but when all this cropped up, I had to take a couple of days to get myself sorted. Everything else fell by the wayside, I'm afraid. You must understand?'

Ronnie's shoulders slumped. 'Trouble is, there's always something with you. You were always taking off on some wild goose chase: a car you just had to view, a business contact you had to visit, a new venture that was going to make your fortune You really haven't changed in the slightest.'

'Ha, well, you're hardly in any position to talk.'

Ronnie brushed off the jibe with a haughty sweep of her head. 'So what are you going to do? Play happy families with this boy and try to be the father you never were to Jackson? Have you actually given any thought to how this might make him feel?'

Jackson narrowed his eyes and shook his head in a quiet reprimand to Ronnie.

'Of course I have,' snapped Rex. 'I've thought of nothing else, but tell me, what am I supposed to do? You don't need to constantly remind me what a shit father I've been. I know that only too well. I can't change the past; all I can do is try to do better now.' His frustration with Ronnie and the whole situation was evident. 'This lad is my son and he wants to get to know me. That's not a lot to ask for, is it?'

'No, it's not,' said Jackson resignedly, jumping in to prevent Ronnie from protesting any further, and chastising her with a stern look. 'We'll support you in whatever it is you want to do.' His reassurance was emphatic and heartfelt, but Pia noticed he didn't give any indication that he might want to get to know Tom himself.

6

Lizzie Baker was busy behind the counter at the Treetops Café, putting together a tray of coffees and toasted teacakes for a group of ramblers when the door opened. Lizzie's face lit up at the sight of a familiar figure that came through the door.

'Hello, Pia! Oh, and Bertie too. How lovely to see you both. Grab yourself a table and I'll be right over.'

Pia wandered off and found herself a window seat that gave panoramic views of the landscape.

'Sit down,' she urged Bertie, who, after a bit of sniffing and a few circles on the spot, settled down beside her.

From her vantage point, she gazed out at the towering redwoods, pines and monkey puzzle trees, a sight that always lifted her mood and one she would never grow tired of.

It was mid-morning on a Tuesday and although there were a few customers dotted around the café, there weren't so many to prove too much of a distraction for the inquisitive dog. Besides, it wasn't long before Lizzie came over with her notepad and a couple of gravy bones tucked in her apron.

'How are you?' she said to Pia, as she continued to make a

fuss of Bertie. 'I don't think I've seen you properly since the wedding. What a day that was! I can't stop thinking about it.'

'Me neither. We were just pleased that Sam and Abbey had the day they were hoping for.'

'You did them proud. It was such a special moment for Bill seeing his only daughter married and gaining a super son-in-law in the process. As a parent you want your children to be as happy as you were in your own marriage. Mind you, not everyone is so fortunate. Bill and I realise we've had a double dose of luck, finding love with each other the second time around.' Pia loved the way Lizzie's eyes sparkled with happiness every time she mentioned Bill. 'Anyway, what can I get you?'

While Lizzie went off to see to her order, Pia reflected on her words. It was true. If you were lucky enough to find that special person to spend the rest of your life with, then you were blessed indeed. She'd seen that for herself in her parents' marriage, the mutual support, love and understanding they'd had for each other, which didn't waver even through the difficult times of hardship and illness. It had always been her natural assumption that one day she would have the same: a rock-solid marriage with the man she loved, someone to build a family and future with, to share the good times and bad. Although was that such a realistic expectation these days? Life was very different than in her parents' time.

'Here you go, lovely. One cappuccino and one millionaire's shortbread.' Lizzie was back bearing gifts. She placed the tray on the table and glanced at her watch. 'I was just going to take my break, actually. Do you mind if I join you?'

'Please do,' said Pia with a smile.

Moments later, Lizzie, having fetched herself a coffee, pulled out a seat at the table opposite Pia. 'So, how are you, and Jackson? How's life up at the hall?'

'Yes, great.' An image of Jackson's handsome face popped into her head as a pain twisted in her stomach. 'He's away at the moment, working in London. He has a diary full of public speaking engagements and charity commitments, so I've been left to hold the fort.'

They kept in daily contact through emails, texts and brief calls, but it made it hard for Pia to gauge how Jackson was really feeling. Was he really just busy, preoccupied with work, or was there something more serious behind his quiet detachment?

'Well, we were all saying what a great team you make,' Lizzie went on. 'What the pair of you are doing over at the hall is fantastic. When you think how many years that house lay derelict, just an overgrown ruin, and now look at it. It's been transformed. What's so lovely is that we can all get to use it, in one way or other.'

'Well, that was always Jackson's vision, putting Primrose Hall right at the centre of the community. He's done a fabulous job, but this really is just the beginning. There are so many great ideas that we're looking at for future events, so watch this space.'

'Yes, but it's not only down to Jackson. You are very much the face of Primrose Hall.'

'Thanks.' Pia felt her cheeks tinge pink, taken aback by the unexpected compliment. It was one of the things she loved the most about her job, meeting and working with such a wide range of people, a job Jackson had been only too happy to offload. 'To be honest with you, most of the time it doesn't feel like work at all. I realise how lucky I am.'

Lizzie put down her mug and raised an eyebrow, a smile playing on lips. 'The two of you look very happy together and long may it continue.'

Pia would drink to that. She picked up her mug and took a mouthful of the creamy, frothy coffee. Lizzie was right in her assertion. Pia was very happy, and she'd have said Jackson was happy too until recent discoveries had come to light. Although Jackson hadn't admitted as much, she sensed that Tom's arrival in their world had unsettled him much more than he was prepared to admit.

'Anyway,' said Pia, suddenly remembering the purpose of her visit. 'I've got some more posters for you, if that's okay?' She reached inside her backpack and pulled out two laminated A4 sheets, handing them over to Lizzie.

'Ah, the literary festival? Definitely. I'll put them straight up.'

There was a noticeboard in the covered entrance to the café near the coat stand, and a glass-encased information box outside where everything from dog-walking services, ramblers' groups, yoga classes and so much more was advertised. It was where Pia had first spotted the ad for her job at the hall.

'I'm looking forward to it.' Lizzie's gaze scanned the details. 'I've booked into the talk by Joanna De Vere. I've read a couple of her novels so I'm interested to hear what she has to say. And little Rosie is signed up for the kiddies' storytime session. She adores her books; she won't go to sleep without having a story or four read to her.' Lizzie laughed. 'I've sent a lot of my customers over to the book exchange at the stables so I know a few people who might be interested.'

The book exchange had been one of Pia's ideas when she realised that the local library would be closed indefinitely due to asbestos being found in the village hall. She thought it might provide a temporary solution for those villagers who relied on the local facility to borrow books and who were unable to travel into town. The library had been a godsend to her when her parents had been ill and she knew that other people valued it in the same way. She hadn't banked on it being quite so popular, though, with people making a special trip to visit the book exchange on the Sundays when the stables were open, so much so that they'd taken the opportunity to open up on Wednesday afternoons as well. Pia would take her laptop and work from the stables on those days and she enjoyed greeting any visitors, particularly the children who would come in with their parents on their way home from school.

'There are still a few spaces on each of the sessions so I'm hoping we can fill those with a last-minute push.'

'Well, leave it with me. I shall definitely do what I can to spread the word.'

Pia was grateful for Lizzie's support. The literary festival was Pia's baby. She'd come up with the idea following the success of the book exchange, but now that it was fast approaching, the nerves were beginning to kick in. What if nobody turned up? What if the events she'd chosen to put on weren't popular with the visitors, and what if it was a complete and utter disaster?

On the way out, Pia hugged Lizzie goodbye, thanking her for her help. Bertie wagged his tail, happy to have another couple of gravy bones for his good behaviour. Pia pulled back her shoulders and stepped outside, soaking up the late summer sunshine as it filtered through the canopies of the trees. There was no room for doubt. She would do her utmost to make the festival the success it deserved to be. To prove to herself that she could do it and, more importantly, to prove to Jackson that his faith in her was entirely justified.

7

Pia walked deep into the woods, where she slipped off Bertie's lead and he trotted off happily, his snout to the ground, exploring every scent that took his fancy. The children had recently returned to school after the long summer holidays so the park was peaceful and quiet apart from the occasional other dog-walker with whom she would share a friendly greeting. The days were still sunny and warm but there was a note in the air, a wisp of a breeze and the leaves beginning to fall from the trees, of cooler autumn days preparing to move in. For Pia, every visit to the woods was an opportunity to notice something new, to appreciate the change in the season.

It was never time wasted because not only did Bertie get his much-loved walk, but it gave Pia the opportunity to get her thoughts in order. It was also where she was at her most creative, taking inspiration from the scenery around her, the natural, rugged landscape feeding her imagination. As soon as she got back to the office, she would jot down in her notebook any ideas that had come to her, so as not to forget them.

When the old wrought-iron gate tucked away on the far

boundary of the grounds of the hall came into view, Pia experienced that familiar sensation of excitable anticipation. The entrance, hidden away behind the trees, always reminded her of a secret passage that led into another world. In a way, that's exactly what Primrose Hall represented to her. A magical destination that she still couldn't really believe she got to call home.

'Hi, Mateo.'

She spotted him, on his haunches in one of the flower beds, a wheelbarrow at his side, and Bertie went bounding across to say hello.

'Bert-o, no! My flowers!'

Trust Bertie to let the side down. Pia gave a short and sharp instruction to the dog, knowing that Mateo didn't appreciate any canine help with his digging or weeding and thankfully, for once, Bertie looked up, listened and obeyed, padding off around the grass instead.

'Sorry, Mateo. I have to say it's looking beautiful.'

'Thank you.' He stood up, slowly uncurling, resting his hands on his hips to admire his handiwork. 'I am tidying, putting in bulbs for springtime. Mr Moody, I think he is very happy today.'

Pia's gaze cast over to the direction of the house. 'Is he back, then?'

'Yes, yes, we talk about planting.' Mateo gestured to the tended beds. 'He come here, just now. I tell him you walk with Bertie. He is in good mood.'

That was a relief. Mateo was always so eager to please his boss and Pia could relate to that feeling entirely. A happy Jackson was a much better prospect than a grumpy, downcast one. His trip away had obviously done him the power of good.

'Thanks, Mateo. I'll go and find him. Catch up with you later.'

She found Jackson in the kitchen, pacing up and down as he always did when he was speaking on the phone. His face lit up to see her and he held an arm wide for her to walk into his embrace. He pulled her close as he continued with his call, and she snuggled up against his chest, revelling in his familiar earthy, masculine scent. Meanwhile, Bertie nudged Jackson's leg, desperate for some attention too.

With his call finished, Jackson could no longer ignore Bertie's demands and he bent down to give the dog a proper fuss before he turned his attention to Pia. 'Hey, I've missed you.'

'Well, I'm pleased to hear that.' She reached up to stroke his face, feeling a heat swirl in the base of her stomach as his gaze roamed her face. 'I've missed you too. How was the trip?'

'Busy. The speaking gigs went down well. Lots of meetings and formal dinners, which tend to get very dull towards the end of the week, but I guess these things have to be done.'

'Honestly, it must be so difficult for you – all those Michelin-starred restaurants and five-star hotel rooms,' she teased. 'I really don't know how you do it.'

'Hey.' Jackson grabbed her around the waist, pulling her body up close to his, his lips hovering over hers. 'I'll have you know, it's extremely demanding work.'

'I'm sure it is,' she said, catching the glint in his eye, and that sexy half-smile on his full lips.

He silenced her gentle mockery with a kiss that was long, tender and deliciously addictive. His arms ran along her sides and over her shoulder blades, his touch making her squirm so that she arched her body up against his, feeling his strength and evident desire.

He pulled away, resting his hands on her hips. 'The only good thing about working away is coming home again to you.'

That was exactly what she needed to hear. She definitely

wanted to make up for the time and intimacy they'd missed out on this week, but she sensed she might have to wait a little longer. Jackson glanced at his watch.

'We'll have a proper debrief later; there's some dates we need putting in the diary and some emails to see to, but first I need to speak to Dad. Have you heard from him at all?'

Pia shook her head. Not since that day he'd turned up with news of Tom.

Jackson sighed. 'I've lost count of how many messages and calls I've had from him.'

'What does he want?'

'To talk about Tom, of course.' Jackson shook his head ruefully.

'You're not avoiding him, are you?'

'I've been busy, Pia, and I'm not entirely sure what he expects me to say to him. What does he want from me in all of this?'

'Just to be there for him, Jackson,' she said softly. 'Your dad was missing from your life for years, and it's been so lovely seeing you two getting to know each other, rebuilding your relationship. It's clear your dad adores you. Tom turning up on the scene shouldn't make any difference to that.'

'Honestly, sometimes I think family are more trouble than they're worth. You try your best but then they only end up hurting and disappointing you.'

Pia felt Jackson's pain as though it was her own. Jackson was no longer the young boy who had idolised his father, confused about why he was only a fleeting, transient presence in his life, but the hurt from those times obviously still lingered.

'Don't say that.' Pia stepped towards Jackson to offer a consoling hug, but he brushed her aside.

'Not everyone had the same traditional, idyllic childhood as you. You look at family through rose-coloured glasses, but it's not all hearts and flowers.'

Pia flinched at Jackson's harsh words.

'Tom has turned up, and I can't do anything about that, but you don't really expect me to get along with him, just because you think we can all be the perfect family now. It doesn't work like that.'

'No, but you could at least try; that's all anyone is asking of you.' She took a breath, biting on her lip to hide her irritation. 'I'll admit Connor and I had a very happy family life at Meadow Cottages, but that doesn't mean we didn't have our fair share of difficulties and falling-outs.' She cast him a sharp glance. 'I'm not completely naïve, Jackson. I know families can be hard work at times, but I just so happen to think it's worth the effort.'

Jackson turned away, and she noticed the imperceptible shake of his head. 'Look, I should go. I'll call Dad, see what he has to say.'

* * *

In the office, Pia sat at her desk and contemplated the pile of post in front of her, trying not to let Jackson's words upset her. She knew he was struggling. Despite his outwardly confident and self-assured appearance, he was a complicated and highly sensitive person. During his childhood years, he'd spent a lot of time with his late aunt, who he'd adored, but the comings and goings of his parents had stirred an insecurity in Jackson that had never left him. Jackson had a tough shell but an instinct to walk away if things became too intense or emotionally tough to handle. Pia suspected Jackson might feel threatened by Tom's unexpected arrival, although she knew him well enough by now to know that he would never admit to any such thing.

Pia idly pulled off the wrappings on the brochures and catalogues, depositing those she knew would be of no interest straight into the bin, putting aside anything she knew Jackson had specifically requested into a separate file. She marked up the invoices received and popped them in Jackson's folder for approval. It was only when she reached the last envelope in the pile that she recoiled. She knew immediately that this particular letter wasn't anything to do with Primrose Hall business. It was private correspondence for her. The sight of the imprinted company logo on the front of the envelope caused her stomach to roll over. She knew exactly who it was from and what it was about. She was only pleased she was alone in the office so no one could witness her opening it. She pulled out the contents reluctantly, her body reacting to the official-looking document.

The solicitors R. P. Westeralls were 'now in a position to finalise matters regarding the probate of Mrs Julia Temple'. Pia had known it was coming. She'd been impatient to get everything resolved as quickly as possible but seeing it there in black and white gave her no sense of satisfaction. It only sent waves of sadness through her body.

Bertie, sensing the change in her breathing, stuck his head up over his bed and after a few moments uncurled his limbs. Curiously, he padded over, nudging her with his wet nose, looking up at her with concern. Pia gave a sigh and a smile, grateful for the dog's support.

'Oh Bertie,' she said, finding comfort in his presence as she buried her head in his fur. He seemed to have the knack of knowing exactly when she needed a cuddle. 'I'm fine. It's okay to be sad sometimes, isn't it?'

She honestly wasn't sure what she would have done without Bertie at her side these last few months. He was her constant companion and emotional support dog. When her neighbour

Wendy, at Meadow Cottages, had suffered a bad fall and needed to be hospitalised, Pia had immediately offered to take care of the goofy Dalmatian. She hadn't given any thought to how she would take a big dog with her when she moved out of the family home in only a few weeks' time, though. Luckily the job at Primrose Hall had materialised and Jackson had welcomed both Pia and Bertie into the household. What had started out as a temporary solution became a permanent arrangement when Wendy moved into Rushgrove Lodge for the Elderly, and Pia and Jackson had been more than delighted to have Bertie on a full-time basis.

Now, Pia's phone pinged on her desk. She reached for her mobile and smiled, seeing Connor's name flash up on the screen.

Hey, sis! Good news, eh? Great to get everything sorted at last. Mum would be pleased to know we're in the money! So what will you do with this new-found wealth 😉 Catch up soon over a drink?

Pia's gaze had flittered over the statement included with the solicitors' letter, but it had given her little comfort to know that she now had more money in her bank account than she might ever know what to do with. She would trade it in a heartbeat to have her mum back at her side, to have one final chat over a cup of tea, but she couldn't deny what was staring her in the face. All the paperwork had now been finalised and she needed to move on. It was what her mum would have wanted.

What exactly would she do with the money, though? It was a good question from Connor. This was her security blanket. She'd taken on the job at Primrose Hall because it offered her a quick solution to her dilemma at the time. She hadn't been thinking long-term, but then she hadn't banked on letting down her guard and falling in love with Jackson Moody all over again, making a heap of new friends at Primrose Hall and finding a happiness that she could never have anticipated. Was this her forever home, though? She didn't know about that.

As much as she loved Jackson, and her job, she had no real security to speak of. If he should ever tire of her or their situation, and he was notoriously mercurial, then she could be looking for a new job and a place to live at a moment's notice. After all, he'd left her in the lurch once before, so what was to say he wouldn't do it again?

'Just as I expected!' Jackson's entrance into the office made Pia jump in her chair, and she was only relieved he couldn't read her mind. She hastily tidied away her letter into its envelope before turning to look up at him.

'What?'

'I've spoken to Dad. He wants me to go with him when he next meets up with Tom.'

'Right... and...?'

'Well, I told him no initially, but you should have seen the look on his face.' Jackson rolled his eyes. 'He said how much it would mean to him for me to go along, so I could hardly refuse. Dad is really keen, and I suppose I didn't want to let him down.'

'And you're really not feeling it?'

'It's difficult to know what I feel.' Jackson ran a hand through his dark hair. 'It's weird being told you have a half-brother out there. I guess, beyond a natural curiosity to see what he looks like, I can't say I have any burning desire to meet him.'

Pia nodded, trying to understand. How might she feel in the same situation?

'Maybe you should just view it as something you need to do for your dad. You know how happy it will make him to see his two sons together.'

Jackson flashed her a disgruntled look.

'You never know, once you've met Tom you might feel differently. And if you don't, well, then it will be up to you to decide whether you want to continue seeing him. Your dad can't argue with that.'

'Yeah, you're right.' Jackson perched on the edge of her desk. 'Look, I'm sorry for what I said earlier, about your family.' He rested his hand on her shoulder, giving it a gentle squeeze. 'I didn't mean it. I guess I'm just a bit frustrated at the moment.'

She accepted his apology with a nod of understanding.

'I only wish you could come with me,' Jackson said in a plaintive tone.

'This is something you have to do with your dad, but if there's another time, then I'll definitely come along, if you want me to.'

'Families, eh? Who'd have them?' said Jackson with a resigned sigh, before his gaze snagged on Pia's hand, which had been resting on the letter from the solicitors the entire time she'd been speaking to him. 'What's that?'

She paused a moment, considering his throwaway comment. Actually, she'd do anything to have her close-knit family back again, but then as Jackson had been only too keen to point out, she and Jackson had very different experiences of family life.

'It's some stuff from my bank,' she said airily. Jackson had enough on his plate at the moment without burdening him with her own issues. This windfall was her security and she needed to make sure she used it in absolutely the right way, a way her mum would have wanted her to. She would give it some serious thought, and if she wanted the idyllic family life that she'd always dreamt of, the one Jackson doubted even existed, then she would need to give her future at Primrose Hall some serious thought too.

8

'It sounds amazing, and probably just the escape you needed after the hectic run-up to the wedding.'

Pia had popped round to see Abbey at her pretty little cottage in Wishwell and her friend was telling her all about their honeymoon on the stunning Northumbrian coast.

'We had a beautiful cottage just a few steps away from the beach. Lady loved it. We'd wake up early and head straight outside and walk for a couple of hours. The coastline is so beautiful there and stretches for miles and miles. Then we'd return to the cottage for a big breakfast before heading out to visit a castle or an antiques fair or a bookshop. The great thing about that part of the world is that dogs are welcome in most places, even bar and restaurants, so we never had to leave Lady behind. We spent most of our time looking at our photos and talking about the wedding. You know how grateful we are to you and Jackson for everything that you've done for us.'

'We do.' Pia smiled. 'And it was our absolute pleasure.'

'So tell me, how are you? How's life at the hall? Sam and I

were saying how good you and Jackson are together. It's as though you've been together forever.'

'I sometimes think that too. In some ways, it's as though I'm finding out about him for the first time and then there are certain mannerisms or expressions of his that take me right back to when we were teenagers.'

'So this is it now? You've really found your vocation at Primrose Hall?'

'It feels that way, although...' She shrugged. 'It's still early days for us, and I have this fear, I suppose, that something might happen to spoil what we have.'

'Like what?' Abbey sat forward in her seat, her attention fully fixed on Pia.

'I don't know. As I say, it's just a feeling. He broke my heart once before. I don't want it to happen again.'

'I can understand that.' Pia was grateful that Abbey didn't immediately try to reassure her, but instead listened intently. 'Do you have any reason to think that could be on the cards?'

'Not really. It's just living, working, sharing a bed together, it's sometimes difficult to draw a line between those different roles, and where being an employee ends and being his partner starts.'

'You should talk to Jackson, tell him how you feel.'

Pia shook her head. 'I don't want to. He's so busy with all his work commitments at the moment, and there's some other stuff he's preoccupied with too.'

'What other stuff?' Pia might have known she wouldn't get anything past Abbey.

'Well...' Pia took a breath, knowing she could trust Abbey implicitly. 'Please don't mention this to anyone, but he's just found out that he has a long-lost half-brother. He's about eighteen months older than Jackson. His dad has only just found out about his existence too so it's been a bit of a shock all round.'

'I can imagine.' Abbey shook her head. 'How does Jackson feel about it?'

'I must admit he's not overjoyed. I think if it was down to him, he wouldn't bother getting to know Tom, that's his brother's name, but Rex is obviously keen to make up for lost time. I think Jackson feels a bit torn. He doesn't really talk too much about it, but I know it's worrying him because he withdraws into himself. Sometimes, I find it hard to reach him.'

'It must be a lot to process, but Jackson shouldn't be pushing you away. You don't want this to come between you, but you shouldn't feel that you can't go to Jackson with any worries or concerns that you might have of your own. You should be there to support each other.'

Pia nodded. It felt good to be able to talk freely with Abbey away from the confines of Primrose Hall. 'I don't want to put any pressure on him, not when he's battling with these different emotions. He's been working away a lot and...' Pia's voice trailed away.

'And... what?'

'Well, it's just that I know he's run into his ex, Tara, recently at a work event. And it got me thinking that all of this has happened so quickly. Me finding a job there, moving into the hall and getting back with Jackson. I just wonder if we would we have got back together if I'd just bumped into him in the pub. Are we together because it's simply convenient? Will there be another woman living at the hall this time next year?'

'No, don't say that. You love Jackson, right?'

'More than anything.'

'And from what I can tell he loves you as much too. Don't worry about the length of time you've been together. That doesn't mean a thing. Look at me and my ex. We were together almost ten years and it counted for nothing. Then I met Sam within a matter of weeks and it was as though we were always destined to be together, that this was meant to be.' She played with the ring on her left hand.

That was true now Pia came to think about it, and it went someway to making her feel better.

'What did Jackson have to say about seeing Tara again?'

'Well, that's the thing. He didn't mention it. I found out through some promotional materials that came through to the office. There was a photo of them together.'

'What, just the two of them?'

'No, it was a group photo, but don't you think it's odd that he wouldn't have mentioned it?'

Abbey pondered on that for a moment. 'I'm not sure, but what's important is that it's troubling you, and that's what really matters. You must ask him. You have every right to know, as his assistant and his girlfriend. Don't be apologetic; just come straight out with it and see what he has to say for himself, or else you'll just torment yourself with all sorts of scenarios.'

Pia had known that Abbey would understand, and she was right, it was simply a case of finding the right time to ask Jackson about it, without sounding like the possessive, needy girlfriend she would never want to be.

9

The weekend of the literary festival arrived, bringing with it the angry storm that the weather forecasters had been predicting. The wind howled around the hall, making the tall trees in Primrose Woods sway like leggy poppies, and whipped across the grounds, making the fallen leaves dance across the paths. Pia had peered out of the kitchen window first thing, marvelling at the ferocity of the weather, watching the rain as it bounced off the plant pots, depositing glossy puddles all around. Thankfully, she'd taken the precaution of stabling Little Star, the Shetland pony, and Twinkle, the donkey, overnight so they were out of harm's way should any of the trees topple over, and to prevent the animals from becoming spooked by the rumbling thunder and lightning that threatened in the sky. She would check on them in a little while, and then regularly throughout the day. After throwing on some clothes, Pia dashed outside with Bertie and quickly walked him around the gardens, keeping him on the lead close to her side, knowing how he could easily be frightened too. The last thing she needed was for him to perform one of his escape acts on today of all days. He'd looked up at her, his ears flapping comically, his doubtful expression suggesting that he thought it was a bad idea too, and there were no complaints from him when Pia decided to quickly return to the safety of the house. After eating his breakfast, Bertie quickly snuggled up in his bed in front of the Aga, where Pia suspected he might stay for the rest of the day.

Over at the stables, Pia gave a last-minute check to each of the units where the participating authors would be selling their books. One end of the stables was being used for the various workshops being held over the weekend and Pia couldn't wait to see the place abuzz with visitors. She just hoped the squally weather wouldn't put too many people off attending.

'How's it going? Have you got everything you need?'

Pia turned to see Jackson, who had joined her in the barn where the main sessions would be taking place. The schedule of author talks and crime and romance panels looked impressive in the day's programme.

'I guess so,' she said, so pleased to see him. His dark hair, soaked from the elements, clung to his head, and raindrops dotted his face and shoulders. He was wearing a black-and-white-flecked cable-knit jumper and she thought how handsome he looked.

'You don't sound sure.'

'No, I am.' She managed a small laugh. 'It's just so nerve-wracking. The thought of all those people about to turn up. I just hope everything goes to plan.' Just at that moment, a crack of lightning flashed in the sky. 'This wild weather isn't helping either. I hope everyone can get here safely.'

'It'll be fine. This looks great,' he said, gesturing to the room in front of them. There was a long table on a raised platform at the front of the room where the speakers would be seated, and rows of chairs were lined up neatly for the audience. 'Once people start arriving, there won't be time for nerves. I saw Ronnie on the way out and she said she'll be over in a few minutes.'

'Great.' She was thankful, and surprised, that Ronnie had volunteered to oversee the catering assistants who would be providing hot and cold drinks, and a small selection of sandwiches, wraps, salads, cakes and pastries, although she suspected she had an ulterior motive in wanting to see the speakers attending.

Just then the double doors to the barn opened and a woman tumbled through the entrance, holding a bag over her head as she struggled with the umbrella in her hands, flapping it around in the air and proceeding to deposit rain all over the barn floor.

'At last, I've arrived!' The woman dumped her belongings on the ground. 'This really is in the arse end of nowhere, isn't it? Beautiful, but right out in the sticks. At one point we thought we might never make it, didn't we, Kevin?' She gestured to a man who was just coming through the doors now. His small, balding and bespectacled appearance was almost entirely covered by the big brown box he was holding in his arms. He nodded at the woman's statement, and Jackson jumped in to relieve him of the package he was carrying.

'I'm Joanna, and this is Kevin, my long-suffering assistant. And the poor man just so happens to be my husband too. Some people have no luck whatsoever!' Joanna had a big, booming laugh that matched her personality. She fell silent for the briefest moment as her gaze snagged on Jackson's, and Pia quickly made the introductions, welcoming them both to Primrose Hall. Jackson took the opportunity to slip away while Pia showed their visiting guests where they could leave their wet coats and where they would be setting up for Joanna's talk, and she took them across to the stables as well to show them the space for signing and selling books.

Back in the barn, Pia was relieved to see that Ronnie and her helpers had arrived, especially as Joanna had announced that she wouldn't be able to do another thing until she had at least two coffees inside of her. Leaving Joanna in what she hoped were the capable hands of Ronnie, Pia took up position at the front table to welcome and register the attendees. Chatting to the people as they arrived, hearing about their journeys, and their enthusiasm for the day ahead, Pia was buoyed by the air of goodwill and, as Jackson had predicted, her nerves soon disappeared.

Pia was compere for the day. It was her job to introduce the different participants onto the stage and it gave her the ideal opportunity afterwards to slip into a front row and listen to the various talks. They were all fascinating; she loved hearing the authors read from their books, bringing their characters to life, and then discussing their motivation for writing the story. After each session, the floor was opened up to questions from the audience, which was Pia's favourite part as it gave even more insight into the authors' ways of working.

The last session of the morning was from Joanna De Vere and she was met with a huge round of applause as she made her way up onto the stage. She was a natural orator who punctuated her words with a deep throaty laugh and soon had the entire audience hanging on her every word. She held up a hardback copy of her book and a respectful hush descended over the room as she prepared to read aloud from the first chapter.

She'd barely got to the end of one paragraph when she let out a heartfelt groan. 'Eugh!' She held her palms up to the sky. 'What is that?' Her face crumpled in disgust and she stretched her neck to look upwards. As she did, a big fat raindrop plopped straight into her eye, quickly followed by another and then another, before she jumped out of her seat, as quickly as her broad frame would allow. 'Kevin!' she hollered, much to the alarm of her long-suffering husband, who was already on his feet, looking perturbed as to how he might be able to help in such a situation. 'Would you do something please?'

10

'I am so sorry, Joanna!'

After a frantic ten minutes where Kevin quickly ran to his wife's aid and steered her aside, Pia moved the pile of books out of the way of what was now a persistent stream of rain coming through the ceiling and the audience took the opportunity to chatter amongst themselves about the actual source of the leak, Pia hoped that they might be in a position to resume the session. She was running on adrenalin, and with the help of a couple of men from the audience had moved the chairs and table to the other side of the room, hoping that Joanna would be happy to carry on where she'd left off. Thankfully, she'd laughed it away with remarkable good humour.

'Don't worry, you'll probably read about it in one of my future books. No experience is ever wasted.'

Joanna brushed herself down with a towel provided by Kevin, zhuzhed up her hair, and did a quick re-application of mascara and lip gloss. Like the true professional that she was, she carried on as if nothing had ever happened, much to the relief of Pia and the audience, and soon Joanna was holding forth as though there had been no interruption at all. Though she tried not to show it, Pia's anxiety had gone through that hole in the roof, and there'd been one point where she'd had a real moment of panic and wondered if the whole weekend would need to be called off. What a disaster that would have been. Pia had visions of having to send everyone home and issuing refunds, and with it the possibility of ever running another literary festival at the hall.

With Joanna centre stage once more, Pia slipped out of the main barn and into the front reception area, taking a few deep breaths to steady herself. She was relieved when she finally spotted Jackson and Frank coming over from the main house.

'What's happened?'

'A big hole in the roof, Jackson, that's what happened. Poor Joanna, one of our leading authors, got drenched just as she was reading from her book. It was so embarrassing. We've put a saucepan down to collect the rain, but it's almost full already. We've had to move Joanna to a different spot. It's not ideal, but it got us over the immediate problem.' The words came out in a torrent of worry. She knew it wasn't Jackson's fault, but she needed to release all her frustration. 'This isn't supposed to happen, not on a newly renovated building. Not on my very first event.'

Jackson put an arm around her shoulder and pulled her close into his side, but she pushed him away, not wanting his reassurance, not now, especially when there was every likelihood that she would dissolve into tears in the warm safety of his embrace. She couldn't afford to wobble. This was her project and she was determined to make it a success, whatever it took.

'Can we get this sorted please? As soon as possible. It hardly looks very professional with a big leak in the roof.'

'It's one of those things that can't be helped. I'm sure people will understand. I suspect some of the roof tiles have been dislodged in the storm. I'll have a proper look later when the room's free. We might need to get the roofer in to come and do the repair, but that's not going to happen until this weather passes. In the meantime, we can reconfigure the room and find a couple of big buckets, if that's any help?'

'Really?' Pia grimaced. 'Buckets? Is that the best thing we can come up with?'

'It's going to have to be,' said Jackson with a shrug. 'Come on, it's a small hitch. These things happen. Don't let it spoil your day.' He peered through the glazed door into the main barn area. 'It doesn't look as though anyone's too bothered by the leak. Besides, it's one of the joys of being out in the countryside.' He held up his hands to the sky, that charming grin spreading over his face and for a moment she thought she might throttle him. She shook her head resignedly. It was hard to stay annoyed in the face of Jackson's tireless positivity, and she couldn't help herself smiling too. It was easy for him to be so relaxed about the situation. He had nothing to prove to anyone, but she had really wanted this weekend to go off without any hitches, not only for the attendees, but also for herself so that she could demonstrate to Jackson that she could successfully implement her own events.

Jackson was right, of course, and once her initial annoyance had worn off, Pia was able to relax into the day and enjoy herself a bit more. Over lunch, she chatted with some of the visitors and they all enthused at how inspiring the morning sessions had been. The small hiccup with the leak was barely mentioned, and if it was, it was only in passing and with good humour. Towards the end of lunch, Pia grabbed one of the few remaining sandwiches, a cup of coffee and an apple and sat on one of the long benches, where she was shortly joined by Ronnie, and then a few minutes later, Joanna de Vere politely asked if she could come and join them.

'Of course! We were just saying how much we enjoyed your talk.' Pia shuffled up the bench to make room for Joanna. 'I can only apologise again for the interruption. I really hope it didn't put you off your stride too much?'

'Not at all. And don't worry. I've experienced much worse. I've arrived for talks where no one has turned up to see me, only the organiser. Then I've had people nodding off as I've been speaking, which is never a good sign. This festival has a lot going for it. A beautiful location, a great venue and a really good turn-out. I'm looking forward to my next session.'

'What will it be about?' asked Ronnie, who'd been enjoying the day much more than she'd expected to.

'How I create my romantic heroes, which is always one of my favourite topics to talk about,' she said gleefully. 'People love to know how I come up with my characters, if they're ever based on real people. The truth is that sometimes they are. Now, take that gorgeous workman that was in here earlier, the one who brought the buckets across; he has all the ideal physical attributes for a leading man. He's tall and sexy with come-to-bed eyes and I might borrow some of those characteristics when I'm drawing up my next character.'

Ronnie looked at Pia and spluttered with laughter. 'You mean Jackson. That's my son you're talking about. He's actually the owner of the hall, and Pia's partner too.'

'Oops, apologies, no offence intended.'

'None taken,' said Pia, laughing.

'Well, aren't you the lucky one,' Joanna said, raising an eyebrow. 'Although please don't tell Jackson what I said. But that's the thing, romantic heroes come in all shapes and sizes. It just so happens that your Jackson fits into the mould of a conventional romantic hero.'

Pia smiled and nodded. She couldn't disagree with Joanna's assessment, but she wasn't sure that she liked the idea of others viewing Jackson in the same way. Was that how Tara still saw him? Pia could understand why. Once seen, those come-to-bed eyes were not easily forgotten.

'He's just like his father,' said Ronnie. 'Good-looking and charismatic, but not the easiest person to live with.' She gave a wry chuckle.

'All romantic heroes have their flaws, and that's an important part of their character make-up,' Joanna added.

'Rex was definitely a charmer in his day,' Ronnie went on, 'but we were never love's young dream, even though I was madly infatuated. Oh, the rows we used to have! When I look back, I wonder what that was all about. We never did get our happy ending.' She gave a rucful shake of her head. 'Anyway, what am I talking about? Rex is still a charmer, even these days; we were just never meant to be. Some people, like us, bring out the worst in each other.' There was no denying the note of regret in Ronnie's voice.

'Look at Kevin,' Joanna continued, and both Ronnie and Pia glanced across the other side of the room, where the unassuming man was rifling through a holdall, clearly looking for something. 'He might not look like your typical romantic hero' – she giggled – 'but I can't imagine my life without him. What he lacks in conventional good looks, he certainly makes up for in kindness, respect and understanding. He's infinitely patient and takes care of all the domestic arrangements at home. We've been married twenty-five years this year. He always says his main purpose in life is to make sure I'm happy. Now, isn't that lovely? It's what love is all about, isn't it? Finding that special person whose happiness you want to put before your own. So, I take those lovely qualities from my Kev, along with a few vulnerabilities too, and just enhance the wrapping a little bit – well, quite a lot, actually.' There was that big, infectious laugh again and Ronnie and Pia couldn't help but join in. 'I'll give him a full head of hair, add a few inches to his height, put a twinkle in his eye and I'll be halfway there to creating my next romantic hero.'

Just at that moment, Jackson bowled through the door, his attention taken by the hole in the roof as he strode across the room to inspect it, hands on his hips, his neck craned upwards, and as one, Joanna, Ronnie and Pia turned to watch his distinctive figure, falling silent as they did. Pia suspected Joanna might be taking mental notes for her next book. Ronnie was lost in thought, probably reminded of Rex when he was a young man. As for Pia, Joanna had certainly given her plenty of food for thought. To her, Jackson really was her ideal romantic lead, but whether she would find her happy ever after ending with him, if they would still be together in twenty-five years' time – she still wasn't certain.

11

Sunday dawned and Pia was heartily relieved when she peered out of the bedroom window to see that the storm had finally passed. Aside from the hole in the barn roof, there were some fallen trees in the grounds of the hall, but fortunately they weren't close enough to have caused damage to any of the buildings.

'We've got a bit of a clean-up job on our hands, but it could have been much worse. Thankfully no one was hurt. Mateo and I will get out there today and clear the debris, but don't worry, we'll be well out of the way of the barn. I've been over there this morning and done a temporary repair on those slates until the roofer can get here tomorrow. It should be fine and means we can get away without the buckets today.'

'Thanks, Jackson.' She reached up to kiss him on the lips. 'What would I do without you?'

'Well, I hope you won't need to.' He ran a hand over her jawline, his dark eyes snagging on hers, and her body reacted as it always did when he was within touching distance. If she wasn't rushing off to open up the barn for the second day of the literary festival then they might have decided to fall back into bed for the morning, but that would have to wait until another day. 'You know I always aim to please.'

Pia appreciated Jackson's innate masculine practicality and his throwaway comment struck a chord. Wasn't that what Joanna had been saying yesterday about Kevin? That he tried to make her life easier by taking care of those mundane issues in her life. Isn't that what Jackson did in his own way? Pia couldn't compare her relationship with theirs as they'd been happily married for years, but Pia loved the way Jackson was always keen to find a solution to any problem.

'Look, I'll have my phone on me so give me a call if there's anything you need,' Jackson called on his way out of the house. Through the window, she watched him stride through the grounds, looking every inch a romantic lead in his brown cords, tattersall-check shirt and cable-knit jumper.

Over at the barn, Pia was happy to welcome the day's speakers and visitors, ticking them off on her list and handing them each a lanyard. She loved chatting with everyone and hearing where they'd travelled from, whether they were readers or writers themselves, or if they had come purely out of curiosity. Everyone commented on the beauty of the location.

'Do you hold any other events here?' asked a lady who had just arrived with a couple of her friends.

'Yes we do.' Pia never missed an opportunity to spread the word about Primrose Hall. 'Every month the stables are open on a Sunday for the craft fair. We have a wide selection of local craftspeople selling their wares. Jewellery makers, artists, natural beauty providers, a silversmith and wood sculptor. There really is something for everyone. Then we had a big classic car show in the summer that we're hoping to repeat next year. Coming up we have our Bonfire Night display and then the big date on the calendar is in December with our Christmas carols by candlelight in the courtyard. This year's will be bigger and better than ever with a Christmas market, a nativity display and a tunnel of lights. It's going to be a real spectacle.'

'I can just imagine that now. We'll have to come,' the woman said, turning to her friends.

'Well, I can put your name on our mailing list if you're interested and then you'll be the first to hear what we have going on.'

Pia was pleased that so many people were keen to sign up to the Primrose Hall newsletter. It gave her a sense of pride to talk about everything they had planned at the hall.

Over in the stables, the children's workshops were underway and, judging by the rapt faces of the children as they listened to the stories being told, they were proving very popular.

Pia whispered a hello to Lizzie, who was standing to one side, holding coats and bags. 'Hey, how's it going?'

Lizzie gestured to her granddaughter, who was sitting cross-legged on the floor. 'Rosie's having the best time. She's joining in with the stories, making all the noises and laughing away. She can be a little bit shy at times so it's great to see her really coming out of her shell and enjoying herself.'

There were so many more happy faces too, which came as a huge relief to Pia.

She slipped out, leaving the storytelling in progress, and went through to the other end of the stables where the authors were signing and selling their books. Yesterday, Pia had bought four books and she wasn't going to miss the opportunity to buy more from today's participating authors. She liked to read a wide range of genres so she picked up a psychological thriller, a cosy crime story set in a country mansion and a non-fiction book on walks, pubs and landmarks in the local area. Usually after Pia had read books, she would put them into the book exchange at the stables, but with these specially autographed editions she would keep them on the shelves at the hall and treasure them. There was one particular thriller she couldn't wait to get her hands on.

Martin D. Sayers, a celebrated crime author with over twenty books in his catalogue and a number of awards to his name, was just taking to the main stage in the barn. He cut a distinctive figure in cream linen trousers, a white shirt and a bold floral waistcoat with a fedora sitting jauntily on his head. He was gregarious, a natural storyteller and he paced up and down the stage, gesticulating as he spoke about his writing routine. He sounded incredibly focused and would be at his desk at eight o'clock in the morning and would stay there until he had completed at least fifteen hundred words. He spoke about his latest book, his publisher and how he came up with his ideas before inviting questions from the audience, which he handled with grace and good humour, especially as Pia suspected he had answered the same questions dozens of times before.

The best part of the session was when Martin suggested to the crowd that they come up with an idea for a crime novel together.

'Ooh yes,' said Stella Darling, who was sitting in the front row along with some fellow residents from Rushgrove Lodge. Abbey, the manager at the home, had organised the visit as a lot of the residents were keen readers, and she'd been thrilled to see them so engaged listening to Martin's talk. Stella clapped her hands delightedly.

'I can think of a few people I'd like to murder,' she said with a mischievous grin.

'Why are you looking at me?' exclaimed Reg Catling, who

was sitting alongside her and cast an alarmed look, much to the amusement of the rest of the room.

Martin galvanised the crowd so that it was a truly interactive experience with everyone coming up with suggestions about where their fictional murder might take place. The residents from Rushgrove Lodge insisted it should be at a residential home, and they were also quick to come up with a cast of characters, some of whom were based, not that loosely, on people they all knew, but it was all done with a great deal of laughter and with no bad will intended. As they continued to brainstorm, they came up with a murder victim and possible motives for all the other characters, and within a short time they had an outline for a novel that gave the budding writers amongst them plenty of inspiration for their own novels. For the rest of the audience, it was a fun and enjoyable task.

'Thanks, Pia,' said Abbey on the way out. 'That was brilliant. Everyone had such a great time, and what a brilliant speaker Martin was.'

'I loved it,' chipped in Stella, who came alongside them. 'It really stirred my imagination. Martin made it sound so easy, as though you could go off and write your own novel. Now, if only I was ten years younger.'

'Don't let age be a barrier to your writing aspirations.' None of them had known that Martin had followed them out and overheard their conversation. He placed an arm around Stella's shoulder and she positively beamed, looking up at him. 'I've known debut novelists in their sixties, seventies and beyond. So if you want to write, then just do it. Don't let anything hold you back. That's one of the many things I love about my job. The idea that I might still be tapping away on my keyboard in twenty or thirty years' time. I really can't imagine a time when I wouldn't want to write, and if I physically couldn't do it, then I like the idea of reclining on a chaise longue and dictating my stories.'

'Ooh, like whatshername? Her with the pink hair. Barbara Cartland!'

'Exactly. You know, I might even adopt the pink look one of these days. Do you think it would suit me?' Martin zhuzhed up his hair with his hands and Pia, Abbey and Stella all burst into laughter at the very idea.

Abbey herded her charges from Rushgrove Lodge onto the minibus to take them the short distance home and Pia said goodbye to each of the residents in turn, thanking them for coming. She reserved an especially big hug for Wendy, her old neighbour from Meadow Cottages, who had recently moved into the lodge after her nasty fall at home earlier in the year. Despite Wendy's initial reluctance, she had admitted to Pia several times since that it had been the best thing she could ever have done in the circumstances. Of course, she'd been incredibly sad at leaving her beloved Bertie behind, but knowing he was living in splendour with Pia and Jackson at Primrose Hall made that particular loss much easier to bear.

'Honestly, Pia, look at you and what you've achieved here. Didn't I always say how capable you were and how you just needed to find the right position to show off your skills? Your mum and dad would be very proud to see how well you're doing.'

'I'm only doing my job,' said Pia, feeling a swell of emotion rise in her chest.

'I know, but it's lovely to see how you've blossomed and grown in confidence. Seeing you so happy, well, that makes me happy too.'

'Thanks, Wendy. Now get on that bus before you make me

cry.' Pia laughed, but bit on her lip at the same time to stop the tears gathering in her eyes. 'I'll come and see you very soon.'

'Thanks again,' said Abbey to Pia, once everyone was safely seated on the minibus. 'Before I forget, Sam is going away for the weekend, on the eleventh, so I thought I'd have a small get-together round at ours. Just some drinks and a bite to eat. I'll ask Lizzie and Katy to come along. And Rhi is back that weekend too so it would be a great opportunity to have a girls-only get-together.'

'Sounds great. Count me in.'

'Brilliant.' Abbey paused a moment, as she appraised Pia's features searchingly. 'How are things?'

'Good, yeah.' Pia knew exactly what, or rather who Abbey was referring to, but now wasn't the time or place for that kind of catch-up. Instead she plastered on a big smile and waved as the minibus pulled away. 'We'll have a proper catch-up soon,' she called.

In truth, she'd been so busy preparing for the festival that she hadn't had the opportunity to speak to Jackson about his trip away or about her money coming through. She'd put those niggling concerns to the back of her mind. Besides, Jackson had been preoccupied too. She suspected it was because he was wary and apprehensive about meeting his brother for the first time, which was perfectly understandable. Pia could only hope that it would turn out to be a much more positive experience than he might ever expect it to be.

12

After the last of the visitors had left, Mateo, Jackson and Pia were all hands on deck to clear the barn and the stables. While Mateo and Jackson put away the tables and chairs, Pia collected the rubbish into a black bag before sweeping the floors and clearing the small kitchen.

'Come on. I think we've done enough here, don't you?' Jackson said, once they were done. 'Let's get back to the house for a well-deserved glass of wine.'

Mateo politely declined the offer and went off to his own living quarters in the hall, while Pia and Jackson wandered across to the house, where they received their usual effusive welcome from Bertie. The dog skidded across the kitchen floor, ran around in circles and nudged his snout against their legs, demanding the attention he'd missed out on all day.

Pia laughed. 'Oh, Bertie, I know. We've missed you too. Come on, let's get you fed.'

'I'll do it. Sit,' said Jackson forcefully, and although he hadn't been talking to Bertie, the dog immediately obeyed his master and sat to attention, his ears pricked, waiting for his next command.

Pia certainly wasn't going to argue with Jackson so she did as she was told too and pulled out a chair at the kitchen table.

'Talking of food, I'll get the dinner on as well. I don't know about you, but I'm starving. There's some fresh linguine and a packet of seafood in the freezer. How does that sound?'

Pia nodded. It sounded perfect. With a glass of wine in hand, she could finally relax after what had been a demanding but hugely satisfying weekend. Moments like these, when it was just the two of them alone together, were the ones Pia savoured the most, when Jackson seemed to be at his most relaxed.

As she watched him move effortlessly about the kitchen, highlights from the two days kept popping into her head, the people she'd met, the conversations she'd had, the books that had been recommended and the sessions she'd attended. She'd come away feeling inspired. All of the authors, without exception, had been incredibly generous and had left copies of their books for the book exchange at the stables.

'You okay?' asked Jackson as he turned from where he was standing over the cooker, as the aromas of sauteing garlic wafted in her direction.

'Great,' she said with a satisfied sigh. 'I'm only relieved the weekend went off as well as it did. Everyone seemed to enjoy themselves.'

'I heard only good things, but then I'm not surprised. All your hard work and effort that went into preparing for the weekend really paid off.'

'Thanks, Jackson.' She felt her cheeks redden. 'That means a lot. And I'm sorry if I was a bit scratchy yesterday about the hole in the roof. I know that wasn't your fault. I was just frustrated when I so wanted everything to be perfect.'

Jackson looked over his shoulder as he jiggled the frying pan over the hob, that familiar half-smile on his lips. 'I think perfection might be a tall order. The very nature of what we do here means that we will inevitably run into problems, but we can only strive to do our best and I think we more than managed that this weekend.'

Pia nodded. What she had to remember was that Jackson had years of experience in business and had his fair share of successes and failures behind him. For Pia, this was her first proper job, and she was still finding her way, learning as she went along.

'Sometimes, in the moment, my emotions get the better of me. I have to stop taking things so personally,' she added, only realising as she said it that she could probably do with applying that to her private life too. 'Really, I just wanted to prove to you that I could do it.'

'What?' Jackson immediately spun round, brandishing a spatula in his hand. His face furrowed in confusion.

'Well, the literary festival was my idea, wasn't it? I didn't want to fall flat on my face. And while it really appealed to me because I love anything to do with books, I wasn't sure how it would be received by other people.'

'Listen.' Jackson pushed the pan off the heat and came over to where Pia was sitting. He pulled her up onto her feet and placed his hands on her shoulders. 'You don't have anything to prove to me. I'd hate for you to think that you did. I would never have thought of running a book festival, but I had every confidence that you could make it work. And you did. But if it hadn't, for any reason, then it wouldn't have been the end of the world. It's still early days for Primrose Hall. Discovering what works and what doesn't. I've always said that it has got to be something one of us feels passionate about rather than it being simply a money-making venture. I'm super proud of you, Pia. You absolutely smashed it this weekend.'

Pia smiled, buoyed by Jackson's reassurance and the kindness she saw reflected in his dark eyes. She'd wanted this weekend to be a success for everyone but she couldn't deny that most of all she'd wanted to impress Jackson, to show that his faith in her was justified.

'So... same time next year?' he said, pulling away and returning to the cooker, putting the pan back on the heat.

'I hope so. Lots of people were asking if we would be making it an annual event.' It had always been her intention, assuming that the first weekend was a success.

'We can't not do it, then,' he said, turning to see her with a wide smile. Pia felt an ache in her arms where she wanted to reach out to him, to feel the form of his body in her arms, to hear him whisper in her ear how much he loved her, but she pushed her need for reassurance aside. Trying to navigate her personal relationship with Jackson alongside their working one was something that she was still trying to figure out.

13

On Monday morning, Pia was brimming with enthusiasm and eager to get to work. Already she'd walked Bertie, seen to Little Star and Twinkle over in the paddock, stopped to chat to Mateo and Frank, and was now ready, with a frothy coffee in her hands, to open up her laptop. She paused a moment as she settled herself at her desk, while Bertie came to join her, collapsing in a heap at her feet. It was a surprise she got any work done in the office because the view through the French doors was entrancing. She could see the extensive grounds of the hall, with its sweeping lawns, vast array of ornamental shrubs and bushes and the backdrop of the towering trees of Primrose Woods beyond. If she was lucky, she might catch sight of some wildlife such as woodpeckers, herons, squirrels and the occasional muntjac deer, but today the only sight catching her eye was the distinctive figure of Jackson. Dressed in jeans, checked shirt, a gilet and safety equipment, he had a chainsaw in his hands and was clearing the debris and cutting up the trees that had fallen in the storm at the weekend. Pia couldn't help but smile, knowing he was absolutely in his element.

As much as she would have liked to sit there all morning and admire the view, she had jobs to do. She opened up her laptop and set to work, updating her mailing list and spreadsheets with the information gathered at the weekend. She looked on her calendar and booked in the same weekend for the literary festival for the following year. She had so many ideas about possible future panels and authors that she jotted them down in a dedicated notebook. As well as her own thoughts, she wanted to hear back from those who had attended this year to find out what they had particularly enjoyed about the weekend, what they thought could be improved and what they would like to see on the programme in future. She drafted an email to send out later in the day once she'd finished making all the changes to the mailing list.

It was a couple of hours later before Jackson wandered in, peeling off his jumper as he came into the office and depositing random bits of twigs and leaves all over the floor. His hair was mussed up and there were black streaks over his face and hands. She thought perhaps she'd never seen him looking more attractive.

'That's a good job done,' he said, perching his backside on her desk, bringing an earthy aroma of the great outdoors with him. 'We've moved all the fallen branches that we can use onto the site ready for Bonfire Night.'

'Ah... yes.' However much she tried, she really couldn't muster up much enthusiasm. 'That's reminded me, the guy from the firework display company is coming in tomorrow morning.'

'Yeah, I saw that on my calendar.'

'He does know we want a silent display, doesn't he?'

'Absolutely.' Jackson's eyes widened at her question. 'Like we discussed... don't worry, it's all in hand.'

From the start, Pia hadn't been keen on the idea of a Bonfire

Night event at Primrose Hall, primarily because she was worried about Bertie, knowing how spooked he would be by the loud bangs and whistles. She wasn't sure how Little Star and Twinkle might react either. Not to mention the wildlife in the surrounding woods. It didn't seem right to inflict that kind of trauma on defenceless animals.

'Come on, Pia, don't be a killjoy,' Jackson had said when they first started to draw up the plans in their weekly meeting. 'It will be fine. We can get Poppy along and she can babysit the animals for the night.' Poppy was the teenager who helped out looking after Little Star and Twinkle.

'It's not a case of just babysitting the animals. I remember how Bertie was last year when he was still with Wendy at Meadow Cottages. He was a nervous wreck, poor thing. I went round there and sat with them both, but Bertie paced up and down the whole evening. There was no comforting him.'

Jackson, however, had his heart set on it. He'd told Pia how he'd loved Bonfire Night as a kid, watching from a distance as the flames of the bonfire roared and crackled a bright orange against the night sky. He'd recounted how, in the run-up to 5 November, he and his mates would make guys, using old clothes cadged from home, then they'd take them round the village to see if they could get some pennies for them. He'd wanted to recapture that sense of excitement and anticipation from when he was a child.

'I promise you, it will be fine. There'll only be a few fireworks and I'll speak to the display company and make sure we don't have any loud bangers or rockets. Silent firework displays are a genuine thing, I promise you.'

So they'd come to a truce, although in reality, despite voicing her reservations, Pia was never going to be able to stop Jackson from doing what he wanted to do. At the end of the day, she was still Jackson's employee and, although their personal relationship might make her a lot closer to her boss than most other employees, it was he who had the final say.

Now, he looked at her, the warm smile in his dark eyes reaching his lips. 'It will be great; I'm really looking forward to it. The main focus of the evening will be the bonfire, and the guy competition for the children, and the activities going on in the stables. Plus, we'll have those glow-stick bracelets and necklaces, remember those? And what about hot dogs and mugs of hot chocolate? Come on, Pia,' he said, laying a hand on her shoulder. 'Can't you at least pretend to be looking forward to it?'

It was hard not to in the face of Jackson's enthusiasm.

'As long as the animals are safe and well looked after then I'll be happy.' She wouldn't admit that she couldn't wait for it all to be over. 'Listen, I've pencilled in next year's writing festival.' She pulled up the calendar on her laptop. 'I can't see it clashing with anything, but just wanted to check that you're okay with those dates?'

Jackson gave a cursory glance. 'Looks fine to me.' He fell silent as his gaze drifted out of the window, before returning to the moment. 'You know, we're a pretty good team, Pia,' he said, fixing her with a smile. 'It's made a big difference you being here. Last year, after we'd finished the renovations, I wanted to put on the Christmas carols gathering so that we could introduce ourselves to the local community. The welcome we received was so heartening, but I could never have believed then that we would come so far in such a short space of time.'

Pia had heard a lot about last year's Christmas event, not only from Jackson, but also from Connor and several of her friends who'd been there on the night. Mostly, she'd heard about Jackson's girlfriend at the time, Tara, who, by all accounts, was gorgeous and charming, the glamorous couple winning over their visitors just as much as the beautiful house and location had. It troubled Pia to think that she had stepped into someone else's shoes, even if Jackson and Tara's relationship had ended before Pia had arrived on the scene. She'd met Tara once briefly when she'd called into the hall to speak to Jackson, and Tara was every bit as glamorous as everyone had made her out to be. Jackson had been quite honest with Pia then, explaining that Tara had wanted to see if Jackson might want to give their relationship another go. He'd quickly reassured Pia that there was no possibility of that, but she had still been unsettled by Tara's return to the hall. Even now, she could sometimes sense Tara's presence within the fabric of the house, which was hardly surprising when Tara had been the creative talent behind the interior renovation and decoration of Primrose Hall.

Still, it didn't stop Pia feeling a pang of sympathy for Jackson's ex, imagining how she might feel if her own relationship with Jackson was to falter in the same way.

'In fact, I was thinking,' Jackson went on, bringing Pia's attention back to the moment. 'Maybe next year we should extend the Christmas fair to cover more days, say three or four nights.'

'That's a great idea,' said Pia.

Pia admired Jackson's vision and enthusiasm. He was a great ideas man and she was a good organiser so she could make sure the foundations were in place to ensure Jackson's plans came to fruition. As he spoke, Pia made copious notes in her notebook and she would transfer those scribblings into specific tasks to add to her to-do list a bit later. Jackson was right, they were a good team.

'We also need to think about what we want to do for Christmas Day. Ideally if it was up to me then I would love our first Christmas together to be a quiet, romantic affair, but, in reality, that's not going to happen.' He gave a wry chuckle. 'Having this big house, I feel it's our duty to invite whoever wants to come along or who might be at a loose end. I love Christmas, always have done, but I know for a lot of people it can be a difficult time. Ronnie, of course, will be here and probably Mateo, although I need to ask him if he has any plans. I'll invite Dad too, as long as he and Ronnie can promise to behave themselves. What are your thoughts?'

'Honestly, that sounds ideal.' Spending Christmas with Jackson in this beautiful house would be enough for her. Last year's holiday had passed her by as it had been the first one without her mum, and she hadn't felt inclined to celebrate. She hadn't even got round to putting a tree up. Their family Christmases at Meadow Cottages before then had been full of joy and laughter and her mum's legendary cooking, so at least she had her happy memories. Now she was ready to move on and make new memories at Primrose Hall. 'Obviously it would be good to see Connor and Ruby at some point.'

'Well, invite them here. They'd be more than welcome. Have a word with Connor and see what he says.'

'There's a party right there,' said Pia, laughing, imagining all of them sitting around the kitchen table. Or maybe they would use the formal dining room for the special occasion, with the fire crackling in the hearth, swathed with garlands. Her thoughts drifted to the Christmas preparations and how amazing the hall would look once it was dressed for the season. She might not have the keen design eye of Tara, but she knew what to do with a string of tinsel. Already she'd put in an order with Sam Finnegan at Primrose Woods for four trees: two ten-feet ones to go outside, one in front of the house and one by the stables, and then two smaller varieties for the interior of the hall. Although Pia suspected, knowing Jackson, that number might increase the closer they got to Christmas.

'Honestly,' he said now, 'Christmas is going to be so much fun this year. I can feel it in my bones.'

Pia smiled, hoping that might be true, but failing to rid her head of the thoughts taunting her mind. If Tara could be here one year and gone the next, what was to say the same thing couldn't happen to Pia? Was she as indispensable to Jackson as she would hope to be? And if so, why hadn't he been entirely honest with her about meeting up again with Tara recently?

14

On a rainy Wednesday afternoon, Jackson sat in the back bar of the Three Feathers, nursing a pint. He could think of a dozen places he would rather be, and so many other things he could be doing, but he'd promised his dad he would turn up today and he wasn't one to break his promises. He glanced at his watch. With any luck this meeting wouldn't take too long and then he could put the whole episode to one side and get on with his life. He had no desire to get to know Tom. Family was just a word. It didn't mean you necessarily had any special or instinctive feelings for someone just because you shared a parent. Especially someone you hadn't known existed for the entirety of your life.

'Hey!' Jackson pressed on a smile when his dad arrived and stood up from his seat to greet him with a hug. Standing beside him was his half-brother, Tom, and Jackson had been totally unprepared for the gut punch of emotion he experienced at seeing him for the first time. There was a moment of awkwardness where it seemed as though neither of them knew quite what to do. Jackson had imagined they would shake hands, but instead they fell into a hug like the long-lost brothers they were.

With the introductions over, the three men remained seated at the table, and for the first few minutes, there wasn't a great deal of conversation, just a few exclamations and shaking of heads. At any other time, it might have been rude to stare, but not here when they were seeing themselves reflected in each other. There was no denying the family resemblance. They all shared the same strong Roman nose and the same jawline, but it was the mannerisms that caught Jackson by surprise. The way Tom held his head to one side and the way he twisted his mouth when he was thinking were all entirely recognisable to Jackson, evoking a sensation that he'd known this stranger for much longer than the few minutes since they'd been introduced.

'I hope this isn't too weird,' said Tom. 'Thanks for agreeing to meet me. You were under no obligation to do so, so I'm grateful to you for turning up. I'm not sure what my reaction would have been in the same circumstances.'

'Hey, I'm pleased to be here.' Jackson surprised himself by saying the words aloud and realising they were true.

'You know what's great for me,' said Tom, his gaze flitting between Rex and Jackson, 'is to see you both and see someone that actually looks like me. That's incredible. I didn't take after my mum, she was blonde with fine features, but then I didn't look like my father either, well, the man I thought was my father for all those years. We were never close and after he left and started a new family I barely saw him. I thought there must have been something wrong with me, for him not to want to know me. It made so much sense when I found out that he wasn't my biological father after all.'

'A big shock, though, I'm guessing?'

'Yeah, it was, but it stirred my desire to find my real father. I never really felt as though I belonged growing up. I always felt like an outsider so I wanted to make that connection with my real family to see where I came from. To help me understand more about myself, really. I'm sorry if it's thrown a spanner into your world. I'm sure it was the last thing you were expecting or hoping for.'

'I'm glad you came and found us,' said Rex.

'Yeah, admittedly it was a surprise,' said Jackson with a wry smile. 'I've gone all my life believing I was an only child so to find out that I've actually got a big brother is a bit mind-blowing.'

The three men sat around the table trading stories, filling in the details of all those absent years. It continued to intrigue Jackson that he and Tom shared some traits. They both had the same way of clasping their hands, steepling their fingers together while they were listening, and when they caught each other doing it, at the same time, they laughed, enjoying the moment of synchronicity. Like Jackson, Tom's years at school hadn't been happy ones and he'd been suspended several times, much to the despair of his poor mum. It was unexpected. Jackson hadn't expected to feel any kind of connection to Tom. He was a stranger after all, but he couldn't deny the feeling deep down inside that he was reconnecting with an old friend.

'I must admit that I did a bit of googling when I learnt about you.' Tom shook his head. 'You've done pretty well for yourself. Fair play.'

'I've had a bit of luck along the way. Made a few good investments.'

Rex gave an imperceptible lift of his eyebrows, knowing that Jackson was downplaying his success, pretending that it had all come easily to him, when Rex knew that everything he'd achieved had come through determination and hard work.

'What about you, Tom? What's your trade?'

'I was in pharmaceutical sales for years. It was a job I fell into when I was quite young and made it up through the ranks to regional sales manager. Good pay and good perks, but with everything that's being going on recently, I realised it wasn't what I wanted to be doing for the rest of my life, so I quit.' Tom gave a resigned shrug. 'Seems a bit reckless now, but my head wasn't in the right place and I don't regret the decision for a moment. I needed some time out to get myself together. To be honest, I had a bit of a breakdown.' He paused to look up at Jackson and Rex. 'It's fine. I've seen my doctor and she's helping me through this. It's just strange to have your whole world and what you believed to be the truth about who you are and where you've come from upended like that.'

Jackson nodded. His own upbringing had been unconventional, but at least he knew who his parents were, for all their failings.

'I'm sorry, Tom, for what you've been through,' said Rex. 'You know, I can't make up for not being there when you were a kid, but I'm here now,' he said with a sheepish smile.

'I know. And that means a lot... Rex. Look, I'm not here demanding to be part of your lives, wanting to play happy families. I know it's not as simple as that. I'm just really glad that I've got to meet you both and to have made that connection. I mean, if we can stay in touch and get to know each other better, then that would be a bonus.'

'I'd like that,' Rex said to his sons, laying a hand on each of theirs. 'You know you can call me "Dad",' he reassured Tom, before adding, 'only if you want to, of course.'

Tom's face lit up. 'Yep, I'd like that. As long as you're okay with it too, Jackson?'

'Sure, I mean, he's our dad, so what else are you going to call him?' said Jackson with a gracious smile.

There were no awkward silences for the rest of the afternoon because there was so much to talk about. It was strange to think that Tom had grown up in a village barely ten miles away from Primrose Woods. He knew the local area well, and he and Jackson had many shared reference points from their youth.

'So do you have a wife or a girlfriend?' asked Jackson, quickly correcting himself. 'I mean a partner.'

'I did.' Tom grimaced. 'Anna. We split quite recently. We'd been together since we were teenagers; she's a great girl but I guess our relationship was another casualty of... all of this. It was my decision. Not her fault at all. I had this overwhelming need to clear my life and effectively start all over again.'

Jackson nodded in understanding, knowing Tom was speaking from the heart, his sadness all too discernible. Every now and then he would rally, plastering on a wide smile, lifting his voice to sound more upbeat, but it was evident that discovering the truth about his parentage had impacted hugely on his life.

'Anyway, don't let me bore you with the sorry state of my life.' He laughed, rather too loudly, and not altogether convincingly. 'What about you? Is there someone special in your life?'

'Yes, her name is Pia,' said Jackson with a smile. He found it hard not to smile when he thought about Pia. 'Funnily enough we were teenage sweethearts as well.' Another similarity he shared with Tom. 'Although it's only recently that we've got back together again.'

When Jackson had left the village suddenly, turning his back on his plans to go to university, as well as on his friends and family, he hadn't thought twice about his decision. The only thing he was certain of at the time was that he had to get away and fast, but his one big regret was leaving behind his young, sweet girlfriend. It wasn't as though he hadn't thought about her over the years. He had, on several occasions, but it was only when he'd confronted his own personal demons and returned to the village, to repay his dues to the community, that he was able to reconnect with his teenage love.

'We live and work together at Primrose Hall. We're very happy.'

Now it was Tom's turn to nod, his gaze running over Jackson's features. 'That's great,' he said with a twisted smile. 'You really have done well. It sounds as though you've really got this whole life business sorted out.' And if there was a bitter edge to Tom's words, Jackson either didn't notice or chose to ignore it.

15

Later that same evening, Pia was cooking dinner for a change. Jackson usually liked to take charge in the kitchen as it was his way of unwinding and relaxing, and Pia was always more than happy to act as sous chef, which most of the time involved sitting at the kitchen table, drinking wine and chatting, and only occasionally leaping up from her chair to find a missing ingredient or a certain cooking utensil. Today, though, while Jackson was out with his dad, meeting his brother for the first time, Pia had made a lasagne, prepared a salad and had a cheesy garlic bread ready to pop into the oven.

All afternoon Ronnie had been restless, drifting around aimlessly, popping in and out of the kitchen, peering out of the window to see if there was any sign of Jackson.

'You know that's not going to make him arrive any sooner, Ronnie. Sit down, you're making me nervous. Let me fix us a drink.' Pia pulled out a bottle of white wine from the fridge and poured them each a glass.

'I wonder how they're getting on. It must be strange, mustn't it?' said Ronnie, sitting on the edge of her seat at the kitchen table, as though she might spring up at any moment. 'Meeting a family member you didn't know about for the first time. I'm not sure how I'd feel in the same situation. I think Jackson is very good to agree to go along in the first place.'

'I'm sure Rex will appreciate the moral support.' Pia didn't mention how Jackson had been dreading the meeting and was only doing it for his dad's sake. She didn't want to give any more ammunition to Ronnie than she already had. As she joined Ronnie at the table, Pia steered the conversation away from Jackson and Rex, and spoke instead about the upcoming Bonfire Night and the plans for Christmas.

'I'm looking forward to it. For the first time in my life, I've found a place that I'm happy to call home. It's funny. Must be something about the old walls of this building. They do seem to wrap you up in a hug. And being back living alongside Jackson, well, that's the icing on the cake. I think our relationship is better these days than it's ever been, even if I still drive him to distraction.' Ronnie held up a hand to stop any defence Pia might present. 'Although me living out the back is probably a good thing for everyone concerned.' Ronnie's distinctive warm laugh tinkled out around the kitchen. She fell silent for a moment. 'Mind you, it's been an awfully long time since I've been off on one of my adventures. I was thinking I might take a trip in the new year. Just jump in the van and go.'

Pia felt a pang of concern, not for herself, but more for Jackson. She knew how bruised he was from Ronnie's constant departures when he was a kid. Apparently, she'd been a free spirit, taking off in the van and heading for the continent whenever the responsibilities of life got too much for her.

'I thought you'd got the wanderlust out of your system.'

'I don't mean like in the old days, but I reckon I've still got time for a few more short trips. There's nothing to beat the excitement of setting out on the open road, not knowing where you might end up.'

Pia smiled indulgently as Ronnie's expression took on a dreamy quality. She'd often spoken of her love of travelling around in her camper van, which was a bit of a mystery to Pia, who was a proper home bird and never happier than with all her creature comforts around her.

'I'm getting itchy feet,' Ronnie went on. 'Besides, those first few months of the year are pretty miserable. It might be nice to go in search of some sun.'

'Well, make sure you give Jackson plenty of notice, won't you? You know what he's like.'

'Stop looking at me like that, Pia. If I do go, it will only be for a month or two. Besides, Jackson's no longer a child; I'm sure he'd barely notice I was gone.'

'You know that's not true.' Pia wondered if that was the crux of the matter. Had Tom's arrival unsettled Ronnie more than she was letting on? She seemed to be forever angling for Jackson's attention, and Rex's too since he'd been back on the scene, and maybe by announcing she might up and leave, she would receive the consideration she felt she needed. Or perhaps that was uncharitable of Pia.

'He's back!' Ronnie jumped out of her seat and dashed across to the kitchen window, hearing the throaty rumble of Jackson's motorbike. 'Oh, and he's got someone on the back. He wouldn't bring Tom here, would he?' she said. 'Not before warning us first.'

'No, it's more likely to be Rex,' Pia said, getting up to look for herself, Ronnie's curiosity rubbing off on her.

Immediately Ronnie stood tall, pushed her shoulders back, smoothed down her dress and ran her hands through her hair. She checked her reflection in a glass cabinet door, running her tongue around her lips. 'I wish they'd hurry up.'

Minutes later, Jackson and Rex came through the door and before they were able to take off their coats, Ronnie had ambushed them with hugs, eager to know every detail.

'So come on, don't keep us in suspense. How did it go?'

'Give them a chance,' Pia rebuked her gently. 'Let me sort a drink first. What would you like, Rex?'

'Anything soft for me will do.'

'I'll have a beer,' said Jackson. 'That looks good. My favourite,' he said, spotting the lasagne on the side, which was exactly why she'd chosen it in the first place. Jackson kissed Pia tenderly on the forehead, and it was almost as though she could feel the tension seep from his body. 'I invited Dad to stay, if that's okay.'

'Of course, there's plenty to go round.'

'I must admit it looks absolutely delicious,' said Ronnie pointedly as she watched Pia pop the dish into the oven, who then went off to find some drinks for the boys. She also took the opportunity to top up her and Ronnie's wine glasses.

'Well, why don't you stay too,' said Jackson, and Pia smiled to herself seeing the look of satisfaction on Ronnie's face, knowing it was what she'd been angling for all along.

While Rex took a seat at the kitchen table where Ronnie joined him, Jackson, never one to sit still for long, rested his backside on the edge of the worktop, taking a swig from his bottle of beer.

'Well?' prompted Ronnie again, who was growing ever more impatient by the moment.

'Yeah, it was…' Jackson glanced at Rex as he searched for the right word to explain. '...great.' He gave a wry smile, realising that he'd come nowhere close, but continued all the same. 'It went much better than I expected. I thought it might be awkward, that we wouldn't have anything in common, but we didn't stop talking the whole time.'

'The two of them hit it off right away,' said Rex, with more than a hint of pride. 'He's a good lad, isn't he?'

'Yeah, he seems like a decent guy, although he's obviously had a rough time of it in recent months. It's really messed him up, all this business, which is understandable. He mentioned he's seeing a counsellor who's helping him to make sense of what's happened, but I don't think it's been easy. It's even caused him to walk away from his job and his relationship.'

'Well, it's his mother's fault,' said Ronnie, bristling with indignation. 'She should never have lied to him like that. Denying the boy the chance to know his real father – what was she thinking?'

'Who knows? And I think that's part of the problem. She's not around now to answer the questions he has. He's left wondering why she couldn't have told him the truth about the man he thought was his father, especially after she separated from him, when she would have known the reason why he showed little interest in seeing Tom.'

'I expect she had her reasons,' said Rex sadly. 'I don't think we can blame Diane; it was a different time. I think about what my reaction would have been if she'd come to me at the time. I hope I would have offered my support, but I certainly didn't have any money then and I wasn't ready to settle down. It was one of those brief, fleeting love affairs, neither of us expecting it to go anywhere. Sounds to me as though Diane simply wanted to do the right thing by Tom.'

'Huh, have you ever been ready to settle down, Rex? You certainly weren't when you were with me.'

Rex ignored the slight.

'I think it's sad,' Pia muttered.

'Well, I can't imagine doing anything like that, whatever the circumstances. It's not fair on the child.'

'Well, we can't all be as perfect as you, Ronnie,' Jackson said, casting her a sharp glance.

'What do you mean by that?' she snapped, her hackles immediately rising. 'You never miss an opportunity to have a swipe at me. I might not have been the best mother, but I tried my hardest. I would never have lied to you like that.'

'I'm not having a go at you, but you're not being helpful. That's Tom's mother you're talking about and she's no longer here to defend herself. Besides, it's really none of our business. How can we judge when none of us are perfect?'

Ronnie puffed out her cheeks and huffed. 'Well, it seems to me that you're always quick to defend other people, but you still blame me for all my shortcomings as a parent. Your father turns up, out of the blue, and it's like he can do no wrong. And yet he was missing from a great deal of your childhood too.'

'Blimey, Ronnie, don't drag me and all my misdemeanours into this. I'm very aware of my failings. I know it's a bit late, but I'm trying to make amends. I wasn't there for Jackson as much as I should have been and I certainly wasn't there for Tom, but hopefully I can make up for that now.'

'Dad, you have nothing to apologise for. The main thing is we're back in touch. That's all that matters.'

'Ha, you've proved my point exactly,' said Ronnie crossly. 'You think I have something to apologise for, though?' She took another sip of her wine, her cheeks flushed from alcohol and emotion.

'I didn't say that,' said Jackson, his exasperation evident in his tone.

Pia laid the table for four, humming a light tune, trying to ease the tense atmosphere within the kitchen. She pulled out four bowls from the cupboard, and filled a jug with some cold water, placing it in the centre of the table.

'So will you be seeing this Tom again, do you think?' Ronnie persisted.

'Probably, yes.' Jackson glanced across at Rex. 'He doesn't live a million miles away from here. He's renting a flat in Popplesham until he decides what he's going to do next. Dad will obviously want to see him and I've said he's always welcome to come here, so we'll have to see how it works out.' They fell silent for a moment, each of them lost in their own thoughts. Pia was surprised but heartened that Jackson had seemingly had a change of heart about the new family member. 'You know, Ronnie, you'd like him, if you got to meet him. He's just an ordinary guy.'

'Hmm. Well, maybe. If I happen to still be here,' she said airily, waving a hand in an expansive manner. 'I was telling Pia that I might go on a trip soon. It's been a while since I've been on the road. Maybe I'll go to Spain or the French Riviera or maybe I'll just head out of the village and see where the fancy takes me.'

'Oh, Ronnie! Where's this come from?' Rex didn't look impressed at all. 'You told me you'd had enough of that lifestyle. That you were happy, settled. You've got a beautiful spot here, with your family around you; why would you want to leave? Aren't you too old for that nomadic lifestyle?'

Ronnie was certainly mercurial, one minute saying she'd finally found a peace and contentment living in the grounds of the hall, and the next announcing she wanted to take off.

'Old?' she blustered at Rex. 'I'm still in my prime, I'll have you know, even if I seem to be invisible to you lot. That's why I feel I have to get away. To live and breathe again. To feel the sun on my skin and the wind in my hair, to discover new sights. To be noticed. Who knows, maybe fall in love again.'

'You've always been such a romantic,' Rex said, with a kindly shake of his head.

'Where's the harm in that? Not that it's ever got me terribly far. Just broken my heart a couple of times. I don't fancy doing that again.'

Pia knew that Ronnie's comments were directed at Rex, even if he hadn't picked up on the inference. Ronnie had already admitted to Pia how Rex had been the love of her life, despite him breaking her heart on several occasions. What was it about the Moody men? And the way in which they got beneath your skin and squeezed your heart dry. Pia could see so many similarities in the way she felt about Jackson. Would she be lamenting her broken heart in thirty years' time? She really hoped not. She sometimes wondered if loving Jackson was too big of a risk to take.

Everyone was relieved when Pia brought the lasagne out of the oven, the aromas of rich ragu, garlic and a bubbling cheese sauce creating a collective swoon of delight from around the table. Jackson stood up and scooped out portions into bowls, while Pia took off the cling film from the salad and pulled the garlic bread into chunks.

Over dinner, the earlier tension evaporated and was replaced with laughter and chatter. Ronnie might be noisy and confrontational on occasion, but her bad moods never lasted for long and soon she would be regaling her audience with amusing anecdotes, her hazel eyes shining with mischievousness, which made it extremely difficult to stay annoyed with her for any length of time.

'We could get down to the coast soon if you still wanted to go?' Rex ventured. 'That's if you'll still be here, of course.'

'Of course I still want to go, but how will I know that you won't let me down again? I wasn't the one to bail out at the last moment.'

'Aw, come on, cut a man a bit of a slack. Let's get a date in the diary, then? We could go down to Brighton. We used to love it there. A walk along the pier. Fish and chips. A mooch around the Lanes.'

Pia noticed the smile that Ronnie was trying to suppress and the way she lifted her gaze to the ceiling as though she actually needed to think about his offer, when everyone around that table knew that she wanted to jump at the chance. She managed to hold out for a matter of moments, before she clapped her hands together delightedly.

'You promise you won't let me down again?'

'No, of course I won't. You have my word.' Rex placed his hand on his heart, his dark eyes twinkling, and Pia could see why Ronnie found him so hard to resist. He had the same cheeky smile and innate charm as Jackson. 'I'm looking forward to it. It'll be just like old times.'

'I hope not,' said Ronnie sharply. 'Or else we'll end up not speaking to each other all day!'

'You know, I think we should have a toast.' Jackson raised his glass and the others followed suit. 'To family. In all its shape and guises, but particularly to our Primrose Hall family, which seems to be growing by the day.'

Pia was more than happy to drink to that. Apart from Connor, her family was a little thin on the ground these days, and she was glad to be a small part of this tribe who she adored, every one of them, despite, or even because of their idiosyncrasies. Pia cast her gaze at Ronnie and Rex, who were already hashing out the details of their upcoming day trip, and Jackson, whose first meeting with his brother had gone much better than any of them could have expected. She only hoped that the relative peace and goodwill permeating though Primrose Hall was destined to last.

16

Pia climbed out of the car, turned to wave at Jackson and hurried down the front path to Abbey's cottage, where the front door was immediately opened and she was swept inside by her friend, who had a big smile on her face.

'Come on in, everyone's here. What can I get you to drink?'

While Abbey saw to the drinks, Pia said hello to the others: Lizzie and her daughter, Katy, and Abbey's other friend Rhi, who was here for the weekend from her home in Dashford-Upon-Avon.

Pia perched on the edge of Abbey's sofa, enjoying the chatter, the glass of Prosecco she held in her hand and being amongst friends. Life at Primrose Hall was great but it was all-encompassing. From the moment she woke up to the moment she went to sleep, she was preoccupied with jobs that needed doing, whether it was seeing to the animals, or working through her to-do list in the office, or ordering items for the house, or dealing with any employee issues, as, although that wasn't her remit, everyone came to her first, rather than speaking to their boss, Jackson. She also spent a great deal of pre-empting what

Jackson might need or want to do next, anticipating his moods, even if that wasn't part of the job description either. She loved being at the heart of the hall, the first point of contact, and she wouldn't have it any other way but it was refreshing to have a moment to get some perspective as well as an opportunity to relax and unwind.

'We didn't expect to see you back here quite so soon,' Lizzie said to Rhi. 'Not that I'm complaining. It feels just like old times when we're all together.' Lizzie, Abbey and Rhi had become good friends since meeting at Primrose Woods, and they'd formed a lovely friendship group along with their respective partners too. Pia was grateful that she and Jackson had been so warmly welcomed into it.

'Well, we've been looking at flats,' Rhi said, her excitement evident in the way her dark brown eyes sparkled as she spoke. 'Around here.' She clapped her hands together excitedly. 'When we came back for Abbey's wedding, it brought home to us just how much we missed living here: being near to our families, having Primrose Woods and the pub on our doorstep and, most of all, we missed you guys. I mean, Dashford-Upon-Avon is a beautiful place to live and it's a great place to visit, but it isn't home. I thought it was just a time thing, that we would come to love it, but we both realised that we would prefer to live round here if we could.'

'At least you gave it a try. And as far as we're concerned, it will be lovely to have you back again. What about Luke's job, though?' Lizzie asked.

'That's the thing. He's on the road a lot of the time and can work from home a couple of days a week so he doesn't need to go into the office that often. It was actually Luke's idea; it hadn't even occurred to me to move back, but it makes sense. My business is home-based, I can work from anywhere, and at least here

I'll have my friends and family around me. I'm looking forward to going back to the pub too, to do a few shifts each week. I've missed it.'

'That is good news. I've missed seeing you in the café and at quiz nights, haven't we, Abbey?' said Lizzie.

'Definitely. And all our walks over at Primrose Woods, putting the world to rights.'

'The good thing is that it feels like a proper next step in our relationship. When we moved to Dashford, Luke already had the flat and his job organised and in some ways, I felt as though I was tagging along with him. Now, we're making plans together for our future. It will be our flat, not just Luke's, and that feels good. Does that make sense?' Rhi asked.

'I understand completely,' agreed Pia, recognising the feeling exactly. She felt a pang of... what was it, jealousy perhaps, that she wasn't making plans with Jackson – well, not personal ones at least. She'd joined Primrose Hall as his assistant and although their relationship had quickly developed into something more intimate and personal, she couldn't help feeling insecure in her position, as though it could be snatched away from her at any moment. Jackson was the one who held the control in their relationship and while that might be expected professionally, it made her uncertain where she stood sometimes in their personal relationship. She shook her head, bringing herself back to the moment. This wasn't about her, this was about Rhi and Luke. 'Well, I hope that means we'll get to see you both up at Primrose Hall soon.'

'Too true you will. We'd planned to come back for the Christmas carols. We don't want to miss that, not after last year, but we're also looking forward to going to the craft days at the stables. Anyway, how are you settling into the hall? I only found out recently that you and Jackson are together.' Rhi had a mischievous look on her face. 'I had no idea. How's it going?'

'Yes, great,' said Pia, feeling a heat rise to her cheeks. 'There's never a dull moment at the hall, that's for sure.'

'I can imagine, and Jackson Moody is quite the catch, isn't he?'

'Rhi, stop it!' Abbey chided.

'Well, he is. You said so yourself.'

'Oops.' Abbey held a finger to her lips, looking guilty as charged. 'Did I really?'

'It's fine.' Pia laughed, enjoying the good-natured teasing.

'Because when we visited the hall last year at Christmas, he was with someone else.' There was no malice behind Rhi's words, only a genuine curiosity. 'What was her name?' The question was directed to the whole group, not just Pia.

'Tara,' said Abbey, glancing across at Pia with a sympathetic look.

'Yes, I remember now. Was she Scandinavian?' Rhi didn't wait for a reply. 'She looked as though she'd just come from the ski slopes with her blonde plaits and fur-trimmed hat. Very glamorous and she seemed very nice too. Oh...' Rhi's face crumpled as she stopped herself, realising that she might be talking out of turn. 'She wasn't nearly as lovely as you, though,' she added with a reassuring smile.

'Yes, they broke up just before I started at the hall. Then we got together a few months later, although Jackson and I knew each other as teenagers. We had a brief fling.' She hoped that sounded suitably casual. She didn't want to admit that the brief romance had broken her heart. 'He was the local bad boy then.'

'Really? And now you're back together again? That's so romantic. It was obviously meant to be.'

'Maybe,' she said lightly, hoping that might be true. She

didn't resent Rhi's interest. Living at Primrose Hall with Jackson Moody was bound to attract speculation. With his undoubtable good looks, his undeniable wealth and his habit of riding the lanes around the woods on his monster of his bike, he struck a glamorous and intriguing figure and there was no denying his local celebrity status.

Pia was relieved when the conversation moved on to another topic and, to the sound of laughter ringing around the cottage, Abbey fetched some plates of food: warm sausage rolls and homemade cheese straws straight from the oven, smoked salmon whirls and bowls of savoury snacks, placing them on the oak coffee table. She gave a stern warning to Lady, the springer spaniel, who circled the table as though she might pounce at any moment and help herself to a sausage roll.

'Not for you. Go to your bed!'

Lady slunk off, but she didn't get as far as her basket. Instead, she lay down on the floor beside Pia's chair, sensing an ally.

The conversation flowed freely, the friends exchanging news and stories, sometimes talking over one another and punctuated by much laughter, until Abbey drew everyone's attention.

'Now, I may have had an ulterior motive in bringing you all together tonight, although of course I don't really need an excuse to spend time with my best friends, but there is something I wanted to tell you all.'

Lizzie's eyes widened and then swept around the room, snagging on Pia's, and it was as though they both came to the same realisation at the same moment. An air of expectation rippled around the room as they waited for Abbey to go on.

'Well, the thing is...' Abbey paused deliberately, revelling in the moment, taking in all the rapt faces. 'Sam and I are expecting a baby.' There was a collective whoop of joy from

Lizzie, Katy, Rhi and Pia, and everyone jumped to their feet to congratulate Abbey, whose smile lit up her entire face. 'I wanted you to hear it from me.'

'How wonderful,' gushed Lizzie.

'I did tell Dad today, but I swore him to secrecy. I didn't want it to spoil the surprise tonight. I hope you won't be too cross with him, or me?'

'Not at all. Although it does explain why he was acting strangely before I left. I even said to him, "What's got into you?" He was walking around like the cat who'd got the cream. I thought it might be because he had the house to himself for the evening, but now I know better. I can just imagine how delighted he was, how delighted we all are.'

'Let me top up our drinks,' said Abbey.

'You sit down,' said Katy, laughing. 'I'll do it. You need to get all the rest while you can because you won't get any when the baby arrives.'

'I'm on the sparkling elderflower,' Abbey called as Katy went in the direction of the kitchen in search of the drinks. 'Honestly, I can't believe not one of you noticed.'

Pia went across to Abbey and wrapped her in a hug. 'Honestly, I'm so happy for you and Sam. That's the best news ever.'

'Thanks, Pia. It's exciting and scary. It happened much quicker than we were expecting, but we're thrilled. Sam is a bit punch drunk by the whole thing. I'm not sure it's actually sunk in yet, but I guess we'll be getting used to the idea very soon.'

'How are you feeling?' Pia paused to look at Abbey properly for the first time this evening. Although it was far too early to see any bump (Abbey's tummy was as annoyingly flat as ever), the freckles on her face seemed much more noticeable, giving her a healthy glow, and her eyes shone as though she held the answer to a mysterious secret. 'You look... beautiful.'

'Aw, thanks. I feel great. No early-morning sickness yet, just very tender boobs. They're a strictly no-go area at the moment, much to Sam's disappointment.' Abbey laughed. 'Anyway' – she lowered her voice – 'how's life with you and Jackson? I hope Rhi didn't put her foot in it mentioning Tara; she doesn't mean to be rude. She's just very direct at times.'

'No, not at all. Besides, I'm always happy to talk about the hall and Jackson. I can see why people might be interested.'

'Did you get to the bottom of what happened with Tara, on Jackson's recent work trip?'

'Oh, that was something of nothing.' She wasn't deliberately lying, just glossing over the truth. 'It's all fine. He's got a lot on his plate at the moment. The events at the hall seem to have taken on a life force of their own so no sooner do we have one out of the way, then we're working towards the next one, and then there's all his public speaking and charity engagements too. I think he's just been a bit preoccupied.'

Abbey nodded. 'I knew it would be something like that. You two are so good together, but I can imagine Jackson may not always be the easiest person in the world to live with. Am I right?' There was a smile on Abbey's face, and a glint in her eye.

Pia grinned. 'He can be demanding, admittedly, but he's actually a really good boss, despite what his surname may suggest. Most of the time he's a real sweetie, does nearly all of the cooking, and as long as we do everything his way, then he's entirely happy.' Her laughter rang out, but it wasn't that far from the truth.

'Well, it's wonderful to see you looking so happy.'

'I am happy. I love Jackson. I think I probably have done ever since we were teenagers, but I'd pushed those feelings to one side, never thinking that we would actually see each other again, let alone get back together.' She locked eyes with Abbey, and her friend clasped her in a hug again. It didn't matter that she hadn't confronted Jackson over Tara. She trusted him implicitly, she'd come to realise. It was only her own insecurity that played with her mind occasionally and caused her to doubt the happiness she'd found at the hall. She thought of her mum and what she would counsel in this situation. *Stop worrying and just enjoy the moment*, she could hear her saying, and that's exactly what she intended to do.

She only hoped her gut instinct wouldn't let her down this time.

17

Pia peered out of the window to see Jackson's car waiting. She gave Abbey one last hug, with a promise that they would get together soon, and said her goodbyes to the others.

'Hope we'll see you all on Bonfire Night up at the hall?' she called on the way out.

'We're looking forward to it.'

In the car, Pia leant over to kiss Jackson on the cheek, catching a whiff of his subtle aftershave, and glimpsing the lazy half-smile on his lips, together a dangerous combination. She suppressed a smile, wondering if his ears had been burning tonight and what his reaction might be if he knew exactly what they'd been saying.

'Good time?'

'Yes, it was fun.' In all the years she'd been caring for her parents, she'd turned down so many social invitations, either because she was worried about leaving her mum or dad behind, or knowing that she probably wouldn't enjoy herself anyway. Now, she was grateful to have the opportunity to make up for lost time. Not that she would ever call herself a social butterfly.

She was too much of a home-bird for that. Sometimes, though, like tonight, it was good to get out and have a laugh and she felt reenergised from the occasion.

'Rhi wanted all the gossip on what it was like living at the hall with you. She seemed to think you were some kind of really cool country squire and...' She paused, making a gesture of quote marks in the air. '...quite the catch.'

'Spot on, then, eh? What did you tell her?'

'That you were a really demanding and a terrible boss.'

'Great. That'll fuel the local gossip at least,' he said with an eye-roll.

Pia laughed at his dramatic response. 'No, I said how lovely you were and how lucky I was to have ended up living and working at Primrose Hall.'

'Luck has nothing to do with it. You're working at the hall based purely on merit, although one of the perks, of course, is sleeping with the boss.' Jackson laughed, before noticing the horrified expression that spread over Pia's face. 'I am joking.'

'Rhi said she remembered meeting Tara and mentioned how glamorous and friendly she was.' Pia had tried to keep her tone light, and she glanced across at Jackson's profile as he steered the car around the country lanes but wasn't sure she'd succeeded.

'What?' He felt the weight of her gaze and briefly took his eyes off the road to look at her. He leant across and laid a hand on her knee. 'Don't let the local rumour mill get to you. Some people have far too much time on their hands. That was then and this is now, right?'

'Yeah,' she said, with a smile that didn't feel entirely natural. Jackson could have mentioned right then that he'd recently met up with Tara, but he'd chosen not to. She couldn't help wondering why. 'You'll never guess what.'

'What?' Jackson's face lit up, probably as relieved as Pia for the change in subject.

'Abbey's pregnant!'

'Wow.' A smile spread across Jackson's face.

'That's why she got us all round there tonight so that she could tell us all together. Honestly, it was such a surprise. I didn't know they were trying, but I can just imagine them with a little one, can't you? They'll make the best parents. Apparently, it hasn't sunk in properly with Sam yet. He's walking around with a daft grin on his face.'

'That's great news,' said Jackson, chuckling. 'I'll make a point of going over to Primrose Woods in the next couple of days to pass on my congrats to Sam.'

Back at the house, Jackson led the way into the kitchen, the low-level lighting creating a warm and cosy welcome, and there was an even more effusive greeting from Bertie, who acted as though he'd been left alone for hours and not a matter of minutes.

'Come here.' Jackson pulled her into a hug. 'We missed you tonight, didn't we, Bertie? The place isn't the same without you here.' His gaze lingered on her face for a moment. 'What do you fancy to drink? More wine? A coffee?'

She slipped off her coat and shoes, tidying them away in the entrance lobby and then pulled out a seat at the kitchen table. 'Do you know what I really fancy? One of your yummy hot chocolates. Is that true that you both missed me, Bertie?' she said, her attention distracted by the dog, who was insisting on some attention.

'Coming right up, madame.' Jackson gave an elaborate flourish of his arm, making Pia laugh. It was hardly her fault she'd grown accustomed to the decadent late-night treat he'd made for her once and that she'd quickly acquired a taste for.

Everything Jackson did was executed with a fine attention to detail and creative flair, and that even extended to making a hot chocolate. She was happy to watch him now as he spooned chocolate mix into a mug, then warmed up some milk in the frother before combining the two, stirring them well. Then he frothed the remaining milk to form a creamy head for the drink. He wasn't finished yet, though, and fetched the spray cream from the fridge, bought especially, and expertly swirled a generous topping of cream on top of the mug. The finishing touches were a handful of bite-size marshmallows and a covering of chocolates flakes, grated from a chocolate bar.

'Wow, that looks seriously wicked. I really hope this is the low-calorie version?'

She took the mug carefully so as not to spill the hot chocolate, the heady aromas making her mouth water. She couldn't resist any longer, and her tongue swept the top of the mug, collecting a mix of cream, marshmallows and chocolate.

'Of course, no calories whatsoever.' Jackson swiped a finger through the cream, depositing a blob on her nose.

'Hey, don't do that, I don't want to waste any,' she said, her tongue performing contortions to attempt to retrieve the cream, which was just out of reach. Jackson laughed and helped her out by wiping the cream off her nose and smearing it messily over her mouth.

'You know, I keep thinking about Abbey and Sam, and their good news. I remember how unhappy she was when she went through that break-up with her ex. Who would have thought that within eighteen months she would be happily married and expecting a baby? It's as though it was always meant to be.' She paused as she heard the words leave her mouth, the same expression that Rhi had used this evening about her and Jackson. 'It's funny how these things work out, isn't it?'

Jackson poured himself a glass of red wine and joined Pia at the table, where she was savouring every mouthful of her hot chocolate. 'I mean, who would have thought that I would reconnect with that skinny, freckly girl I met as a teenager and she would end up making herself indispensable.' A smile played at his lips, and Pia smiled in return, ignoring the niggle of doubt in her stomach that was making a habit of turning up whenever he spoke about how useful she was at his side. He often referred to her as his right-hand woman, how he wouldn't be able to manage without her, but she would much rather hear him say that she was his soulmate, and that he couldn't imagine a life without her.

'I know, it's mad, isn't it? Mind you, had I known it would be you interviewing me that day, I would never have turned up in the first place. So perhaps it's just as well I didn't know.'

'That doesn't bear thinking about, and I'm very pleased that you gave me a second chance and forgave me for my teenage misdemeanours. I mean, you have forgiven me, haven't you?'

'You know I have.' She would need a heart of stone not to have forgiven Jackson when she finally found out the reason for his abrupt departure from the village. He'd confided in her, a few months ago now, that he'd been with his friend Ryan on the night of the accident that had claimed his life. The friends had been out on their mopeds, riding across the fields and lanes, and it was as they went on their separate journeys home that the accident occurred. Jackson had been wracked with guilt, wondering if he could have done anything to prevent it, and, unable to face the rumours and speculation that spread around the village, and the grief of Ryan's parents and family, Jackson did the only thing he felt able to. He walked away, turning his back on his plans, his family and his girlfriend, to start a new life in London.

She reached across the table and took Jackson's hand in her own. If anything, hearing how that night's events had tormented Jackson for years had only increased her love and understanding for the man.

'Hey, Abbey was saying that the four of us must get together soon for a drink or dinner.'

Jackson groaned.

'What? It'll be fun. You like Abbey and Sam, don't you?'

'I do, but I really hope they're not going to turn into one of those awful smug couples who talk about nothing but babies. I don't know what happens to people when they have kids, but they change. It's as though a few brain cells die in the process and they seem to be hijacked by this little monster, who isn't nearly half as cute as their parents insist.'

'I'm certain Abbey and Sam won't be like that,' Pia said, laughing, 'but you could hardly blame them if they were. It must be such an exciting time to be preparing for the arrival of their first child together, don't you think?'

'I guess,' he said with a reluctant smile.

'Can't you imagine that for yourself one day? Having a couple of little Jacksons running about the place?' Pia wasn't about to admit it to him, but she'd certainly imagined that scenario herself. She'd spent far too much time, in those quiet lulls in the office, when her gaze had drifted out of the window and she'd wondered what their children together might look like. They'd have the same dark colouring they shared, with big brown eyes, but would they take after Jackson, or might they be more like her in personality? She imagined they would have a girl and a boy, and she had a growing list of possible names in her head for their future children. Amelia and Jack were top of the list at the moment.

'Ha, I'm not sure about that,' he said dismissively. 'Would it be fair to pass my hang-ups and insecurities on to any offspring? Besides, I've not the first idea on what makes a good parent. I wouldn't know where to start.'

Pia smiled across at Jackson, doing a good job at hiding her disappointment. It was as though she was continually discovering ways in which she and Jackson had different hopes and dreams for the future. Then again, they'd had very different experiences of growing up and maybe that had shaped Jackson's views towards having children.

'That's a shame. I think you'd make a great dad.' And of course, Jackson was in the enviable position of having a beautiful home and the wealth to provide any children he might have with a carefree and idyllic childhood.

'Do you?' He dropped his head to one side as though contemplating that thought. 'It seems like a lot of hassle and worry to me, being a parent. I'm not sure I even like kids. From what I've seen they're noisy, expensive and disruptive. Can you imagine what they'd do this place? Hey, I remember what I was like.'

'No? You don't mean that?' So much for Pia keeping a lid on her emotions. She was aware that her mouth had fallen open and her eyes had widened as she heard the pang of dismay in her own voice.

'I've got everything I want here. The house. My folks. My motorbikes. You.' There was a discernible pause when she couldn't help noticing that she'd come bottom of that list.

'Why? Do you want kids?' he asked, as though the thought had only just occurred to him. He shifted forward in his chair and rested his forearms on the table. It felt like a loaded question coming from Jackson, especially when his gaze wandered her face.

'One day. Yes.' Why should she lie? She wanted to recreate

the happy family life they'd had at Meadow Cottages. It wasn't the worst aspiration to have in the world.

'Right, I see.' He nodded, still observing her closely and she felt her toes curl under the scrutiny of his gaze. She found solace in the remainder of her hot chocolate, lifting the mug to her mouth and slurping up every last trace of chocolate and cream.

Jackson was giving her a none-too-subtle message that he wasn't interested in ever having children and he'd already made his views on marriage very clear. He was laying out his cards so she could be under no misapprehension about his real feelings on the subject and what she could reasonably expect from their relationship. *Fair enough.*

There was a smile on his face as he leant across to wipe away the wayward traces of chocolate and cream from her face with his thumb.

'Look, don't worry. I promise when I see Abbey and Sam, I will pretend to be overjoyed at their news. I mean, I am happy for them. I will ask all the relevant questions and show a genuine interest in the little sprog. How does that sound?'

She nodded and forced a smile. It sounded as though she knew exactly where she stood.

18

'Don't wait up!'

Ronnie had steered the motorhome from its usual space at the rear of Primrose Hall around to the front of the house. The camper rumbled its agreement and Ronnie rested one arm on the opened driver's window, a big smile on her face. Rex leant across from the passenger seat and gave a wave.

'Wish me luck.' He chuckled.

'Drive carefully,' said Jackson, who stood on the gravel driveway, with one arm around Pia.

'Ooh, I hope they have a lovely time, and they don't fall out with each other before they've even left the village,' said Pia as they watched the camper rumble slowly down the long private road.

'Well, there's no guarantee of that.' Jackson laughed.

* * *

Ronnie had been a ball of excitement for weeks, anticipating her trip to Brighton with Rex. She'd given the van a good clean from top to bottom, washing all the cushion covers and fabrics, polishing the woodwork and restocking the supplies. She'd bought in some special teas and biscuits for when they stopped for a break so she was mightily relieved when Rex actually turned up that morning, grabbing him in a grateful hug.

'Well, that's what I call a warm welcome.' Rex staggered backwards exaggeratedly under the weight of Ronnie's effusive greeting.

'I was worried you weren't going to turn up,' she said honestly.

'Would I ever let you down, Ron?'

She bit back on the sharp retort hovering on her tongue. She'd already given herself a stern talking to. There would be no sniping, goading or arguing today. This marked a new step in their relationship and she was determined they wouldn't fall into those old patterns of behaviour.

They took the scenic route avoiding the motorways and pootled through the countryside, stopping to look at some of the villages, taking photos of anything that caught their eye. They chatted the whole way, laughed as though they were kids and ate ham and piccalilli sandwiches that were more delicious than they really should have been. It was a good few hours before they reached the outskirts of Brighton, where they left the camper van in a park and ride facility and hopped onto a bus to take them into the town centre.

'First one to spot the sea wins a prize,' said Rex, peering out of the window of the bus.

'Me, me, me!' sang Ronnie a little later, who had been determined to be the one to catch the first glimpse as they began to make the descent over the hill.

With their rucksacks on their backs, they climbed off the bus and Ronnie shook out her legs and stretched her arms high above her head. Seagulls, on the search for food from unsuspecting visitors, squawked in the sky above them, as though welcoming them to the town.

'It's so lovely to be here,' she said, grabbing hold of Rex's hand. 'I can taste the sea already. What do we want to do first?'

'I am entirely in your hands. Whatever you want to do is fine with me.'

They walked arm in arm down the hill to the seafront, with Ronnie's attention distracted by almost every shop that they passed. She stopped to peer into the restaurants, swooning over the menus, then dragged Rex into a couple of gift shops, handling the trinkets with delight, and she even hovered over the threshold of a tattoo parlour at one point, trying to entice Rex inside with the idea that they should get matching tattoos.

'Don't be daft,' he chided her, dragging her away. 'Now we're here, we want to enjoy the sea air and the sights.'

'Aw, but you used to be so spontaneous. Where's your sense of adventure gone?' she teased him, only half-jokingly.

'Ha! But wasn't that exactly what you complained about back in the day? That you wanted me to be more responsible and reliable. And now that I am, well, I can't win. I'm a reformed man these days, Ronnie.'

They reached the seafront and Ronnie grasped hold of the ornate metal ironwork that ran the length of the promenade, her hair flowing behind her as she looked out onto the horizon. It was a beautifully sunny day, but the cold air whipping off the sea made her cheeks sting and her eyes water.

'Isn't it wonderful? It makes me feel like a teenager again. There's something about being by the coast that is deeply energising and rejuvenating, don't you think?'

'I do. Come on, shall we get down there?'

They wandered, hand in hand, down onto the beach, where

they found a lovely spot that had the old Victorian pier to one side of them and the sea in front of them. Ronnie pulled out a tartan travel rug and laid it on the pebbles, where they sat down and Rex opened up his rucksack and reached for the flask of tea. He poured two cupfuls, handing one to Ronnie.

'This is the life!'

They must have whiled away an hour just sitting there, watching the world go by, chatting about anything and everything until the topic of conversation turned to Jackson.

'You know, despite all our differences over the years, I think we must have done something right to produce that boy. When I think about everything he's achieved, well, it makes me very proud, especially when I remember what he was like as a teenager. Honestly, Rex, I used to despair. He'd be out all night, drinking, smoking, tearing up the lanes on his moped, and then I used to have the school on the phone, either asking where he was or telling me he'd been suspended again. You won't remember those times.' It wasn't meant as a criticism. 'I honestly believed he was destined to end up in a ditch or a prison cell. Of course, he never ever listened to me.' She shuddered, reliving those years. 'Mind you, that's one thing that hasn't changed. He still doesn't listen to me.'

Rex nodded and picked up one of the shiny, glossy pebbles at his side, examining it closely, his hands running over its smooth contours with his thoughts in a different place and time. 'I should have been around to help you. Teenage boys need a positive male role model in their life. It's easy to look back and think how you should have done things differently, but at the time, well, I suppose I thought I was doing him and you a favour by staying away. Mind you, as you say, he's managed to do okay, in spite of us.' He gave a low chuckle. 'Everything he's achieved, though, the man he is today, that has to be down, in no small part, to you, Ronnie. At least you were there for him.'

'Not all of the time,' she said wistfully. 'Not enough of the time, I'm sure Jackson would say. Marie was more like a mother to him than I ever was. Do you know, I sometimes look at Jackson now, with Pia, and it reminds me of you and me when we were that age. Don't you think?'

That caused Rex to laugh out loud. 'Not at all. She's a sweet, calming presence and brings out the best in Jackson. I'm not sure I've ever known them to have an argument. Not like us. We only brought the worst out in each other.'

'Hmm, so you're saying I wasn't sweet and good-natured?'

'Definitely not. More like fiery and passionate, I'd say.'

'Was that such a bad thing? Of course, Jackson is much more handsome than you ever were,' she said disingenuously, with an airy sideways glance. 'But I adored you, Rex. You were the love of my life; that's what I always tell everyone.'

'I know, Ronnie.' Rex took hold of her hand and squeezed it tight. 'I felt the same, but we weren't good for each other. Not then. We had too many bad habits; we were too selfish and too stubborn. It's a wonder we're still talking to each other now.'

'Yeah, but I'm very thankful that we're back in each other's lives.'

'I look back and realise that I wasted too much time on the unimportant things. Like chasing after dodgy business deals or dreams or women,' he said with a raised eyebrow. 'When the most important things in life are your family and friends. It's good, us being together as old friends.'

She nodded, nursing a hope that they were something more than just friends. All those years they'd known each other must count for something.

'I hope you'll want to meet Tom too, one of these days. He's a good kid, although he's really not a kid any more. He's a lot like Jackson. I think the two of you would get on well together. We're the only family he has now so I want him to feel as though he can come to me if he needs to.'

'Thanks, Rex. I'd like that,' she said sheepishly, knowing that she hadn't exactly been overjoyed at the discovery of Tom's existence. 'I wasn't sure you'd want me to be a part of this new stage in your life. You seemed so excited. I suppose I felt threatened by Tom, and how his arrival might impact on your relationship with me and Jackson.'

'You've always been a daft bugger. Why would you worry about that?' He put an arm round Ronnie's shoulder and pulled her into his side, her head dropping onto his chest. It was easier to talk as they sat side by side, their attention taken by the ebbing and flowing of the waves, their gazes lost in the distance.

'It's nice that you've got this opportunity to get to know each other better. It's never too late to reconnect and you're right, family is the most important thing of all. I sometimes wish I had a bigger family, that I'd had more children, but it wasn't to be.' Ronnie fell quiet for a moment. 'Do you think Jackson and Pia will stay together?'

'I jolly well hope so. He'd be a fool to let her go. Pia's good for him, and he seems to adore her too.'

'As long as Jackson doesn't take her for granted or turn his back on her for whatever reason. I've seen him do it before. Poor Tara was heartbroken when he finished with her. None of us saw it coming.'

'I'm sure this time is different, though. Pia and Jackson make a great team and it looks to me as though they're utterly devoted to each other. I'll have a quiet word with him, urge him not to make the same mistakes I did. Although I don't think Jackson needs any advice from me. He's much more sensible and switched on than I was at his age.'

A little later they walked into town and to the Lanes, with Ronnie determined to go into all the gift shops that took her fancy. Rex tagged along, more than happy to wander aimlessly behind, soaking up the atmosphere. When she got distracted in a clothes shop, pulling out all the scarves and draping them around her shoulders in front of a mirror, Rex slipped off to one of the previous shops they'd visited. It only took him a moment or two because he'd known exactly what he was looking for and a little later he returned to Ronnie, who hadn't even noticed that he'd been missing.

'What do you think?' she said. 'This one or this one?' She held two silky, floaty scarves in her hands, one in a bold animal-print design and the other a deep purple floral. She took them in turns to drape over her chest.

'They both look great and suit your colouring. They're not too expensive, are they? Why don't you get them both?'

'That's exactly the right answer,' she said gleefully, rewarding Rex with a kiss on the cheek and then taking both scarves to the till.

After a slow walk along the pier and a visit to the amusement arcades, where they lost all their change in the slot machines, they went in search of their tea and bought fish and chips from one of the shops on the front. They took their paper-wrapped fish supper and found a bench to sit on to eat it.

'Oh my goodness, is there anything better?' said Ronnie, unwrapping the warm package as the aromas of salt, vinegar and crispy batter mingled with sea air. She popped a hot, fat chip into her mouth and savoured its deliciousness. They huddled together, the sky dark now, the lights of the pier creating a magical effect.

'I've got something for you.' After they'd eaten, Rex delved into the pocket of his coat and pulled out a brown paper bag, handing it to Ronnie.

'What's this?' Her hazel eyes lit up with curiosity as she opened the top of the bag and peered inside. 'Oh, Rex, you didn't? What a sweetheart you are. Thank you.'

'Well, you spent enough time looking at them in the shop. It seemed a shame not to take some home with you.'

'Do you know what these are?' she asked with a sidewards smile.

Rex shrugged and shook his head.

'They're rose quartz crystals.' Ronnie pulled a couple of the pink crystals from the bag and showed them to Rex. 'They're beautiful, don't you think? I will cherish these.' She cupped them in her hands and held them up to her chest. 'I've got a little bowl next to my bed that I'll keep them in. Rose quartz symbolises unconditional love and its gentle healing properties are supposed to promote intimacy and help in the rekindling of relationships.' She looked up from the stones in her hands and into Rex's eyes. 'It seems quite fitting that you bought these for me.'

Rex beamed. He knew nothing about crystals or stones and wasn't sure how they could have any special powers, but he was pleased that Ronnie was so delighted with the gift.

'It's getting blimming cold sitting here; do you think we ought to make a move?' Rex wriggled his body with a shiver. 'That chill is just about reaching my bones.'

They walked arm in arm towards the bus stop to wait for the ride that would take them back to the motorhome, but Ronnie didn't want this day to end. It had been the best time she'd had in ages, making her feel alive and young and attractive again. She wanted to savour every possible moment that she could.

'You know, we don't have to go back tonight. We could find a spot to park up and spend the night beneath the stars.'

'Ronnie Moody! I do hope you're not trying to lead me astray.' Rex's faux outrage made Ronnie laugh. 'It wouldn't be the first time. You're forgetting, I know you of old.'

'I think, if I remember correctly, it was you who was always leading me astray back in the day, but I promise to be on my best behaviour tonight if that will make you feel any better. I was thinking it won't be a lot of fun driving home in the dark so we could get a good night's sleep and set off in the morning.'

'Well, there's nowhere else I need to be and I could do with warming up, so it might be nice to get back to the van and have a cuppa.' He held out his arms to Ronnie and she walked into his embrace, and they hugged so tightly that soon the cold night air was forgotten about. She eased herself back from his hold to look into Rex's eyes and she was instantly transported to when she was a young woman and how she had fallen for the young, handsome and wayward man he'd been back then. He was still handsome now, not quite so young and thankfully no longer wayward, but he still had the ability to send goosebumps along her body and make her heart sing.

19

It was late morning and already Pia had visited the dentist for a check-up, had a trim of her long, dark hair at the salon and visited her friend Wendy at Rushgrove Lodge for coffee and cake. She had booked the entire day away from the office, for the purpose of catching up with all those personal tasks that had been building at the bottom of her to-do list.

'Hey, sis. How are you doing?' Connor bowled through the front door of the café, a big smile on his face, and pulled out a chair opposite Pia, after gracing her with a kiss on her cheek.

'Great.' It always lifted her spirits to see her brother. 'Thanks for coming.'

'It's good to see you. How could I turn down an invitation for lunch and an afternoon touring the delights of town.'

'Honestly, I really do appreciate it. What are we having to eat?' she said, handing a copy of the menu to Connor.

They ordered sausage and caramelised red onion toasties and mugs of tea, and chatted easily, catching up on each other's news. Even though he only lived ten minutes away from the hall and she saw him on a regular basis, she missed those times when she was still at Meadow Cottages and he would pop in on his way home from work, and they would natter about anything and everything. Usually, he would get on at her, in a kindly, brotherly way, chivvying her along to get things done, to move forward in her life. There was no need for that now. She'd done exactly what he'd been badgering her to do for months. She'd made a new life for herself at Primrose Hall, but that didn't mean to say that she didn't look back fondly on her old life with all its familiar comforts.

'Do you miss home?' she asked him as he tucked into his sandwich.

'Well, I suppose it's easier for me because I'd left years before you did, but it's strange knowing that another family are now living there. I drive past most days and always look at the house to see how it's doing. They've put new windows and front door in. I suppose it had to happen at some point.'

'Yeah, and I guess it wouldn't be the same there now anyway, with Wendy having moved out too. Still, it's lovely to have such happy memories of the place.'

'And now that our inheritance has come through we can both use that money for our future, which is what Mum would have wanted.'

'That's true. She would be pleased to know that she's helping us out. So have you spent yours yet?' Pia joked.

'No, but it's a big relief knowing it's there. We're going to use some of it as a deposit for a house and the rest we're going to put to one side as a nest egg for when we have a baby. To buy all the paraphernalia you need.'

'That's exciting.' Pia's face lit up. 'I can't wait to be an auntie.' She knew Connor and Ruby were trying for a baby, but to hear her brother talk about it so matter-of-factly made it seem as though it might be within touching distance. 'And might that be soon?'

'Hopefully. We'll just keep on practising until we get it right,' he said, with his familiar chuckle. 'But with Mum's money it means we can do it sooner than we might otherwise have been able to.'

'You've heard Abbey's pregnant, haven't you?'

'I did. That's really good news.'

'It really is,' said Pia wistfully, her attention drifting off to the people sitting in the café.

All around her, people were making plans. Abbey and Sam were having a baby. Rhi and Luke were moving back to the area and choosing a place to live together, and Connor and Ruby were looking at houses and trying for a baby. She was delighted for them all, but it brought home to her that she didn't have as much control over her own life as she wanted to have. She was being swept along on a huge and exciting wave of new opportunities at Primrose Hall and while she was enjoying the ride immensely, she knew that if the wave was to spectacularly crash at any time in the future then she would be left floundering with no idea of what to do or where to go next.

'So tell me, what are we going to see this afternoon?'

'Well, I've got three properties lined up. They're all flats in the same area of town. The estate agent will be showing us around.'

'Okay…' There was a hesitation in Connor's voice. 'And what's your thinking behind this, then?'

'I'm looking on it as an investment. Don't they say you can't lose with property? I want to put Mum's money into something that's a safe bet and will hopefully increase in value over the years.'

'So, what will you do, rent it out?'

'Yes, I think so.' To be honest she hadn't thought much beyond buying a property. She saw it as a bolt-hole, somewhere that she could call her own, her plan B if things didn't work out. Only Connor's questions were making her nervous, a realisation dawning on her that she hadn't given this idea as much thought as she should have done.

'Well, I'm sure you know that there's quite a lot to being a landlord and you would need to get the necessary insurances and contracts in place.' It was as though Connor could read her mind. 'Although I guess if you do it through an agent, they might take care of those things? I expect Jackson knows about this kind of stuff, doesn't he?'

'Er, yes, probably.' Suddenly she felt unnerved, a heavy weight pressing on her chest. 'As I say, it's early days so I'm just investigating the possibility at the moment.' The mention of Jackson troubled her even more. She hadn't told him that the probate had been finalised or of her plans to buy a flat. It wasn't as though she was deliberately hiding it from him. It was just that she wasn't sure she was ready for that conversation even if she knew Jackson would only be supportive of her plans.

After lunch, they met up with the estate agent, who took them along to the first property, a two-bedroomed first-floor flat in a block of twelve. As soon as Pia walked through the outer doors, she knew this place wasn't for her. There was nothing wrong with the flat. It was nice and airy, with spacious bedrooms, and would only need a lick of paint to refresh it, but there was no way she would be spending her mum's precious money on a soulless flat that she felt no connection to.

The two other flats they visited evoked the same feelings in Pia. She couldn't imagine living in either of the properties, and she certainly couldn't imagine Bertie settling there either. Would it be fair to keep a big dog like Bertie in a flat, and perhaps there were regulations that might prevent her from doing so anyway? She had no intention of moving out of Primrose Hall any time soon, but she had to consider the possibility that she might need to one day, and wouldn't it be better to have a place ready and waiting? An anxiety spread around her body and her head was a rush of conflicting thoughts. Had she given this idea the proper thought and research it required? she wondered.

The trouble was she'd been spoilt. Living in a country manor house that had been completely refurbished meant she had every comfort and luxury at her fingertips. The kitchen, although light and spacious, was the cosy hub of the house where everyone congregated. There was a drawing room with big comfy sofas that they used if they had guests, a formal dining room, a cosy snug where Jackson, Pia and Bertie snuggled up together of an evening to watch TV, and there was the office too, not to mention the guest suites. How could the properties she was viewing today ever compare to the hall?

'So, what are your thoughts?' the estate agent asked keenly after they'd seen all three flats. 'Do you have a favourite? You know, it's always worth making an offer. All three buyers are keen to sell.'

Her thoughts were that she really didn't want to be here right now, doing this, because her heart wasn't in it. She didn't want to live alone in a flat in a busy street with only Bertie for company. And she certainly didn't want to be a landlord with all the associated problems that might bring. For all the warm grandeur of the hall, it wasn't the house and all its well-appointed luxuries that she would miss so much as the sense of belonging that came from being part of the Primrose Hall family. She couldn't even contemplate the thought of not living and working with Jackson. She turned towards the estate agent.

'You know, I'm not entirely sure that they're quite what I'm looking for at the moment. I think I need to have a rethink about my requirements if that's okay?'

He nodded and gave a tight smile, and she actually felt sorry for him. She hadn't intended to waste anyone's time, but at least the afternoon had been helpful in making her realise what she didn't want, even if she was no further forward in what she should do with her inheritance.

'Thanks for coming, Connor. I really appreciate it, even if it turned out to be a bit of a wasted afternoon.'

'Not at all. It's not often we have brother/sister bonding time, just the two of us. To be fair, I don't think any of those places would have been right for you. Perhaps you need to sit down with Jackson and decide between you the best way to proceed.'

Yes, perhaps she should, but Jackson was incredibly busy and had much more important matters on his mind. Besides, this wasn't business-related. It was a personal affair and she wanted to get it straight in her own head before she spoke to Jackson about it.

'That reminds me. Jackson and I were chatting about Christmas. How do you feel about coming to us this year? Ronnie and Mateo will be there, and there could be some others too so it should be fun with all of us mucking in on the day.'

'Yeah, that sounds great.'

She'd never spent a Christmas without Connor popping in and she didn't want to start this year, so she was relieved at his positive response.

'I'd love to. Obviously I'll need to run it past Ruby first, but I'm sure she'll be up for it.'

'I can't wait. Can you imagine what the hall will be like at Christmas? Just magical. We've already got four Christmas trees ordered and I may have gone a bit mad ordering in the decorations too.' She grimaced and lifted her shoulders to her ears. 'Jackson's talking about getting a goose and a turkey, and a ham, so there'll be plenty of food, but I've told him while I don't mind helping out, he'll have to wrangle all those birds in the oven.' She laughed. 'I've offered my services on veg duty.'

Connor laughed too, looking at his sister with an indulgent smile on his face. 'You've always loved Christmas, haven't you?'

'Yep. It's my favourite time of year. It just reminds me of being a kid, peering out of the bedroom window, hoping to catch a glimpse of Santa on his sleigh, finding a stocking at the end of the bed and having all the family and neighbours round on Christmas Day. Mum and Dad always made it so special, didn't they, and I want to continue that tradition going forward.'

Suddenly her mood felt lighter, and she realised that she needed to put the idea of buying an investment property onto the back burner until the new year at least. Her energies would be much better focused on something more positive and uplifting, like preparing for the upcoming festive season. That seemed to Pia a much better proposition.

20

'Didn't I tell you it would be fine?' Jackson squeezed Pia into his side as they stood behind the cordon, watching the flames of the bonfire as it crackled and blazed into the air. It was bitterly cold but it didn't seem to matter when they were wrapped up in their big coats and hats and woolly mittens, watching the display. The fireworks were mesmerising, making coloured rainfall in the sky and, as Jackson had promised, there were no loud bangs or roars, just a few fizzes and whooshes, which Pia was sure wouldn't disturb the animals at all. Poppy had come along tonight to keep an eye on Little Star and Twinkle all the same, and Ronnie had volunteered to dog-sit Bertie in the house as she was quite happy being inside in the warm rather than standing outside in the cold.

'Wheee!' Little Rosie and her brother, Pip, had come along with their parents, Katy and Brad, to join in the fun.

'Make sure you keep your sparkler at arm's length,' Lizzie told her granddaughter, while Katy bent down on her haunches and held Pip's sparkler with him, waving it around in the air.

The children's faces were rapt as they watched the fireworks glow and spark in their hands.

Abbey and Sam were there too, enjoying the spectacle, while gathering some warmth from the mugs of fruit punch in their hands.

'How are you feeling now?' Pia asked her friend.

'Eugh.' Abbey groaned. 'I knew I was tempting fate when I last saw you. The morning sickness has arrived with a vengeance, which is no fun whatsoever. Lizzie assures me it won't last for long and I'm keeping my fingers crossed she's right. I can't complain too much, though, because Sam is taking good care of me.'

Pia was thrilled to hear her friend sounding so happy and positive, despite the sickness.

'Abbey!' Jackson finished his conversation with some friends, and then turned to greet Abbey and Sam. 'Congratulations. What wonderful news. I'm delighted for you both. You must be incredibly excited; Sam was telling me that it took you a little by surprise, but the best possible surprise, eh?'

Pia smiled as Jackson and Abbey hugged. She hadn't doubted for one moment that Jackson would be absolutely charming and show delight in their friends' news even if he'd admitted that babies weren't his favourite topic of conversation.

Later, they wandered over to the stables, which were decorated with strings of fairy lights. The aromas of hot dogs and onions wafted in the air from the nearby food stalls, stirring Pia's appetite. She was sorely tempted but they had pumpkin soup, jacket potatoes and sausages waiting for them back at home so she decided to save herself for supper.

It was encouraging to see such a good turnout of people: families, couples and teenagers all enjoying the ambience and the food. Jackson and Pia made slow progress across the grounds of the hall as they stopped to speak to so many friends and neighbours on the way. Jackson had always wanted to share the restored and renovated hall with their neighbours, creating this sense of a community hub, and it was on nights like tonight that it was clear that he had well and truly achieved his aim.

'I haven't seen Rex yet,' Pia said, looking around the throng to see if she could spot him.

'He was here earlier, but he bumped into some old mates. I think they went off for a coffee and a catch-up. I told him we'd see him back at the hall.'

'Mr Jackson?'

Pia looked down to see little Rosie tugging on Jackson's trouser leg, while her dad, Brad, was trying to divert her in the opposite direction, but Rosie was persistent.

'But Mr Jackson, where is the pony and the donkey, Little Star and Twinkle? They're not in the field.'

'Ahh, Rosie, how lovely to see you again.' Jackson nodded hello to Brad before bending down to talk to Rosie. 'I'm afraid they're tucked up in the barn for the night. Sorry about that.'

The little girl pushed out her bottom lip, looking disappointed.

'You know you can always ask your mum or dad to ring us and arrange to come and see the animals on the weekend if you'd like to?'

Rosie nodded with serious intent. 'Will they be here for the Christmas show?'

Jackson smiled.

'You bet they will.'

The little girl clapped her hands together excitedly. 'Because I did name them. Little Star and Twinkle,' she said gleefully, before breaking into a tuneful rendition of 'Twinkle, Twinkle, Little Star'.

'I know you did. And that was very helpful. I'm very grateful, Rosie.'

'Will Santa Claus be at the Christmas show too?' Rosie gazed up at Jackson with wide eyes and an expectant look on her face.

'Santa Claus?' said Jackson, an expression of mild alarm spreading across his features as he turned to look at Pia. She was of no help whatsoever as she simply shrugged and cast him the same wide-eyed look as little Rosie. He blustered for a moment before saying, 'Well, of course Santa Claus will be there, because you can't have a Christmas event without an appearance by the main man himself.'

'Yippee! We can see Santa Claus,' she said, peering around the buggy to tell her little brother, Pip. 'Can't we, Daddy?'

With Rosie suitably satisfied with Jackson's answers, she and her family wandered off in the direction of the sweet stall where they were selling toffee apples, popcorn and marshmallow cakes.

Jackson grimaced. 'I mean, that's something we can organise, right?'

Pia looked doubtful. 'Well, I'm not entirely sure about that,' she said airily. 'From what I've heard, December is Santa's busiest time of the year. I wonder if we've left it too late to get him booked in. You know you really shouldn't go round making big promises to little children when you can't be certain that you can keep those promises. You could be at risk of breaking little Rosie's heart.'

'Hey.' He took Pia's face in his hands, looking intently into her eyes. 'Now, you know I'm not in the habit of breaking people's hearts.' Those dark, attentive eyes that roamed her face now told another story entirely. He kissed her lightly on the lips and she felt the ripples travel the length of her spine. 'Besides, I have the best executive assistant in the country, so if there's anyone who can get Santa Claus to fit us into his schedule, then I know just the right woman for the job.'

'Hmm, you think a bit of sweet-talking will work in this instance? I'm not so sure, you know.'

'Really? Are you telling me I'm losing my touch?' he said, nuzzling his face into her neck and leaving a barrage of kisses there.

'Stop it! No,' she squealed, laughing, enjoying the sensations far too much in the circumstances. Although the evening was as much fun as Jackson had promised it to be, Pia was very conscious that they were working and needed to present a professional front. She extracted herself from Jackson's embrace. 'I can vouch that your touch is just as persuasive as it's ever been.'

'That's just what I wanted to hear,' he said, with a smile that was deliciously flirtatious. 'Really, though? It's a good idea, isn't it? We've got room at the stables to house Santa's grotto and it will be a great attraction for the kids. We can arrange some presents for them too.'

'It's a brilliant idea,' agreed Pia. 'I don't know why we didn't think of it before. We need to get Rosie on the events team at Primrose Hall.'

'She's a sweet kid,' said Jackson with an indulgent smile, 'and her brother, Pip, is pretty cute too.'

'Hey, wait a minute. I didn't think you liked kids?'

'Did I say that? Well, I guess there are some exceptions and if Rosie wants to see Santa Claus when she comes here, then who am I to refuse her request?'

'Okay...' There was a playful tone to Pia's voice. 'And does that only apply to requests from cute kids or... can any of us put in our special requests?'

'Oh absolutely, especially from you.' His voice dropped an

octave. 'I'm waiting to hear them. Tell me what I can do for you, Pia,' he breathed in her ear.

She laughed, enjoying the moment and the sensation of his body, hard and firm, up against hers. She pulled away, looking into his hooded gaze. What would she ask of him? There was only one thing. That she could stay living, working and loving at Primrose Hall forever more? Although judging by Jackson's intense and seductive expression now, she suspected he had something much more immediate and gratifying on his mind.

'Let me give that some very serious thought,' she said, matching his gaze. 'I'll let you know later my list of needs and desires. Oh, and it's very long…'

21

Over at the house, Ronnie had poured herself a glass of red wine, put on a classical music radio station and had positioned herself close to the Aga with Bertie, who was curled up tight in a ball on his bed, oblivious to the celebrations outside. She'd brought with her the patchwork blanket she was crocheting and the book she was reading, a purchase from the recent literary festival, but she couldn't really settle to anything. Her thoughts kept drifting towards Rex and wondering what time he might arrive. Ever since their jaunt to Brighton, he'd been uppermost in her thoughts, and she'd replayed the day in her head, going over their conversations, laughing over remembered jokes, thinking about what they'd seen and what they'd eaten. Staying over had made a special day even more memorable and they'd had a leisurely drive back home the next day when she really hadn't wanted to say goodbye to Rex. She'd seen him again on a couple more occasions since then. They'd been food shopping together in the big supermarket in town, like the old married couple they might have been if things had worked out differently, and then they went to see a live band at the Three

Feathers in Wishwell, singing along and dancing as though they were young newlyweds.

A knock on the door brought Ronnie out of her reverie and she rushed to open it, certain it must be Rex.

'Hello, can I help you?' she asked, when she realised it wasn't. Bertie, who had followed her to the door, gave his customary upright and scary stance, just to let the visitor know who was in charge here.

'Yes, I was looking for Jackson. Is he around?'

'Um...' Ronnie was momentarily taken aback by the man standing on the doorstep, uncertain what to do. 'He's over at the bonfire. Have you been over there yet?'

'Yes, I did have a quick look, but I couldn't find him. Never mind, if he's not here, I'll wander back over.'

'You're welcome to come in and wait. They won't be long.' She hesitated for a second. 'It's Tom, isn't it?'

The man relaxed his features and smiled. 'That's right. How did you know?'

Ronnie laughed and opened the door wide, inviting him inside. 'How could I not know? It took me a moment, but the similarity to your dad and Jackson is undeniable. You're three of a kind, that's for sure. Can I fix you a drink while you wait?'

'If you're sure that's okay. I don't want to intrude on your evening.'

'Not at all. I was just waiting for the troops to return. Come in and keep me company. I'm on the red wine, but I can offer you a beer or white wine, a cup of tea, whatever you fancy?'

'I'll join you on the red wine, thank you. Are you...?' Tom stopped himself, unsure whether he was about to put his foot in it.

'I'm Ronnie,' she said as she poured the wine into glasses. 'Jackson's mother. And Rex's ex-wife. Don't worry. We're pretty good friends these days, despite what you may have heard.' She chuckled to herself. 'It all seems like such a long time ago. Such a shame that we didn't know about you back then, Tom. Who knows how things might have turned out?'

Tom sat down on the cushioned window seat and Ronnie joined him. 'One thing I've learnt over recent months is that it's not helpful to look back and think what might have been. It doesn't change anything and just fills you with regrets. You have to accept what the reality is, the here and now, and move forward with that.'

'That's easier said than done, though, isn't it? Ooh, I've just remembered. I've got some parkin that I made today. Should we have a slice?'

'Absolutely,' said Tom eagerly. 'Even if I don't have the first idea what parkin is. But I like the sound of it, whatever it is.'

Ronnie laughed and jumped out of her seat, turning off the radio and putting on some pop classics that lifted the mood in the kitchen. She moved her shoulders in time to the music, sashaying across the floor, delighted to have some company. 'Parkin is like a gingerbread cake with golden syrup and treacle, and spices. My mum always used to make it for Bonfire Night.'

'Well, you had me at "cake", so thank you.' Tom looked all around him for the first time, his gaze soaking up the charm of the farmhouse kitchen with its hand-painted cabinets, a rustic old dresser brought to life with an eclectic collection of blue and white pottery, the gleaming Aga, and the overhead oak beams, a wonderful mix of old and new.

'Wow, I knew Jackson had done well for himself, but coming here and seeing the scale of the hall and how stunning everything is, well, it takes your breath away. You must be very proud?'

'I am. Although he's done all this in spite of me.' Ronnie

laughed, before falling silent, her thoughts drifting away. Seeing Jackson and the hall for the first time presented an image of an idyllic lifestyle that didn't show the heartache, hard work and determination that Jackson had put in to reaching his goals. From an outsider's point of view, it might seem that everything Jackson had achieved had come easily, when really the opposite was true.

'This is delicious, by the way,' Tom said, munching on another slice of cake. 'I am definitely a convert to parkin.'

Ronnie beamed under Tom's compliments. Rex had been right. Tom was a genuinely affable guy and she wasn't sure why she'd ever thought he might be a threat to her or their life at the hall.

'Ha, I suppose I must be a bit of a disappointment to Dad,' he said, only half-jokingly. 'I don't have a country mansion or a hugely successful career to show for myself, but one out of two sons isn't bad, is it?' This time Ronnie definitely heard the touch of bitterness in his words.

'Now, don't go thinking like that. I know for a fact that Rex is absolutely delighted to have you in his life. He doesn't stop talking about you. He's really very proud.'

Tom dropped his gaze to study his clasped hands, lost in his own thoughts for a moment until they were interrupted by what sounded like someone trying to barge their way through the front door. It was followed by some insistent knocking.

'Hang on a minute. I'm coming, I'm coming.' Ronnie pulled open the door and a rush of cold air swept in. 'Oh, I might have known it was you. What's the emergency?'

'I was just impatient to see you, that's all my lovely. You can't blame a man for that, can you?'

'Hmm, you old charmer, you! Anyway, you'll need to be on your best behaviour tonight because we have a visitor.'

Rex's face screwed up in confusion briefly and then changed into an expression of delight when he spotted Tom in the kitchen. 'Well, this is a lovely surprise. Glad you could make it, son.'

Tom got up to greet his father and the two men hugged fondly, Rex patting Tom's back.

'Did you get to see the fireworks?'

'I did. It was a brilliant display and I had a wander around the stables too. It's quite the set-up Jackson has here. I had a look out for you both, but couldn't find you, so I decided to come across to the house. Ronnie has been keeping me entertained.'

'That's good to hear.' Rex flashed her a grateful smile. 'Jackson should be back soon. Every time I spotted him, he was talking to someone, so he's probably got waylaid.' He slipped his coat off and rubbed his hands together. 'It's blimmin' freezing out there. Something smells good, though.'

'There's sausages and jacket potatoes in the Aga, and some soup on the hob, so as soon as Jackson and Pia are back we can get supper on the table. There's some parkin, if you fancy some? And what would you like to drink?'

'I've not had this for years,' said Rex, helping himself to a slice of cake. 'I'll have a cuppa if there's one going, please.'

Ronnie popped on the kettle and while she waited for it to boil, she opened another bottle of red wine and topped up her glass and Tom's. They moved across to sit at the kitchen table, close to the warmth of the Aga, the lighting low and the mood relaxed and convivial. Conversation bubbled between them. Ronnie listened interestedly, gleaning snippets about Tom's life and discovering the ways in which he was so similar to his father, and his brother too.

It was a while later when Jackson and Pia came back, their

high spirts outside heralding their arrival even before they'd come through the door.

'Sorry, guys. You must be starving. You should have started without us. We got caught up chatting with everyone.' Jackson took his coat off and helped Pia off with hers, taking them out to the boot room to hang them up, talking all the time. 'Seems like everyone had a good time, though. Another event that will become an annual feature on the Primrose Hall calendar even if my faithful, and very glamorous, assistant here wasn't keen on the idea in the first place.'

'It wasn't that I wasn't keen, it was just that I was worried about the animals and how they might react. Now I know they were absolutely fine,' Pia said, laughing, as Bertie danced around their feet demanding their attention, 'then I'm more than happy to make it an annual event. It was a great evening.'

As they both finished seeing to the demands of Bertie, they looked up together and it was only then that Jackson realised Tom was there, listening to their every word.

'Hey, Tom, what a surprise. It's great to see you. I hoped you'd be able to make it and I even said to Pia out there it was a shame that you hadn't come along, and here you are. Welcome to Primrose Hall,' he said expansively, before going over to shake Tom's hand. 'Where are my manners?' He turned to beckon Pia over. 'You've not met Pia before, have you? Let me introduce you. Pia, this is Tom.'

Tom stood up, a genuine smile on his face. 'Hey, Pia. It's great to see you again.'

22

For a moment Pia was completely flummoxed. She smiled and said hello in return, but she couldn't for the life of her remember where she'd met Tom before. It was like seeing someone you knew only vaguely, like your dentist, out of context in a different setting entirely.

Jackson looked from Tom to Pia, his brow slightly furrowed. 'You two know each other already?'

'Yes.' The realisation came, along with a huge sense of dread, as Jackson looked at her questioningly. She faltered, unable to find the words to explain. She needn't have worried because Tom jumped in to help her out.

'I wouldn't say we really know each other, but I showed Pia around a few flats in town the other day. With...' Tom's voice faded away, just a moment too late, as he realised he might be on the verge of putting his foot in it.

Jackson's expression couldn't have been more puzzled had he said they'd met on a spaceship, but Pia sensed the cloud of tension that suddenly permeated the room.

'With Connor. I was with Connor. My brother,' she added for Tom's benefit.

'Ah, okay, that makes much more sense now,' Tom said, looking relieved.

'You were looking at flats? With Connor?' Jackson repeated.

'You see, that's what I'm doing right now,' Tom explained, 'helping out an estate agent's in town with the viewings. I realised when I jacked in my job that I probably needed something to tide me over until I decide what to do next. It's a casual part-time arrangement, which suits me fine at the moment.'

Jackson nodded, but he hadn't been listening to what Tom was saying. He was focused on Pia and what she wasn't saying.

'Yes, I hadn't got round to mentioning it because...' That stopped her. Why hadn't she mentioned it to Jackson? She'd intended to, but after she'd been to see the properties with Connor, she'd realised that she hadn't thought the idea through properly. Did she really want all the stress and worry that came from being a private landlord? There were probably better ways of using her inheritance to secure her future. She'd put the idea out of her head then and determined to look at it again in the new year. There had been no point in telling Jackson because really there was nothing to tell.

Only right now he was looking at her as if he needed an explanation. How could she possibly explain, with Rex and Ronnie and Tom here, when they should be celebrating Bonfire Night?

'Sorry, I don't understand. Why has Connor been looking for flats? I thought they were looking for something larger. A three-bed property on that new estate on the edge of the village?'

At this point, Rex and Tom discreetly sat back down at the kitchen table, making their own chatter, pretending not to be listening in on the awkward conversation between Jackson and Pia.

'Right. Should I start serving?' Ronnie busied herself taking the sausages, jacket potatoes and fried onions out of the Aga. She clattered bowls onto the table, knives and forks, and a selection of condiments. 'Who would like some soup to start with?'

Jackson held up his hand, as though urging Ronnie to wait. There were clearly more important matters on his mind.

'Yes, they are.' Pia cleared her throat. 'We were actually looking for something for me, would you believe?' She was trying to inject a touch of light-heartedness into her words, but Jackson wasn't smiling. 'I quickly realised, though, that I hadn't thought it through properly. I should have mentioned it...'

Pia squirmed in her boots, annoyed with herself that she felt guilty and ashamed by her own reaction. It wasn't as though she'd done anything wrong, but an uneasy, prickly sensation ran the length of her spine. More than anything it hurt to see the disappointment in Jackson's eyes.

'Yes, you should have mentioned it. What the actual hell?' From the rigid set of his shoulders and the hard glint in his eye, there was no mistaking the quiet anger simmering beneath his words.

'Look, let's talk about this later. It really isn't important.' Pia reached out to touch his arm, but he yanked it away. Her thoughts drifted to earlier that evening, their delicious flirtation with a promise of what was to come when they were finally alone together. 'Come on, let's not spoil a lovely evening.'

'What? And you think it's me who's done that? We're supposed to be partners, Pia. We're not meant to have secrets.'

'It wasn't a secret.'

'Of course it was a bloody secret if I didn't know the first thing about it!'

'Hey, come on, Jackson. Don't give Pia a hard time.' Tom pushed back his seat, stood up and strode across to Jackson and Pia. It was only then that Ronnie noticed the brothers were the same height and build, their evident masculine physicality filling the room.

'It was no big deal,' Tom said. 'We looked at three flats and I couldn't tempt Pia with any of them,' he said, in his own attempt to lighten the mood.

Jackson cast him a sharp glance. 'With all due respect, I think I'll be the judge of whether it's a big deal or not so perhaps you'd do well to keep your nose out of business that you know nothing about.'

'Whoa, hang on. I was only trying to help.' Tom held up his palms to Jackson and placed himself between Jackson and Pia, which only served to rile his brother even further. Standing shoulder to shoulder, Jackson grasped Tom's forearms and forcibly moved him out of the way, causing Tom to stumble sidewards. As he lost his footing, he tripped over Bertie's water bowl and folded over, landing in a heap on the floor.

'Jackson!' Pia chided him and Ronnie rushed to Tom's side.

'What the bloody hell is your problem?' Tom staggered to his feet, looking accusingly at Jackson, and grabbed hold of his lapels, and in a matter of seconds the situation had escalated with the two brothers grappling around the kitchen, hurling insults at each other.

'For goodness' sake,' shouted Rex. 'Will the pair of you stop it. You're acting like a couple of kids.' He pulled them apart, scowling at them both.

'I won't be told what to do or what to think in my own home. Especially from... from...' Jackson stopped himself from saying something he might eternally regret. 'From someone I barely know.'

'Right, cheers for that. Well, I should go. I knew it was a bad idea coming here in the first place.' Tom went back across to the table to collect his wallet and keys.

'No, don't go,' Rex, Ronnie and Pia said as one.

'You can't drive,' said Ronnie, putting her hand over Tom's keys. 'You've had far too much to drink.'

'Don't worry, I'll call a taxi. I'll collect the car tomorrow. If that's all right with you,' Tom said pointedly to Jackson.

'You can't go, not like this,' Rex butted in. 'Come on, boys, please, don't fall out over something stupid.'

'This has got out of hand.' Pia tried to placate Jackson, but she knew that his mood had darkened and there would be no getting through to him now. 'Let's all take a breather and have some dinner. I don't know about anyone else but I'm starving.'

'Don't leave on my account,' Jackson told Tom gruffly. 'Stay for dinner. But if you'll excuse me, I'm not hungry.'

Jackson waltzed out the room. Pia dashed after him. She knew exactly what he had in mind to do, but she wouldn't let him, not tonight, not when they'd worked so hard to put on such a brilliant evening for the community. They should be sitting down with Jackson's family to enjoy the success of their hard work, but instead Jackson wanted to storm out the door, hop on his bike and disappear out into the cold night. The same way he dealt with all his problems. She caught up with him in the boot room, grabbing hold of his arm. This time he didn't pull away.

'Jackson, stop acting like a spoilt child. You're over-reacting. There was no need for all of that!' She gestured to his family in the other room, annoyed that what could have been a lovely evening had turned sour. She hated it when he got like this. She could see him visibly withdraw into himself, could sense his emotional defences come up, but this was no way to deal with their problems. 'We'll talk about this, but not now. Please...' She grabbed his hands. 'Don't go. I'll worry about you, out on the bike on a night like tonight. It's freezing out there.' She could hear the plaintive tone to her voice, but she didn't care. It wasn't fair of Jackson to make her worry like that. And honestly, he should know better. There was already one motorbike accident that had impacted hugely on his life. Did he really want to risk another one? 'Besides, your brother's here. You should make an effort to smooth things over. For your dad's sake.'

'What an idiot. He's no brother of mine. Who the hell does he think he is, turning up here, giving me the benefit of his advice? I've done without him for the last thirty years. I can do without him for the next thirty years. He's nothing to me.'

'Don't be like that. He was only trying to help. I think he feels bad that he was somehow part of something that clearly upset you. None of this is Tom's fault. You need to get back in there now and apologise.'

He exhaled a big sigh, the tension escaping him as he ran a hand through his hair. He grimaced, shaking his head. 'Right, I'll do this for you. For Dad, but I still don't understand why you didn't tell me, Pia. Unless you have some kind of plans that you don't want me to know about? Is that what this is?' He nodded, as though chewing over that possibility in his head, his gaze scrutinising her face.

She felt the weight of his disapproval as if he was seeing her now in a totally different light.

'Are you not happy here? Is that why you're looking for somewhere else to live?'

'No!' She was quick to reassure him. 'I've never been happier, but...' She faltered again, still unable to find the right words. 'I'll explain. We'll sit down together and talk about it later, but it's not important, really it isn't.'

He shrugged and gave a dismissive snort, clearly not believing her protestations for a moment.

'It's important to me,' said Jackson. 'If this relationship has any hope of working, then we can't afford to have secrets between us, don't you see that?'

She understood entirely, but she wasn't the only one with secrets, was she? Annoyance crept beneath her skin. How dare he make her feel bad when she'd done nothing wrong. She was tempted to bring up Tara and why he hadn't mentioned seeing her again, but the cold glint to Jackson's eye and the edge to his voice told her that would only make a bad situation much, much worse.

23

Much to Pia's relief, when they returned to the kitchen, Ronnie and Rex had managed to talk Tom round, and he'd agreed to stay. He was now busy helping himself to two fat sausages from the dishes of food in the centre of the table.

'Look, Jackson,' he said, when he spotted his brother re-entering the room. He stood up from his place. 'If you want me to go, I will. Just say the word.'

'No, it's fine. Stay.' He plastered on a smile. 'You're welcome here. Sorry about earlier. I shouldn't have taken my frustration out on you.'

'No apology required,' said Tom.

Pia glanced across at Jackson and her heart twisted, knowing how much it would have taken for him to admit to such a thing. Her emotions were fluctuating between anger at Jackson's hypocrisy and compassion for the fact that she'd hurt him unintentionally.

'Well,' said Rex, chuckling, 'I suppose you two are only making up for lost time. If you'd grown up as kids together there would have been plenty of scraps. It's what brothers do, isn't it?'

Pia was glad that the food provided something of a distraction and that Ronnie was chatting on gaily, telling Tom all about her and Rex's recent trip to Brighton.

'Ronnie's thinking of heading off to the continent in the new year in the van, aren't you?' Pia said to Tom, desperate to get the conversation onto safe ground.

'Really? That sounds like a proper adventure.'

'Well, it's just in the planning stages at the moment. And I could do with a travelling companion,' she said, looking pointedly in Rex's direction, 'so I shall have to see what I can get organised.'

'Ronnie's always had a case of the wanderlust. She's never liked to stay in one place for too long,' said Rex.

'Ain't that the truth,' Jackson grumbled. 'Ronnie was more often away than she was at home when I was a kid.'

'I'm not sure that's true,' she protested. 'I was probably away six weeks at a time. He's never quite forgiven me, though. Besides you always loved being with Marie.'

'Marie?' Tom looked for answers around the table.

'She was my sister,' Ronnie told Tom. 'She adored Jackson. She never had children of her own, so she looked upon him as her own. She would take him into town most Saturdays and buy him one of those collectible figures, ugly monster things they were, and she'd treat him to lunch. She'd make a proper fuss of him on his birthday and at Christmas too. You liked to get out in the garden and help her with the planting, do you remember, Jackson?'

'I do indeed,' he said, barely giving anything away.

'We lost her a few years ago now to cancer. She left a big hole in our lives.' Ronnie felt able to be candid with Tom. It was as though they were old friends, that this wasn't the first time they'd all sat together around the kitchen table at Primrose Hall.

He was friendly and easy to talk to and she had to wonder why she'd ever felt threatened when she'd first heard about his existence. It was a shame that Jackson wasn't quite so forthcoming, but Pia was only relieved that he was sitting at the table trying to be civil, even if he wasn't quite succeeding at it.

'Sounds as though you had a decent childhood, Jackson?'

'Yeah, Marie was like a second mum to me. Ronnie was away a lot, I barely saw Dad and I hated school, so it was good to have someone I could rely on. I had some good mates around here too.'

Rex sighed at the implicit criticism, and Ronnie gave a resigned shake of her head.

'I know we might not have been the best parents, Jackson, but we always loved you. Both of us. Even when we weren't around. And let's face it, who's childhood was perfect?' Rex stated.

'Not mine for sure,' said Tom. 'I mean, Mum and I were very close, even though she decided not to tell me the truth about my real father. That hurts. I still can't understand why, but she must have had her reasons. I mean, I would have liked to have been part of a big family, but it wasn't to be. When my dad left, he remarried and started a new family. I always wondered why he'd left me behind and now I know. He never really had any real love or felt any obligation towards me.'

'Families come in all shapes and forms, though, don't they? We didn't have a big family, it was just the four of us, but we were very close. Now it's just my brother, Connor, and me, and I do miss that really tight bond that we shared with our parents. I guess nothing stays the same forever. Connor and Ruby are making plans to start their own family, and I suppose I've found my new family here at Primrose Hall, which has been lovely. Of course, I'd like to have a family of my own one day, to recreate the sort of childhood my parents gave to us.' She didn't look at Jackson, but she felt his gaze flash across to her as she spoke. 'What about you, Tom? Would you like to have children one day?' Pia hoped she wasn't being intrusive, but it felt like a natural follow-on to their conversation.

'Not sure,' he sighed. 'I've just split up with my long-term girlfriend so I can't see it happening any time soon. Besides, I would have to be certain that any new relationship was pretty solid, and would go the distance before I even considered bringing children into it. And can you ever be certain about that?'

Tom's question was met with a few mumbles and shrugs from the others, but Pia was determined to put a positive spin on it.

'No, you can never be entirely certain. None of us know what lies ahead for us. But if you meet the right person then taking a chance on love and a future together has to be worth opening your heart up for. Don't you agree?'

Ronnie nodded, but Pia wasn't sure if Jackson's expression was one of wide-eyed bemusement or if it had actually been an eye-roll of incredulity.

It didn't escape Pia's notice that the brothers shared the same sceptical view of marriage and family. She supposed it was understandable knowing that their childhoods had been marred with uncertainty and insecurity, but it made her sad to think that they should both be so cynical about something that could potentially offer them a happy future. Maybe she viewed it in a different light because her own upbringing had been so settled and comforting. Was she looking back with rose-tinted glasses? Perhaps she'd been sheltered from some of the harsher realities of family life, and it could never be as perfect as she imagined it to be, but that wouldn't stop her from trying to recreate that same loving home environment that she'd experienced as a child.

Tom went on. 'I would hate for any kids of my own to go through what I went through. Growing up with that sense of being an outcast, of not being quite good enough, then finding out those feelings of uncertainty were justified, coming from a background of lies and secrets.'

Jackson nodded, his heavy pause and the ensuing silence all too noticeable.

'I understand that totally,' he said, in a moment of brotherly bonding. 'If you haven't got complete openness and honesty in a relationship then what have you got?'

Pia looked up at that moment, locking eyes with Jackson, holding his gaze. She agreed with that sentiment entirely, but it had to be a two-way thing.

24

If Pia had been dreading that unavoidable conversation with Jackson, there was a part of her that wanted to get it all out in the open and the air cleared as soon as possible so they could put the matter to one side and move on with their lives. She'd hoped that they would be able to sit down the following morning over breakfast and chat it through reasonably, but she hadn't reckoned on Jackson having other plans.

'I'm going out on the bike,' he'd told her. It was early, far too early for a Sunday. She'd still been curled up beneath the duvet, looking forward to their usual routine of a slow and lazy start to the day, followed by a walk around Primrose Woods before settling at the kitchen table with the newspapers and a full cooked breakfast.

'When will you be back?'

'Not sure,' he'd called. 'This afternoon probably.'

'Don't go, Jackson. We need to...' But it was too late; her words went unheeded as she heard the door slam on his way out.

He hadn't even kissed her goodbye and her heart had

twisted at the cold edge she'd detected in his voice. Hearing the roar of Jackson's motorbike as it departed the grounds only made her feel worse. All she'd wanted was for him to hold her in his arms, and to tell her that everything would be okay, that they could work things out, but he hadn't and now she was left wondering if something significant had shifted between them.

'Everything okay, sweetie?'

Later that morning, after Pia had showered and dressed and she'd walked Bertie over at Primrose Woods, she'd gravitated to the kitchen. There was no joy in having a cooked breakfast for one so she'd made do with a banana and a slice of toast, which she ate glumly, standing up against the worktop. Her face brightened at seeing Ronnie come into the kitchen.

'Yes, fine,' she said, plastering on a smile that didn't match the way she was feeling inside. 'Coffee?'

Ronnie nodded keenly. 'Where's His Lordship, then, this morning?'

'He went out early. I think he must have taken Rex home, or perhaps Tom did, as he's gone too. Jackson said he might be out for a few hours.'

'That's a shame. I was looking forward to us all having a big breakfast together.'

'You're not the only one,' said Pia resignedly. 'Mind you, after last night's tussle between Tom and Jackson, perhaps it's for the best.'

'What on earth got into Jackson?' Ronnie sat down at the kitchen table, resting her chin on her steepled hands. 'Why was he so cross with you?'

'I'm guessing he found it embarrassing to find out something about me from his new brother. I should have told him that I was looking at properties with Connor, but I wasn't sure he'd understand. I called that right, didn't I?' She gave a wry chuckle. 'I've had the inheritance through from the sale of my parents' place and I was just thinking about what I should do with it. I had this idea that I could buy a small property that I could let out all the time I'm living here, but that would be somewhere of my own.' Pia grimaced, realising too late that perhaps she was being overfamiliar with Ronnie. Sometimes she forgot that Ronnie was Jackson's mother, whose loyalties would lie, quite rightly, with her son.

'A bolt-hole, you mean? I understand entirely. I can't see anything wrong with that and neither should Jackson. My mother always used to tell me that every woman should have a little bit of money stashed away. A running-away fund, she used to call it.'

'Don't get me wrong.' Pia was quick to explain her true intentions. 'You know how much I love living and working here, and I've got no intention of going anywhere, but I have to think of my own security. What happens if Jackson and I were to ever fall out, or if he decides that he doesn't want to be with me any more? I'd need somewhere to go.'

'To be honest,' said Ronnie, 'I can't see that happening. Jackson adores you.' Pia's heart swelled to hear those words from Ronnie. She knew Jackson loved her, but it was reassuring to hear it from Ronnie as well. 'That's clear for anyone to see, but I can understand why you would want to make provisions for your own future. It's why I've always loved having the motorhome. I've never been in a position to afford my own house, but buying the van was the next best thing. It is my home now and no one can ever take that away from me. It gives me a great deal of satisfaction and security to know it's sitting there and I can jump behind the wheel and disappear off if I should ever want to.'

Pia nodded. That was the whole point. Unlike Ronnie, she

didn't want a van that she could escape in, but it was the idea of having somewhere of her own. A back-up plan if things should ever be upended. Wasn't that simply being sensible?

'The trouble with Jackson is that he's a control freak. And I'm not speaking out of turn because I would say exactly the same thing to his face. He likes things done on his terms and if they're not then that's when he can dig his heels in and be very stubborn. Mind you, I'm not telling you anything new. You'll know better than anyone what he's like,' Ronnie continued.

That was true. It might be only eight months since Pia had come to work at the hall, and less than that since they'd rekindled their relationship, but you didn't get to work closely with someone every single day not to know their idiosyncrasies and their moods. Jackson could be kind, caring and altruistic, but equally he could be difficult, demanding and unforgiving too.

'I just hope he and Tom are still good after what happened last night,' said Pia.

Ronnie shrugged. 'Who knows with Jackson, but he'd be a fool if he were to turn his back on his brother. I know how much it means to Rex for them both to get along. They don't need to live in each other's pockets, but like we were saying, neither of them have a lot of family so they need to stick together. Besides, he seems like a nice guy, doesn't he?'

'Yes.' Once she'd got over the shock of seeing Tom the estate agent in the kitchen and realising with dread that he was Jackson's brother. Why she hadn't realised it when she'd first met him, she didn't know, but then she'd had other things on her mind. Tom's likeness to Jackson was uncanny, though. 'I dread to think what Tom must have thought of us all. Secrets, disagreements and fights, and that was only in one evening. He probably felt relieved that he hadn't been part of this family growing up.'

'I don't know about that,' said Ronnie. 'I got the distinct

impression that Tom has been trying to find his tribe and I think he might have done that with Jackson and Rex. Besides, you have to expect a few ups and downs in family life. That's only natural. Admittedly, we might have had a few more ups and downs than most, but we're still here together, supporting each other, and isn't that the most important thing of all?'

Pia nodded.

'Don't worry. Jackson might have thrown his toys out of the pram, but I'm sure you'll sort it out, the pair of you. What is it that they say? The best thing about falling out is the making up,' said Ronnie, with a mischievous twinkle in her eye. 'I remember a few of those times with Rex,' she said, pursing her lips and raising her eyebrows.

Pia could only hope that was true and Jackson would be in the mood for talking, listening and making up, and not turning his back on the situation like he had in the past.

25

Pia had spent a productive day in the office tackling her to-do list and was just thinking about taking a break to make a late afternoon mug of tea when she heard a flurry of activity in the kitchen.

'Pia, are you there?' Frank's voice beckoned her and she went hurrying in to find him.

He was standing alongside Mateo with what seemed like a bundle of rags in his arms.

'What have you got there?' she asked.

'We found him caught up in the fencing. Completely stuck, he was. I had to cut him free. His fur is terribly matted. He must have run off from his owner in the woods. He has a tag on, but the engraving is faded; we can't seem to work out what it says.'

'Oh, let me see.' Pia rushed over to see the fluffball in Frank's arms and the dog looked up at her with big, brown, sorrowful eyes. He looked pitiful with his grubby fur and paws, and wore an expression of guilt. He stank too from where he'd clearly been rolling in something unsavoury. 'Hello, little fella, what have you been up to? Your poor owner will be worried sick somewhere. Let me have a look and see if I can find out who you are.'

Gently, Pia put her hands up to the dog's collar and pulled round the silver metal tag. Frank was right. It was barely decipherable, but if she screwed up her eyes and peered very closely she could just make out a name. 'Teddy!' she said triumphantly, and the dog rewarded her by tilting his head and pricking his ears at hearing his name. 'There's a telephone number here. Do you want to jot it down?' she said to Mateo, grabbing a pen and notepad from the dresser and handing it to him. She read the numbers aloud, then she took Teddy from Frank's arms, talking to the dog the whole time, telling him what a good boy he was and how she would make sure he would be returned safely to his owners.

'You're such a sweet boy, aren't you?' she said, tickling him beneath the chin, which elicited a disapproving bark from Bertie. 'Stop it, Bertie. Say hello to Teddy.'

She placed Teddy on the floor, making sure all the doors were closed so he couldn't escape again, and Bertie gave him a good old sniff before Teddy wandered off, doing a tour of his new surroundings. Bertie was most disgruntled by the new interloper, and followed Teddy around, keeping a watchful eye on his movements. Pia watched Teddy closely too, worried that he may have done himself some damage as he'd tried to negotiate the wire fencing, but he seemed none the worse for his adventures.

'He doesn't appear to be hurt, but it doesn't bear thinking about what might have happened if you hadn't found him. It's dark out there now, and if you hadn't rescued him when you did then he might have spent the whole night in the freezing cold. Goodness knows what might have happened to him then. Just keep an eye on him while I ring this number.'

Only Pia didn't get the effusive relief and thanks she might have expected when she finally got through on the phone.

'Not that bloody dog again,' a man grumbled down the line. 'I've told them. No longer at this address. You'll have to take him to the dogs' home. I don't want anything to do with it.'

'I'm sorry.' Pia faltered, not understanding at all. 'Are you not Teddy's owner? It has this number on his collar.'

'I know it does, but she's not here any more. And I can't be expected to look after that mongrel. If she wanted to keep the dog, she should have taken the damn thing with her. Good riddance to both of them, that's what I say.'

'Right, I see,' said Pia, trying to keep calm and read between the lines. 'So am I right in thinking that the owner has moved away? Does she have a forwarding address or number?'

The man on the other end of the phone gave a mirthless laugh. 'She's gone to the other side of the world, love – Australia. She's followed some fella there. And by all accounts she won't be coming back any time soon.'

With that, he slammed the phone down and Pia was left staring into the handset, not quite believing what she'd just heard.

After filling in the blanks for Frank and Mateo, who had been listening in to the conversation intently, she turned to look at the little dog, who was now eyeing up Bertie's bed beside the Aga. Bertie had got wind of Teddy's possible intention and barged his way past the intruder and slumped heavily onto his bed, eyeing the little dog warily.

'Oh, Teddy,' she said, scooping him up in her arms. 'No wonder you were trying to get away from that horrid man, but what can we do with you?' She glanced at her watch. 'I think we'll need to take you to the vet's to have you checked over, but I'm not sure that they'll still be open.'

'They do have an out-of-hours service. I'm sure there'll be a number on the website,' Frank suggested helpfully. 'Or you could always contact the dog warden. I know Sam at Primrose Woods gets in touch with them whenever they find any strays over there.'

'Hmm.' Pia fell silent for a moment, unable to bear the thought of Teddy having to spend the night in a kennel. 'I think Teddy's had enough trauma for one day, don't you? We've tried to return him to his owner, without any joy, so I can't see any harm in him staying overnight here. The poor thing is probably exhausted and hungry. He probably needs to decompress. I can take him along to the vet's in the morning.'

'But he is very stinky,' said Mateo, screwing up his nose and pulling a face. He wasn't the greatest lover of dogs and just about tolerated Bertie, but Pia agreed he might have a point. There was an awful whiff wafting about the kitchen now and Teddy was covered with some very suspect muddy brown patches all over his fur.

'Well, perhaps I'll give him a bath, and feed him, and then hopefully he'll settle down for the night. That's the best idea, I think,' said Pia, already having made her mind up. 'You get off – I'm more than happy to take care of him now.'

Mateo raised his eyebrows, giving Pia a doubtful look, while Frank gave a cheery wave. 'I'll have my mobile on; give me a call if there are any problems.'

Pia couldn't imagine there would be, although it was probably a good thing that Jackson was away this evening. He'd left early on Monday morning to travel up to London for a couple of days of meetings. She'd already spoken to him today, so it was unlikely he would call again. She gave a thought to what he might be doing right now. There were no drinks or dinner engagements in his diary, but who knew what invitations might crop up or who he might bump into at the hotel bar. She sighed, pushing that thought right away, focusing instead on Teddy, who was enjoying the attention he was receiving in her arms.

Jackson might not have been so keen to have a canine visitor staying overnight and would probably have found a solution to the problem of Teddy already. Still, he wasn't here and Pia was very much in charge tonight so they would make the most of the opportunity and she could give Teddy some much-needed TLC. Hopefully even Bertie might come to enjoy spending time with their houseguest. She would worry about what they were going to do with Teddy on a more permanent basis tomorrow.

26

The following morning, Claire, the vet, gave Teddy a thorough going over. She checked his body for any cuts or grazes, felt his underbelly for lumps, looked at each of his paws, and inside his ears and mouth too.

'Well, he doesn't seem to have any injuries this time.' That came as no surprise to Pia, because after a warm bath last night and a supper of some cooked chicken and dog biscuits, Teddy had settled happily on the sofa next to her and slept contentedly through the night.

'This time?' Pia only then jumped on those words.

'We have seen Teddy in here on a couple of occasions before. It's not the first time he's escaped. The last time he was clipped by a car. No serious damage was done, but obviously if he keeps escaping like he does then he might not always be so lucky.'

'Oh.' Pia's hand flew to her mouth, her stomach tumbling at the thought. 'I did call the number on his tag, but the guy I spoke to wasn't very helpful. Seemed like he wanted nothing to do with Teddy.'

'Yes, from what I understand the couple had quite an acrimonious break-up and poor Teddy has been caught up in the fall-out.'

'That's such a shame,' sighed Pia. 'He's such a sweet little dog. I don't know how anyone could turn their back on him.' She picked Teddy up and he looked up at her with a soulful expression.

'Look, I do have the details of his microchip so I need to make a few phone calls before deciding on the next steps. Thanks so much for bringing him in. If you want to leave him with us, then we can take care of everything from here on.'

Pia's expression must have given away her dismay at that idea.

'Of course, if you want to give us a call in a couple of days' time then we'll be able to give you an update on Teddy's condition and where's he gone.'

'But what will happen to him?' She'd been stroking Teddy the whole time. 'Would he be sent to the dogs' home?'

'That seems like the most natural conclusion,' Claire confirmed. 'But don't worry. They're very good and he will be well looked after. They'll make sure he goes to the best possible home.'

At that moment, Teddy looked up at her, his head tilting to one side, his expression full of love, hope and expectancy.

'But he's been through so much and I can't bear the thought of not knowing where he might end up.' There was only the briefest moment of hesitation before Pia spoke again. 'Well, if he's going to the dogs' home, then he might as well stay with me. I know how pushed they are for space and if he comes home with me then it gives all those other dogs a better chance.'

Claire raised her eyes at Pia's dodgy logic. The two women knew each other well enough by now. Pia brought Bertie in regularly for his jabs and his treatments, and Claire visited the hall to see to Little Star and Twinkle when they needed any care.

'You know you don't have to take him just because you feel sorry for him. He's a lovely little chap and I'm sure he wouldn't stay in that shelter for long. Someone will snap him up.'

Pia nodded. That's what she was worried about. If she was going to offer Teddy a home, then she knew she wouldn't be able to take too long thinking about it. She didn't have the sort of time it would take to sit down with Jackson and explain the situation. If she sent Teddy to the shelter and went to collect him in a few days' time, there was every possibility that he could have already found a new home, and Pia would be left sad, forever wondering where Teddy might have ended up. Besides, the little dog was now sitting upright in her lap, imploring her to take him home with those big, dark, soulful eyes.

'No, really. If it's okay with you, then I would very much like to adopt him.'

'If you're absolutely sure,' said Claire, with an indulgent smile. 'Presumably Jackson is happy with this arrangement too?' she said lightly.

'Yes.' Pia answered rather too quickly. 'He loves dogs.' It was no word of a lie.

'Well, it sounds to me, little fella, that you've fallen right on your feet. You'll have plenty of room at Primrose Hall to go exploring and I know you'll be thoroughly spoilt. First, though, I will need to make a couple of phone calls to ensure that the registered owners really do want to rehome Teddy and then we'll be able to go from there. I can give you a call later this afternoon or...' She paused, looking at Pia and Teddy's impatient and expectant expressions. 'Fine, if you go and take a seat in the waiting room, I'll see if I can get through to them now.'

As Pia sat on a plastic chair in the waiting area, she felt a huge swell of love for the bundle in her arms and a bubble of excitement ran through her veins. It was as though Teddy was always destined to be a part of the Primrose Hall family and she felt certain that he would fit into the household as though he'd always been there.

'You're going to have such a lovely life with us,' she promised, tickling him beneath the chin. Bertie's nose might be put out of joint for a few days, but once Pia had sorted out a proper bed for Teddy with his own water and feeding bowls, then she felt certain Bertie would soon adjust and get to appreciate having Teddy around. She swallowed hard, trying to ignore a feeling of unease that swept over her. Perhaps, in hindsight, it wasn't the best time to bring another dog into the set-up at Primrose Hall. She realised she should have spoken to Jackson first, but events, along with her emotions, had run away from her.

She thought back to when Jackson had first offered her the job at Primrose Hall. She'd been looking for excuses to turn down his offer, not wanting to be anywhere near the man after what had happened when they were teenagers. She'd had the perfect excuse in Bertie, who she'd recently agreed to look after, but when Jackson insisted that Bertie came along too, she'd not been in any position to turn down his offer of a job and accommodation. She smiled, realising she had Bertie to thank for bringing them together again, which had worked out so much better than she could have ever anticipated back then. What on earth he would have to say about this latest development, she didn't know.

Would he tell her to take Teddy straight to the dogs' home? There was no chance of that as far as she was concerned. She sighed, nuzzling her face into his newly shampooed and fresh-smelling fur, and she was rewarded with a kiss. One thing was for certain: none of this was this sweet little dog's fault.

That fuzzy area between her personal and professional life was overlapping again and she could hardly be blamed for finding it an increasingly difficult area to navigate.

27

Pia had been on tenterhooks waiting for Jackson to return. When she heard his car pull up in the driveway, she rushed across to the kitchen window to see him climb out of the driver's door. He was dressed in smart navy chinos and a crisp white shirt, the sleeves rolled up showing off his tanned forearms, and Pia's body reacted as it always did, seeing his familiar figure approaching the house.

'Hey, how are you? Did you have a good trip? I've missed you.' She rushed over to greet him, throwing her arms around his neck and kissing him on the lips, forgetting that there had ever been any tension between them before he'd left.

'Well, I shall have to go away more often if this is the reception I can expect to receive.' He placed his laptop bag down on the table and pulled her into a tight embrace, sighing in contentment as he held her in his arms. Stroking her hair with one hand, the other one caressing her face, the look in his eyes told her that he'd missed her as much as she'd missed him. A hope rose in Pia's chest. Perhaps their misunderstanding was simply that and all that bad feeling between them had been forgotten.

'Where's my boy, then?' He looked around him in search of Bertie, his face expectant.

'He's out in the garden. I'll go and get him, but there is something I need to tell you first.'

'That sounds ominous,' he said, his mouth curling. 'He's all right, isn't he?'

'Yes, he's fine, it's just that we have... well, it's very exciting... we have a new family member.'

Jackson stiffened and his mouth fell open. 'Jeez, please tell me you're kidding.' He lowered his voice. 'I can't cope with any more long-lost relatives.'

Pia spluttered into laughter. 'No, it's nothing like that. The thing is, yesterday, Frank and Mateo rescued this little dog from the fencing onto the woods. His fur was all caught up in the wire and Frank had to cut him free. Anyway, they brought him up to the house and we found a name on his tag, but...' She paused for breath, noticing Jackson's eyes were growing wider with every word that she spoke. '...when I got in touch with the owner he was really rude and said he didn't want anything to do with Teddy.'

'Teddy?'

'Yes. I thought the best thing was to take him to the vet and Claire confirmed that she actually knew the dog. Apparently it wasn't the first time he'd escaped. It was so sad because he was such a lovely little thing.'

'Right...'

'Claire spoke to the owners too, and the woman explained that she'd left her partner, and to be frank I can understand why – he was a right miserable bugger. Anyway, she's found a new man and gone off to Australia with him and there was no way she could take an animal with her. Claire said she would get in touch with the kennels to find a space for him, but the poor little thing had been through so much it didn't seem fair to send him there. I know the girls who work there are really dedicated in caring for the animals, but it must be a cold and unwelcoming environment if you're only little.'

Jackson's brow furrowed and he gave a bemused shake of head, although she sensed he was beginning to realise where this might be leading. Pia was about to explain further when they were interrupted by Ronnie's voice.

'Come on, then. Was your mummy ignoring you? Shall we find you both some treats for being such good boys?' Ronnie waltzed into the kitchen with Bertie and Teddy padding alongside her. 'Ahh, you're back,' she said, spotting Jackson. 'You know these two were out there barking their heads off,' she said, addressing Pia. 'That's why I let them in.'

Bertie went leaping up to Jackson, his excitement evident at the return of his master, and his snout nudged Jackson's hand for attention. Little Teddy, picking up on the excitement, ran round in circles and gave a yap of welcome.

'Sorry?' said Jackson, looking between Ronnie and Pia, and then down at Teddy. 'I'm a little bit lost here. You were telling me something about a little dog that was going to the kennels? That's what normally happens with strays, isn't it?'

Jackson looked at her expectantly with a wide gaze but she was relieved to see the glint in his eye and the hint of a smile he was suppressing at the corners of his lips.

'Yes, that's Teddy,' she said sheepishly, her gaze dropping to the ball of fluff at her feet. 'The thing is, I felt so sorry for him. He was completely traumatised by what happened to him and I couldn't bear the thought of him going into a dark and cold kennel, feeling unloved, waiting for a new home where, who knows, he might suffer the same fate as before. He has so much love to give.'

'He doesn't look very traumatised now,' said Jackson sternly.

Ronnie suppressed a smile as they all watched Teddy, who was now rolling around the floor on his back, legs in the air. Pia may have exaggerated Teddy's distress, although her own had been very real, and she had to wonder now if the dog had known exactly what he had been doing and been playing for sympathy. He was definitely showing off now.

'He seems to really like it here. And Bertie has been so good with him, hasn't he?' Pia said, hoping for some moral support from Ronnie.

'Yes. I think of them as Little and Large,' said Ronnie, chuckling.

'So, what's the plan, then?' asked Jackson.

'Well, I said we'd look after Teddy... you know... for a while. Just until...'

Ronnie cast Pia a doubtful look, which Jackson picked up on immediately. 'Until when exactly...?'

He tilted his head, the unanswered question hung awkwardly in the air and Pia simply shrugged.

'Can we see how it goes? We have this great big house and there must be room for a little one. I bet we won't even notice he's here and he'll be good company for Bertie. You've always told me that one of your main aims in running the hall is to give something back to the local community, to help those less fortunate than ourselves.'

'I was actually talking about the villagers, the kids, those people who are struggling financially, to provide somewhere they can come and appreciate the beauty of the landscape, not every scruffy stray that you're likely to come across in Primrose

Woods. We're not a rescue centre, Pia, although I know it sometimes feels that way.'

'Look, Jackson,' said Ronnie brusquely, 'if you're not prepared to accept this little man into the hall, then I'll take him with me in the motorhome. I think we'd rub along together very well and he'd be good company for me.'

Pia's face dropped, unable to hide her dismay at the idea. 'No, Jackson's only joking,' she said, not entirely sure that he was.

He turned away, shaking his head. 'Well, it looks as though the decision has been made in my absence, and I'm probably outnumbered anyway. Fine. He can stay, as long as he behaves himself. Any nonsense, mate, and you'll be out on your ear on the way to the dogs' home. Do you understand me?'

Teddy wagged his tail and did a mad dash around the kitchen as though he understood completely. Ronnie and Pia exchanged a conspiratorial smile, and Pia was relieved to hear the friendly tone in Jackson's rebuke.

'Thanks, Jackson. I should have run it past you first, but there wasn't time, and I was so worried about him. I promise you it will be fine.'

'I'll have to take your word for that,' he said in a resigned voice. 'Look, I'm going to have a shower, but then I'll be down for a gin and tonic and dinner,' he said, taking the lid off a large frying pan on the hob, releasing the aromas of garlic, onions and mushrooms into the air. Pia would cook the steaks later when Jackson came down from changing. 'Five minutes,' he said, kissing her on the forehead.

When Jackson went upstairs, Pia turned to Ronnie, making a thumbs up motion. 'Thanks for sticking up for Teddy then and offering to give him a home as well. That was so kind of you.'

'I meant every word of it. I quite fancy having a little canine companion in the van, especially one as cute as this little one. Not that I believed for a moment that Jackson would really have turned his back on Teddy. Despite Jackson's grouchy exterior, he really is a big softie underneath.'

'I know but I didn't share your confidence on this one.' She knew Jackson better than most people, but sometimes it was hard to second-guess his moods. Pia went across to the hob to check the sauce bubbling in the pan. She gave it a stir with the wooden spoon. 'Are you staying for dinner?'

'No, Rex is taking me out in town.' She gave a delighted squee. 'We're going to that new Italian tapas place to give it a whirl. I've heard very good things about it.' She looked down at her watch. 'In fact, I should go and make myself beautiful. He'll be here shortly.' Ronnie dashed off and Pia smiled to herself.

'Have a lovely time,' she called.

For the first time in a few days, Pia felt a sense of relief. Jackson was home and he was still talking to her. Calm and normality had been restored to the hall, for the time being at least.

28

When Jackson came back downstairs, his hair was still damp from the shower, the scent of citrus fruits reaching Pia's nose, and he'd changed into a pair of black jeans and a black short-sleeved T-shirt that accentuated his biceps. Her gaze ran up and down his arms, the sight eliciting a swirl of desire through her body.

She picked up the gin and tonic she'd prepared and handed it over to him.

'Perfect,' he said, taking a sip, before slipping an arm around her waist and pulling her into his side, kissing her on the lips, the chemistry between them simmering. If it was down to her, she might take him by the hand and lead him back into the bedroom, but she knew he'd had a long day and, besides, the dinner would be spoilt if she didn't serve it soon. 'Is Ronnie not staying for dinner?'

'Hot date with Rex, apparently.'

'Again? Those two have a better social life than we do. They're spending a hell of a lot of time together recently. Which is great while it's going well, but I'm dreading the fall-out when it all goes horribly wrong.'

'Why would you say that?'

'Because I know them both of old, remember, and I've seen it happen before.'

'But that was years ago, when you were a kid. I think they've both mellowed over the years and they're really enjoying each other's company now. I don't think either of them want that kind of drama in their lives any more. They're making the most of the moment and where's the harm in that?'

'Well, let's hope you're right,' said Jackson, resting his backside against the rail of the Aga, watching her as she seared the steaks in the frying pan, the sizzle as the meat hit the pan matching the heat radiating between the pair of them.

'I think it's really sweet how they're finding love for the second time around,' Pia said. 'It gives hope to us all.'

'What the hell is that supposed to mean?'

Pia shot him a glance. 'Nothing. Only that it's heartening to see that you can still be madly in love and feeling all those wonderful emotions even when you're the wrong side of sixty.'

'Ha! Do you know what your problem is? You're too much of a romantic.'

Pia laughed and held up her hands. 'Guilty as charged.' It wasn't the first time he'd told her that, but was that such a bad thing?

Jackson moved out of the way of Pia as she reached around to grab a tea towel and as he did, he tripped over something and went stumbling across the kitchen floor.

'What the...?' He looked down to see Teddy scoot out from beneath his feet and scamper beneath the kitchen table. Jackson cursed beneath his breath. 'Are you sure that thing's a dog, and not just a big rat?'

'Don't be mean. Close your ears, Teddy. Look, he's frightened of you.' Teddy was cowering beneath the table, looking out at Pia. 'I wonder if his owner used to abuse Teddy; he seems much warier of men. Don't worry, little one,' she called to him. 'You're safe here, and we'll look after you, won't we, Jackson?'

Jackson gave a resigned smile. It wasn't as though he had any say in the matter at all.

* * *

After dinner, Pia cleared the plates away and made coffees, and they wandered through into the snug, where they collapsed down onto the big squashy sofa. Bertie followed and Teddy padded along behind him, watching as Bertie easily climbed up on the other sofa, and his cute little face said he might like to do the same. Pia bent down and scooped Teddy up in her arms, kissing him on the head before placing him alongside Bertie, where he walked around in circles before curling himself up into the tightest ball and snuggling down behind the bigger dog.

'Isn't that the most adorable thing?' Pia looked up as Jackson pulled her into the crook of his arm and she relaxed into his embrace. 'So have you forgiven me yet?' she asked him.

'What for?'

'Well, for bringing Teddy home for a start?'

'Sure. I mean, if I was going to choose to have another dog, then it wouldn't have been a scrap like Teddy. I would have gone for something more befitting a stately home, like a pointer, or a Weimaraner, or a Vizsla, but hey, I guess that decision was taken out of my hands.' He gave her a sidewards glance and although there was a smile on his lips, she wasn't entirely sure that he was joking. He placed his legs up on the coffee table, crossing them. 'Although are you absolutely certain that you've thought through all the ramifications of bringing another dog here? What happens if you decide to move out into a place of your own? A small flat, for example. Not the best place for a couple of dogs.'

'Oh, Jackson,' she sighed. She shot up, tucking her legs beneath her and turning on her knees to face him. 'I thought it was a sensible plan. To buy somewhere as a rental investment. I got my inheritance through from Mum and I suppose it panicked me. I thought, what on earth was I going to do with all that money? I saw it as my pension fund.'

Jackson sat up straighter on the sofa. 'What I don't get is why you didn't mention it to me. I might have been able to offer some advice. I don't care about your money and what you decide to do with it, that's entirely up to you, but I thought you would have at least told me. Do you know what an idiot it made me feel to find out what you were intending to do in front of Tom? I thought we were a team, a partnership, but it wouldn't have appeared that way to him. It was bloody humiliating.'

Jackson never normally cared what people thought about him, but he'd obviously been keen, this one time, to make an impression in front of his brother.

'I never meant to humiliate you.' She'd heard the anger and bitterness behind his words. She'd hurt him without ever intending to.

'This was a big deal for you, and I thought we were close enough that you would want to tell me what's going on in your life. That you would want to confide in me. I tell you everything that's going on in my world.'

'Everything?'

He turned to face her, noticing the edge to her voice. 'Yes, everything,' he said emphatically.

She took a breath. She'd been undecided whether to say

anything, but now she couldn't stop herself. 'You didn't tell me about Tara.'

Pia's comment stopped Jackson in his tracks, his dark eyes latching on to hers. 'Tara? What's she got to do with any of this?'

'When you went to London the other week. You met up with Tara. You didn't mention that to me. She's your ex. The last time she came here, she wanted to get back with you. What am I supposed to think?'

'What the hell?' He shifted back in his seat, putting distance between them. 'Have you been checking up on me?'

'No, I haven't. I have no reason to.' She realised she trusted Jackson. 'The organisers of the charity event sent through a write-up with some photos of those who attended on the night. It's in your inbox if you want to check.'

'Jeez!' He dropped his head in his hands. 'That's an entirely different situation.'

'Is it, though?' Pia pressed.

'Yes. The reason I didn't mention it is because it was inconsequential. It didn't even cross my mind to tell you. We were at the same engagement together, that's all. It's going to happen. We used to mix in the same circles. We had a brief catch-up and that was it. You can't seriously believe that I still have feelings for Tara?' He sounded defensive, but any suspicions or doubts she may have had about Jackson had disappeared in the intervening weeks.

She gave a shrug. 'It would have been nice to have known. Especially as you're the one talking about being transparent with each other.'

He shook his head. 'Okay, I get it. I should have told you, but I promise it was simply an oversight and nothing more.' He reached across and took her hand. 'I promise.'

They fell quiet for a few moments, with Jackson's gaze roaming her features.

'Look, Jackson, I'm sorry I didn't mention my money coming through, but you were preoccupied with work and with Tom turning up.'

'But you always come first. If there's something going on with you, I want to know about it. It's as simple as that.'

She gave a grateful smile, realising she may have misjudged him. 'I wasn't being deliberately secretive. I suppose I wasn't certain in my own head what I should do, and I wasn't sure how you might react.'

He gave a rueful smile. 'Or else you knew exactly how I might react?'

Pia fell silent, knowing it was the truth.

'Look, Pia, I know that we're in an unusual situation in that our personal relationship came out of us working together, but I think we need to be entirely honest with each other about what we want from this arrangement or else it's never going to work between us.'

'Sorry?' Jackson's words filled Pia with dread. 'This arrangement? Is that all this is to you?' Wasn't that one of the reasons she'd been looking at flats in the first place? To have a place of her own should their 'arrangement' fall apart.

'You tell me. I thought we were solid, good together. I thought you were happy living here, so to find out that you were considering putting in a back-up plan, an escape route, whatever you want to call it, makes me question if you're as committed as you say you are.'

'You're being unreasonable, Jackson. You know how much I love my job here, how much I love you.' Her voice was full of tenderness as she clasped his face in her hands. 'This is my whole world now, being here, but I have to be sensible about my future, about my own security.'

'Why, though?'

'This is your house, your dream, your business. The whole success of this place is down to you. It's been your vision and your ambition for years and all your hard work has paid off.'

'You're a central part of its success, though. You've breathed new life into the hall. You're so good at dealing with the staff and our visitors in a way that I'm not. You're a natural. Best of all, you fill in the gaps that I'm missing.'

She smiled, enjoying Jackson's validation that she was a vital part of the team. It would break her heart if she ever had to leave. And wasn't that the one thing she was trying her hardest to avoid – a broken heart?

'That means a lot, but Mum left me the money to secure my future.' If Jackson wanted her honesty, she would give it to him. 'I thought it would be a good idea to have a place of my own so that if anything should ever happen, then...'

'What on earth are you expecting to happen?'

'Worst-case scenario.' How could she express her innermost fears to Jackson? 'If you decided that you wanted to change the way the business is run, or if you ever decided to sell the hall, or if...' She faltered over the one thing that troubled her the most. 'If we were ever to break up.'

Jackson lifted his chin to the ceiling and closed his eyes, his exasperation evident. 'We're not going to break up, unless this is your way of telling me that you're not one hundred per cent committed to this relationship? And I've certainly got no intention of ever selling the hall. This is my forever home. I won't be going anywhere.'

'Yes, but that's my point exactly. This is all yours.' She didn't want to sound demanding or money-grabbing, it wasn't about that, but if they were to split up, Jackson's life wouldn't change in the slightest. He would still run the hall, a different personal assistant would step into Pia's shoes, and it would remain his home for as long as he wanted it to be. For Pia, she would have to look for a new job and a new place to live. 'You can't know how you are going to feel a year or two down the line. Relationships break up all the time, and I don't want to find myself in a situation where I'm suddenly homeless. Where I don't have anywhere to go.'

'So what you're telling me is that you're going to buy your own place and at the first sign of trouble between us, you're going to hotfoot it there.'

'No!'

'Well, that's what it sounds like.'

'It's not unreasonable for me to make plans for my own future.'

'I thought your future was here with me.'

'It is. I hope it will be. I'm just being sensible and investing in something of my own for a rainy day.'

'Pia.' He sat back on the sofa, running his hands through his hair. 'Growing up, I used to live in fear that my mother would walk out the door to go off on one of her adventures, not knowing if perhaps the next time she left, she wouldn't come back again. It was awful, that sense of uncertainty, not feeling as though I was important enough for her to stay. Then I was just a kid and I had no control over what was going on. Now I'm an adult. I don't want or need that kind of uncertainty in my personal relationship. Not with you.'

'This is totally different, Jackson.'

'Is it? Have I got to live with the idea that there's part of you thinking, *Oh, it's okay, if things don't work out, then I can simply take off and leave. Go to my little flat and start again*? Because to me that's not a great sign. If you're in a relationship and you're continually thinking about the get-out clause, then I don't know how that relationship can ever truly work.'

'It isn't like that, I promise.' Her worries and concerns about her own security were valid, but now Jackson was turning the tables on her and she sought to justify herself. 'I'm not Ronnie. I'm not going to leave on a whim. Hopefully, I've shown you in the brief time I've been working at the hall that I'm dependable and reliable, that I would never let you down.'

'I don't need a character reference for your ability to do the job. I know how great you are. This is about us. Our personal relationship.'

'Exactly. I don't know what I can tell you. I love you. You're the only man I've ever loved and while that's exciting and brings me happiness, it leaves me very exposed. You broke my heart once...' she said, her voice fading to a whisper.

'I know, and I've apologised for that. You can't hold that against me forever. I thought you understood?'

'I do. I'm just looking out for myself, that's all.'

'It saddens me that there's a part of you that's holding back from being fully committed to me and to the hall.'

'That's not true.' She was wounded by the accusation. 'I couldn't be more committed if I tried. There's nowhere else I'd rather be. I'm being sensible, that's all. When you think about it, this time last year you were still with Tara. I don't suppose either of you were thinking that you would be breaking up within a matter of months.'

'That was different. I liked Tara, respected her. Admired her talent, but I was never in love with her. I wanted to be. I tried hard to make it work, but I realised that I was never going to love her in the way she wanted to be loved, that she deserved to be loved, and that's when I knew it wasn't fair on either of us to stay in the relationship.' He picked up his glass from the table and took a hearty glug of the red wine. 'She's in a new relationship now and she's happy. I'm pleased for her. We've both moved on. With you, it was different,' he went on. 'I loved you from the start, from when we were kids. When you came back into my life, it was as though I was being given a message from some higher authority. It felt right, Pia. And I don't want it to ever feel wrong again.' He looked at her with a vulnerability that tugged at her heart strings.

'We're saying the same things, Jackson, wanting the same outcome. I'm sorry you were humiliated in front of your brother, but can we move past this, please? I hate falling out with you.'

'Me too. Just remember that, whatever happens, I would never want to do anything that makes you feel insecure or vulnerable. Your job and your home are safe here, for as long as you want. Please believe that.'

Pia nodded, relieved they'd cleared the air. There were no guarantees in life, but she had the next best thing, an assurance from Jackson that they both wanted the same thing from their life at Primrose Hall. Knowing that Tara was settled and happy in a new relationship came as a huge relief too.

29

'Do you think the tree should go in the nook beside the fireplace or in front of the double doors?'

Pia stood with her hands on her hips, surveying the main drawing room, feeling a buzz of excitement at the prospect of putting up the decorations. The tree would be arriving later that day and she couldn't wait to get started. She'd gathered everything she needed together in front of the stone fireplace.

'Definitely in front of the doors, overlooking the garden,' said Ivy. 'It will look really magical when it's lit up, with the dark starry sky behind it.'

'Well, we won't be short of lights.' Pia laughed, looking at the boxes in front of her. She'd bought multi-coloured ones, candle lights and all-singing and dancing flashing lights, along with garlands, sparkling baubles and individual handcrafted decorations. She'd laid them out on the coffee table, along with the holly and berries, mistletoe and pine cones that she'd collected on a recent walk over at Primrose Woods.

They were just unpacking a couple of large brown boxes that Jackson had retrieved from one of the storage cupboards in the garage that contained all last year's decorations when they were interrupted.

'Pia!'

The back door slammed shut and Jackson's call reverberated through the hall, reaching Pia with an urgency that told her something must be wrong. Pia glanced across at Ivy with wide-eyed incredulity and Ivy could only shake her head and shrug.

'Everything okay?' Pia replied, wandering through to greet him in the kitchen.

'No, everything is not okay. I found my slipper,' he said, holding aloft the said item.

'Oh, well, that's good news, isn't it?'

Jackson's leather mule, a designer slipper, no less, had gone missing a couple of days earlier, and they'd both searched high and low to find it, without any success. Jackson had been convinced that Ivy must have scooped it up inadvertently and placed it in the rubbish, but Ivy was adamant that she hadn't. Pia said it was more likely that it had got wedged beneath the bed or the wardrobe, and that it was bound to turn up eventually. Still, it had put Jackson in a bad mood so she was relieved that he'd finally retrieved it.

'No, it's not good news. Do you know where I found it?'

Pia grimaced in anticipation.

'In a big muddy hole in the garden. Look at the state of it. It's sopping wet and has teeth marks in it.'

'Oh dear…'

'That doesn't really cover it, Pia. Do you have any idea how much they cost? They were my favourite slippers and now they're completely ruined. Where is that little beast? TEDDY?' he yelled. 'Come here now!'

If Pia had been addressed in that manner, then she definitely wouldn't have responded, but Teddy had proved himself to be an obedient little dog who came trotting in from the living room, looking inordinately pleased with himself, wondering what all the fuss was about.

'This is bad,' said Jackson sternly, waving the slipper in front of Teddy's face. 'Very bad. Naughty dog! Go to your bed.'

At that moment, Pia made the mistake of glancing across at Ivy, who had just wandered into the room with a triumphant smile on her face.

'I told you it wasn't me. Crikey, he's made a bit of a mess of that, hasn't he? I expect they smell lovely to him.'

Pia turned away for a moment, trying her hardest not to laugh.

'It's ruined. No wonder his previous owners were keen to get rid of him. He's nothing but a pain in the backside. Go to your bed,' Jackson repeated gruffly.

'Bless him, he looks very sad when you say that,' said Ivy, who was definitely on Team Teddy.

'He doesn't realise what he's done. He's just a sweet little dog,' added Pia. 'It's nice that he's so settled here that he feels comfortable enough to have a bit of fun.'

'Yeah. Great. At my bloody expense. He needs to learn a few manners and to realise who's boss around here.' At that, both Ivy and Pia started giggling. 'Look, he doesn't do a thing I tell him. GO TO YOUR BED!' Jackson reiterated, much more loudly this time, waving the soggy slipper around in his hand.

At that, Teddy leapt up, wagging his tail, thinking it was a new game, and grabbed the slipper from Jackson's hand and then went running off to his bed, just as he'd been told to by his master.

'Oh, he thinks you want to play,' sighed Pia.

Jackson shook his head in dismay as he left the room,

knowing when he was most definitely beaten, while Pia and Ivy cooed over Teddy, who was hugging his new favourite toy.

Ten minutes later, Jackson returned with his laptop bag and overnight bag over his shoulder.

'Oh come on, Jackson,' joked Pia. 'It's not that bad. You're not leaving home because of Teddy, I hope?'

'Believe me, I'm seriously tempted,' he said with a tight smile. 'No, I'm going up to town. Just overnight. There are some bits and pieces I need to attend to,' he said casually.

'Really? Well, that sounds very intriguing.' She cast him a questioning look. At the moment, she probably knew his movements better than he did and there was nothing in the calendar. And, after all, hadn't they promised to be absolutely honest with each other? 'Are you going to tell me more?'

'No, not sure I am,' he said coolly, taking in her puzzled expression. 'All I'll say is that I have some preparations to see to for next month.'

Pia couldn't think what he meant. She was pretty certain that all the arrangements were in place for the Christmas carols evening.

'A small occasion known as Christmas?'

'Oh, I get it.' She flung her arms around his neck, standing on tiptoes to kiss him. 'Christmas shopping, for me. How very exciting.'

'Well, it gets me out of drinks tonight with Dad and Tom,' he said with a quirk of his eyebrow.

'Oh, that's a shame. It'll be a good chance to get to know Tom better. Are you sure you can't put off your trip to London?'

'Nope, I don't want to. I'm happy to leave it to the pair of them. It's great Dad has reconnected with Tom but I don't want to play happy families. I can't pretend to feel things I don't.'

Pia pressed her lips together, sad to think that Jackson didn't want to put more effort into his new relationship with Tom. 'Give it time. It's still early days, but please, don't give up on Tom just yet.'

'Right, I ought to get going,' he said, ignoring Pia's comment. 'I'll be back tomorrow afternoon.' He held her arms, kissing her on the lips. 'And please, in my absence, don't take in any more waifs and strays.'

'Do you need any ideas, for presents? I could give you a list if you like?'

Jackson shook his head indulgently.

'You know, you could always pick up a couple of presents for the dogs too, if you see anything special.'

'You think I'm spending money on that scruffy hound after he's demolished my best pair of slippers? I really don't think so.'

'Aww, don't be such a grinch,' she said, laughing as he went out of the door. At least she knew the perfect present to buy him for Christmas.

* * *

With Jackson out of the way, it gave Pia the perfect opportunity to throw herself into decorating the hall. She wanted to take her time over it, savour every moment because it was one of her favourite things to do in the run up to the Christmas festivities. She would put a Christmas film on the telly, one she'd seen a dozen times before, and she'd pour herself a glass of Irish cream liqueur. She wanted to have a bit of a craft session at the kitchen table too, spraying the huge pine cones. She had a tin of gold spray paint and one that promised a snowy effect and she was hopeful they would look suitably festive in a wicker basket in the fireplace. She'd already placed the wreath she'd made on the outside kitchen door, after spending a fun evening at the home of one of Lizzie's friends, Joan, who had shown a small group of them how to make their own wreaths, with an assortment of materials found in the woods including Scots pine sprigs, variegated ivy and holly with berries. There was a lot of laughter and a few glasses of wine and the end result hadn't been bad for a first attempt. Another two bigger wreaths were coming today from Primrose Woods. They would be far more professional-looking and would go on the main front door to the hall and on the entrance to the stables.

First, though, Ivy made a pot of tea and placed a plate of mince pies and shortbread biscuits on the small table by the window seat, sustenance for the job ahead, where they sat and chatted. Bertie and Teddy came over to join the party, sitting obediently in the hope that they might be able to nab a crumb or two. Ivy was more than happy to oblige by feeding the two dogs with a biscuit, which would have annoyed Jackson intently, but Ivy made a valid point.

'Well, it is almost Christmas, and if you can't have a treat at this time of year, then when can you?'

Pia agreed wholeheartedly, even if technically it still was only November.

'Come on,' she said, once they'd had their tea. 'Let's get started on the fireplace in the main drawing room.'

They worked at a leisurely pace, chatting and laughing the whole time, stopping to sing along to the music, and for another cup of tea, until the fireplace was transformed with verdant garlands, white pillar candles on the hearth and a curl of fairy lights entwined across the logs. Pia stood back to admire their handiwork.

'I'd say that's perfect.' Pia was pleased with their efforts. On the mantlepiece there were more candles in varying sizes in glass and antique holders, the overall effect warm and eye-catching.

'That will be the Christmas trees,' said Pia, hearing a loud rat-a-tat on the kitchen door. The dogs went running ahead, barking in welcome.

'Hi, Sam, lovely to see you,' she said, greeting her friend with a kiss. 'Just what we've been waiting for,' she said, eyeing the trailer on the drive that was overflowing with trees, the scent of pine reaching her nostrils. 'Christmas has finally arrived.'

'I love my job all year round, but it's extra special this time of year because everyone is so pleased to see me,' he said, laughing. 'So, where are these going?'

'I'll get Mateo and Frank to come over, and they will show you where we want the two bigger trees to go. One will be by the stables and the other will be at the front of the house. The two smaller ones are going inside the house, one in the drawing room and one in the hall please.'

Sam manhandled the trees for the interior into their positions, with an ease that showed it was something he did on a daily basis, declining the cup of tea that Pia offered. He still had several deliveries to make, but instead would take a couple of the delicious mince pies with him.

'How is Abbey doing?' she asked.

'Really well, she's feeling much better. She's beginning to show as well so it makes it seem so much more real. We're looking forward to Christmas, the last one with just the two of us, before life changes forever, so everyone is keen to remind us.' Sam laughed. 'It can't be that bad, surely?' He widened his eyes and grimaced, before laughing again. 'We really can't wait.'

'It's such an exciting time for you both. You'll have to come over during the holidays and we can celebrate.'

'Definitely. And we'll see you at the Christmas carols event. Looking forward to that one.'

Mateo and Frank came over and Pia called out her thanks to Sam as the three men went off to place the huge Christmas trees in position. Pia had been happy to give the job of decorating the outdoor trees to Mateo and Frank, as she didn't much fancy getting up a ladder in the cold air. Her creative skills were much better utilised inside the hall.

'Why don't you get off home now?' Pia said to Ivy, an hour or so later, when it was already way past Ivy's finishing time.

'Are you sure? There's still so much to do here, and that mess in the kitchen. Do you want me to make a start on clearing it?'

'No, it's fine. I'm happy to potter. And what I don't get done tonight can wait until tomorrow.'

With Ivy gone, Pia poured herself a glass of wine, popped a seasonal film on the telly and continued decorating the trees, wandering between the two, deciding one particular bauble suited one particular tree better. She plumped for a silver and gold theme for the tree in the hall, and an all-white theme for the tree in the drawing room, the festive sparkly effect increasing with each shiny bauble that she placed. The dogs were stretched out on the rug in front of the fire, with one eye on Pia as she drifted between the rooms. Eventually, she was able to stand back and view the room as a whole. A thrill of excitement snaked along her spine. If she said so herself, she'd done a pretty good job.

After tidying away the empty boxes and sweeping up the rogue pine needles from the floor, she went into the kitchen, where it was looking equally festive with candle arches in every window and holly, ivy and mistletoe swathed across the old oak beams. Pia took a moment to sit by the Aga, where she was joined by the dogs. Although Pia had bought Teddy his own bed, he much preferred to curl up next to Bertie in the larger one, and Bertie didn't have much choice but to tolerate the new sleeping arrangements.

It warmed Pia's heart that the dogs had bonded so quickly. Where one of them went, and that was Bertie usually, the other followed, and to see them frolicking around in the garden together was such a delight. Although Bertie may have been suspicious of the scruffy little mutt at first, he quickly adapted to having him around and if Teddy ever became too confident or overstepped the mark, then Bertie would issue him a sharp warning by way of a bark. She looked down at them both now, a feeling of contentment filling her chest at seeing them happily snoozing away.

This time last year she'd been facing a miserable Christmas alone, the first without her mum, and despite Connor's best efforts to get her involved in the festive season, she had been in no mood to celebrate. With her future so scarily uncertain, all she'd wanted was to get through the holidays and then to focus on getting a job and a new home sorted. She would never have believed then that within the year she would be sitting in the kitchen of a swanky manor house that she would call her home, having found a new family. It was a different type of family, living with Jackson, Mateo, the two dogs and Ronnie, but she relished the sense of belonging and love that came from being at the heart of a busy household.

She made herself a sandwich, toasting two slices of bread while quickly frying some streaky bacon, the aroma making her stomach rumble. She cut up some slices of Brie, laying them on one slice of the bread, and popped it beneath the grill. When the cheese was a soft gooey consistency, she removed it, placing it on a plate and then tipped the bacon with its juices onto the other slice of bread. She pressed the two slices of bread together and then cut the sandwich in half, putting it on a plate, taking it across to her favourite spot in the kitchen, the chair right next to the Aga.

As she finished her impromptu dinner, listening now to a phone-in show on the radio, she was interrupted by a knocking at the kitchen door. She was grateful to the dogs for barking as she wondered who it might be calling at that time of night. She peered out of the small side window, spotting Jackson's tall, familiar frame standing outside. Why was he back so soon and why wasn't he using his own key? She flung open the door, excited to see him, but concerned in equal measure.

'Oh,' she said, unable to hide her surprise. 'It's you.'

'Ah,' he said disappointedly. 'Don't sound too pleased to see me, will you?'

'Of course I am,' she said, laughing. 'Come on in. I was just about to make a hot drink. I'll make you one too.'

30

Pia spooned coffee into mugs, poured milk into the frother and flicked the kettle on. When the water boiled, she half-filled the mugs and then topped them up with the steamed milk, before adding the creamy milk topping and a sprinkling of chocolate powder. She placed the mugs on the table, smiling. It was no wonder she'd thought it was Jackson standing outside when in the dark shadows of the night Tom could quite easily be mistaken for his brother.

'Sorry, just turning up like this. I was hoping to see Jackson tonight, but he called off at the last moment. I sent him a couple of texts, but he didn't reply so I thought, *I know, I'll go round, and get it sorted face to face*.' He let out an exasperated sigh. 'Although after what happened last time that probably wasn't one of my better ideas. It's probably just as well Jackson isn't here.'

'Oh, he's terrible at replying to texts. I shouldn't read too much into that. He's had to go to London,' she said, making it sound as though he'd been called away on business.

'Well, I suppose that makes me feel a bit better. I just wanted to clear the air after I put my size tens very squarely in it the other night. I must apologise to you as well. I'm sorry if I made things difficult for you with Jackson. I just didn't realise.'

'Why would you? That misunderstanding was entirely down to me so you have nothing to feel bad about. Besides, it's all forgotten about now.'

'Is it really? It might be with you, but what about Jackson?'

'Honestly, we've talked it through. He's fine.'

Tom looked doubtful and Pia felt a pang of sympathy. She spent enough time herself trying to gauge Jackson's moods and wondering whether she'd upset him or not, so she knew exactly how Tom was feeling.

'I hope so.' Tom clasped his hands together on the table. 'I'd hate for us to fall out before we've got to know each other.'

'I wouldn't read too much into that night. Jackson was upset, and he took that out on you, which he shouldn't have done. Ron was right in what he said, though. It's how brothers are together. They fall out. Have scraps. Then make up again. Please, don't worry about it. Jackson is...'

'Ah, I thought we had visitors.'

Pia and Tom's conversation was interrupted by the arrival of Ronnie, who had an unerring knack of knowing exactly when a visitor had turned up at the hall, and if it was someone that she might be remotely interested in, then she would put in an appearance in her inimitable style. Tonight, she was in a long, pale green, silky nightdress covered up with a patterned kimono, looking ready for her boudoir.

'Tom, how lovely to see you again. I thought it might be you.'

'That's a lovely welcome, Ronnie. Thank you. How are you?'

Despite Ronnie's initial reservations about Tom, it was their relationship that had been the most natural and easy from the outset. They'd clicked right from the first moment that they'd met, chatting and laughing together as though they'd known each other for years.

'I'm very well, as you can hopefully tell,' she said, holding her arms out wide and giving a quite unnecessary twirl in the middle of the kitchen, which made Pia laugh all the same. 'Did I hear you talking about Jackson? What's he done now?'

'Nothing. I wanted to catch up with him, that's all, make sure we were still good.'

'Don't go fretting over Jackson. I love that boy dearly, but he can be an awkward bugger at times. Can't he, Pia?' Ronnie went on, not waiting for Pia's affirmation. 'I dread to think what he says about me, but I'm his mother and he can't do anything about that,' she said gleefully. 'For all his flaws, Jackson has a real sense of duty and responsibility, and for family. He would never turn his back on you. I'd be certain of that.'

Pia nodded, realising, if she hadn't known before, that Ronnie was absolutely right. It was one of the many things she loved about Jackson. His morality, his belief in doing the right thing, even if sometimes he went about it in a peculiar way.

'I hope you're right. There's no self-help guides out there on meeting your father and your brother for the first time as an adult. It's a tricky thing to navigate. You want it to be perfect, to have those deep ties that you would expect with your family, but of course it isn't as straightforward as that. Those bonds are built over the course of years, through mutual honesty and trust. I might have been guilty of expecting too much too soon.'

'All you can do is start from where you are now and continue to build on that. It's easy to look back with regrets and think what might have been, but what's the point in that? It's like me and Rex. If we rake over all that old ground, bringing up all the past grievances, then we only end up hurting each other. Life's too short for that. You've got this opportunity to get to know your dad and Jackson and I think you should all make the most of that.'

'It's lovely having you as part of the family now,' said Pia. 'I mean, I'm not real family, but that's how I've come to consider everyone here at Primrose Hall.'

'It's what I want. I'd like to know how Jackson feels, though. To save us wasting each other's time. It's fine with Dad. I can tell that he's genuinely happy that we've found each other. Jackson, though? I'm sure he's not gone through life thinking, *It would be good to have a brother*, and it's not as though we've got loads in common now. I mean, look at this place. You could probably get my entire flat in this kitchen. If he were to turn around and say to me, *Look, it's been good to have met you, but honestly, I don't want you in my life*, I would respect that. It might sting a bit, but I could understand where he was coming from.'

'Jackson wouldn't do that.' Ronnie was quick to reassure Tom again. 'And it's not about money or having lots in common. It's more about mutual respect, and that's something that will come, given a bit of time.'

Pia nodded reassuringly, agreeing with every word that Ronnie said. It made perfect sense, but whether Jackson would make a real effort to forge a bond with his brother, or simply go through the motions, for appearances' sake, she still wasn't sure.

* * *

'Wow. Look at this place. You've done an amazing job.'

Jackson returned home at lunchtime the next day. He jumped out of the car and went across to look at the Christmas tree outside the stables, stopping to chat with Mateo on the way, then Pia saw him go round to the front of the hall, to view the other tree. The Lord of the Manor had returned and he was surveying his estate.

'I'm not sure I can take any credit for how it looks outside, that was all done by Frank and Mateo, but I am the sole creator of this winter wonderland inside. Come and have a look.' Pia took Jackson by the hand and led him through the kitchen and the hall and then into the drawing room. 'What do you think?'

'It looks great.' Jackson chuckled. He kissed her on the lips and she fell into his arms, relishing the way his embrace made her feel, his body so strong and firm against hers.

They stood for a moment admiring the tree and the fireplace, before Pia was ambushed by a flicker of doubt. 'Are you sure you like it? You're not just saying that? You don't think it's too over-the-top?'

'What? Never, I love it,' he said, pulling her into his side.

She'd had every intention of putting on a classy and traditional display, following the colour schemes she'd chosen for each of the trees, but she'd got carried away and couldn't help putting an extra bauble on here and adding extra sparkle there, which didn't necessarily match with the theme. She had been adamant that she wouldn't add any tinsel, but she'd found a whole bagful of different coloured strings at the bottom of one of the boxes so she couldn't resist adding one or two, until she gave in to the temptation and ended up draping all the tinsel over the trees.

Pia gave a thought to Tara, who would have been standing in this same position last year. She wondered how the decorations might have looked then. Very classy and sophisticated, she didn't doubt. Tara was an interior designer by trade, her work appearing in glossy home magazines and on her Instagram profile, gathering plenty of likes and acclaim. Still, as far as Pia was concerned, *less is more* had no place when it came to Christmas decorating.

Would she and Jackson still be looking at the same Christmas decorations in years to come, feeling a pang of nostalgia as they were reacquainted with the funny little robin with the broken wing? And would that shiny tinsel in all colours of the rainbow be thinning and threadbare, but still an essential part of the Christmas tradition? Pia certainly hoped so.

'You know,' she said with a sigh, seeing the room in a completely different light with Jackson standing at her side, 'I think it might actually be totally over-the-top, but that doesn't matter, does it? I think it's beautiful.'

'It is. Just like Santa's grotto,' said Jackson, still laughing. 'Do you know what you've done, Pia? You've transformed Primrose Hall from a house into a home. That's exactly what I wanted.'

That might have been Jackson's way of saying, politely, that her decorations were on the tacky end of the scale, but she didn't care; his back-handed compliment sent a ripple of satisfaction around her body.

'Come on, let me make us some lunch, and you can tell me how your trip went.'

In the kitchen, Pia quickly cobbled together a ploughman's platter, putting a block of vintage Cheddar, a gooey dolcelatte and a soft Brie onto the wooden board, along with some mini pork pies, some Brussels pâté and some celery sticks and grapes. She cut chunky slices of brown bread and a baguette, placing them in the wicker basket. She pulled out a bottle of chilled white wine from the fridge and a couple of glasses and plates, and cutlery. Lunch was served.

'So, did you get all my presents?' Pia asked cheekily as she watched Jackson pour the wine and then help himself to some cheese.

'Presents? Plural? You're optimistic, aren't you? And besides, I'm not telling you. You'll have to wait until Christmas Day.'

'You're no fun. What about the dogs? Did you pick up anything for them?'

'Those dogs are spoilt enough as it is. They're lucky to have a home here, let alone anything else.' Jackson said this with an entirely straight face, but she knew he couldn't possibly mean it. He and Bertie were best buddies, and she often caught them stretched out on the sofa together, sharing an afternoon nap. She sensed he was warming to Teddy too, because she'd spotted Jackson giving the little dog a cuddle and a motivational speech when he'd thought no one was looking.

'We had a visitor last night.' There was no point in pressing Jackson any further on his shopping trip as he clearly wasn't in the mood for discussing that subject.

'Who was that then?'

'Tom.'

'What did he want?' Jackson bit into a stick of celery.

'He wanted to see you, of course. He still feels that he may have upset you that night.'

'Well, he's right, he did.'

'Come on, that really wasn't his fault. That was down to me. He mentioned that you hadn't responded to his messages.'

'I've been busy, Pia.'

'I know you have, but this is clearly important to him. He's trying to find out about his roots, where he came from, who is family are, so I think he might really appreciate a text from you.'

'I was going to contact him; it just slipped my mind.'

Pia would give him the benefit of the doubt. Maybe Jackson's forgetfulness was simply a cover for his own vulnerability and awkwardness in knowing how to act around his new brother.

'Yes, give him a call. You could go for a pint of something?'

Jackson sighed and sat back in his chair, running a hand through his hair. 'To be honest, I think we've exhausted the whole talking about our crap childhood thing. I'm not interested in those deep and meaningful conversations, going over old ground. I'm not sure it helps. Does that make me sound like a mean bastard?'

'No, I get that, but I think it was probably cathartic for Tom to speak to you about his experience, to explain his history and compare notes with you. I think he's in awe of you, and everything you've achieved. He looks up to you even if you are the younger brother.'

'Terrific,' said Jackson, unable to keep the sarcasm from his voice.

'It's true. Just give him a chance. It's still very early days. You never know what might come from it.'

'Probably a whole lot of drama and disappointment. That's what usually comes from the interactions with my family.'

'Don't say that. You're getting on well with your mum these days, Rex is back in your life and now you've got a brother you can get to know better. I see it as a wonderful opportunity, and you should too.'

'Okay, Pollyanna,' he said, with a roll of his eyes. 'I'll text him, if that's what you want me to do. I'll do it for you, and I'll do it for Dad.'

'You need to do it for yourself, Jackson, not us.'

It was entirely up to him whether he wanted to put the effort into building a relationship with his brother. She couldn't force him, but hopefully he would give Tom another chance.

'Actually, on the subject of family,' Jackson went on, 'there was something I wanted to run past you.'

'Okay?'

'I was going to ask Dad to move in here, to take over the

guest suite that you were in. He's been living with his friends for a few months now and although he always talks about finding his own place, I'm not sure how practical that would be. I'm not even sure what his financial position is, but, as you are keen to point out, we're his family. We've got this great big house. He should be here with us.'

'Exactly. I think it's a great idea... although I'm not sure what Ronnie will have to say about that.' Pia giggled.

'She's bound to have a strong opinion on it, one way or the other. She'll probably be pleased, as she's pretty smitten with Rex again these days. She won't have far to go to find him, although that might not be such a good thing for Rex,' he said with a wry smile. 'Anyway, I'll have a word with Dad and see what he thinks. It would be great to have him here, if it's something he would want, of course.'

Pia smiled to herself, knowing the answer to that one already. Underneath his grumpy exterior, Jackson was much more family-oriented than he was perhaps willing to let on.

31

Pia pulled out a batch of twenty-four mince pies from the Aga, the aromas of buttery pastry and seasonal spices bringing a delicious whiff of Christmas directly into the kitchen.

'Hooray. Third time lucky!

Relief washed over her. Her first batch had collapsed, the unctuous filling leaking out through the pastry, leaving a sticky, gloopy mess over the baking tray. The second lot had been coming along nicely, until she had a call that required her to go to the office to look something up on a spreadsheet, where she'd then got distracted by her inbox. It was only when the bitter scent of burnt fruit caught her nostrils that she leapt out of her seat and went dashing back to the kitchen. It was too late, though, and she'd rescued the burnt pies from the Aga, tipping them straight in the bin.

The third batch had turned out perfectly and just in time. The charity coffee morning at the hall was due to start in an hour's time. She sprinkled them with a light dusting of icing sugar and popped them on a large platter decorated with winter foxes and hares. As well as the mince pies, there was a selection of cakes and cookies laid out on the kitchen table that would put an artisan bakery to shame. Pia had made some Christmas tree cupcakes, some chocolate chip cookies and some cranberry and orange muffins too. Ronnie had baked some gingerbread, Lizzie had provided some traditional shortbread and Ivy had made a number of Christmas cakes, one for Jackson and Pia's personal Christmas celebrations, and a few smaller ones that would be served in slices for today's event. Other villagers who would be attending had indicated that they would be bringing along some sweet goods too, so they certainly wouldn't be short of cakes.

The December charity coffee morning was a long-held tradition that normally took place in the village hall, but with the building out of action after asbestos had been found in the roof in the summer, Pia had offered to host the event at Primrose Hall. It was one of the major fundraising opportunities in the year, raising money for local community groups like the youth club, the animal shelter and for any parishioners in need, so it was vital that the event went ahead. Aside from the obvious charitable benefits, it was an event much looked forward to by the villagers, a chance to see their neighbours and friends, exchange Christmas cards and share plans for the upcoming festive season.

Pia pulled out some extra plates from the cupboard and set out the mugs on the worktop ready for the first of the visitors. The candle arches were lit up in the mullioned windows, and a sweeping rustic fir garland, decorated with pine cones and berries, draped over the oak beams of the kitchen. Ivy had come in early and had given the kitchen and the rest of the hall a thorough clean.

'I think we're about ready, don't you?' said Pia. 'Do you think we need some Christmas tunes as well?'

'Definitely,' said Ivy with a smile. 'It wouldn't be the same without Michael Bublé crooning away in the background, and if anyone complains or we get fed up with his dulcet tones, then we can always find some carols or something.'

'That's good timing,' said Ronnie, swanning in from the corridor to the main house. 'It looks as though all the hard work has been done. Gosh, doesn't that look amazing,' she said, eyeing up the selection of cakes. 'I'm not going to know where to start. Okay, so where do you want me?'

'Well, I think initially if you and Ivy can be on the drinks, people can help themselves to cakes. There are two money tins, and plenty of change. There's a book of raffle tickets on the counter if anyone asks, but don't worry, I'll make a point of going round and trying to persuade people to take a strip or two. Also, if we can remember to remind our visitors that the book exchange is open today in the stables if anyone wants to go and have a look.'

'Good morning. Ahh. I forget. It is cake and coffee today.' Mateo came through the back door as he usually did at this time of day to take his mid-morning break, but he took a step backwards. 'I am sorry. I go now.'

'No, there's no need to go, Mateo. You've got your choice of cakes today. What do you fancy?' Ronnie went across to Mateo and slipped an arm through his, leading him across to the table to show him the selection of goodies. 'People won't be turning up for another fifteen minutes yet so help yourself.'

'It is all right, Pia? I wash my hands.'

'Of course, Mateo. You go right ahead.'

'I can very much recommend the gingerbread as I made it myself,' said Ronnie, laughing. 'And there's some warm mince pies from the oven that Pia made. I'm not sure how much longer I can resist one of those myself.'

Mateo took a plate and helped himself to both, before settling himself on the window seat, looking out over the front aspect of the hall. Ronnie joined him on the seat, biting into the crumbly pastry of one of Pia's mince pies.

The kitchen was the hub for all the team at Primrose Hall. It was where any staff meetings took place and they were encouraged to use the facilities when they were on their breaks. It gave Pia the chance to catch up with them all, one on one, as they made a coffee or a tea, and she enjoyed hearing about the minutiae of their days. If they had any problems or needed any extra supplies, then Pia could make a mental note to sort it when she returned to the office, and she could pick up any bigger problems that she felt she might need to talk through with Jackson.

Pia got on well with every member of the Primrose Hall team and she would be forever grateful to them for going out of their way to make her feel welcome when she'd first joined. Then, she'd been nervous and apprehensive, and wary of working alongside Jackson, not knowing if it might be awkward or embarrassing, in light of the history they shared, but she needn't have worried.

She'd always had a soft spot for Mateo because they'd started at the hall at the same time and they'd always been very close allies, looking out for one another, a friendship that continued to this day.

'Your people, they come to arrive,' said Mateo, peering out of the window and jumping up out of his seat. 'I will go back to work.'

Ronnie smiled. 'All right, Mateo. I will save you an extra piece of gingerbread. How does that sound?'

Pia wasn't the only one to have a soft spot for Mateo. Ronnie did too, and at one time it had looked as though she might have romantic designs on him as well, much to Mateo's alarm. He would go and sit in her motorhome and they'd have a cuppa together, and sometimes Ronnie would cook for him. Although Ronnie might have wanted more from the relationship, Mateo quickly made it clear that he was singularly devoted to the memory of his late wife and was not interested in anything other than a platonic friendship. Ronnie may have been disappointed briefly, but it didn't last for long and when Rex turned up unexpectedly in their lives again, her attentions quickly diverted to him. Still, it didn't stop Ronnie flirting unashamedly with Mateo. She gave him a big hug and a kiss on his way back to work, and he blushed, wiping her attentions away with the back of his hand.

'Mateo,' Pia called, pulling him to one side. 'Did Jackson mention to you about Christmas? I hope you'll be joining us for lunch?'

'He did say. It is very good of you to ask me, but I say thank you and no. You will be with your people and I no want to intrude. Christmas is for the family.'

Pia took hold of Mateo's hand and gave it a squeeze. 'Please say you'll come. You're part of this family now, whether you like it or not, and it simply wouldn't be the same without you.'

32

Within ten minutes, the kitchen was brimming with people, full of goodwill and Christmas spirit, chatter and laughter ringing up in the eaves of the kitchen. Almost everyone brought something with them: cakes or biscuits, a Christmas card, or a bottle or some posh toiletries for the raffle. A queue formed quickly for the cakes and Ivy and Ronnie were in their element, serving the visitors and enjoying the occasion. Pia made it her mission to talk to everyone who walked through the doors, even if only in passing.

'Pia, this place is amazing.'

She spun round to see Rhi standing there, alongside Lizzie.

'Rhi! I wasn't expecting to see you today. What a lovely surprise.' Pia embraced her friend in a hug. 'How's things?'

'Good. We've found a new flat in town. We'll be moving in before Christmas so I've come down to do some measuring up.'

'That's amazing. It must feel great to be back?'

'It really does. We've had a great year in Dashford-Upon-Avon, but there's no doubt that this area is home. All our friends and family are here.' Rhi cast a glance over at Lizzie, smiling.

'It's great to get a sneaky peek of the inside of the hall. It's stunning. How on earth do you manage to get anything done here? I'd spend my whole time simply admiring the view.' Her eyes widened. 'Talking of which, is Jackson here today?'

Pia threw back her head and laughed. 'He might be along later.' She followed Rhi's gaze as she took in her surroundings. 'It's tough working here, but someone has to do it. I was still living in the cottage where I was born this time last year and dreading having to move out so coming here has been a massive change. I feel very fortunate.'

Lizzie put an arm around her shoulder and pulled her into her side. 'I know you always say that, Pia, but...' And Lizzie gave a surreptitious look around to make sure there were no listening ears. 'I've told you before, it's Jackson who's the lucky one. Don't they say, *behind every successful man there's a strong woman*, and that's certainly true with you two.'

'I think we make a good team, but really the hall was on the road to success long before I arrived.' She took a moment to appreciate how far she'd come in less than a year. She'd gained so much experience in running the office, been on various training courses and grown in confidence hugely. More than those tangible skills, she'd learnt so much about herself and what she wanted from her life. She'd be forever grateful to Jackson and the hall for showing her that.

'Well, Jackson is looking a happy man these days, so you're clearly doing something right.'

'What will you be doing for Christmas, Lizzie?'

'Bill and I will be hosting at mine, the whole family will be coming over and the neighbours will be in for a pre-lunch drink. We're looking forward to it, especially now Rosie is of an age where she can really appreciate what's going on, and Pip is such a happy little fella that he's bound to enjoy all the excitement. Mind you, there's a part of me that thinks we'll never be able to top last year's Christmas.'

'That was mad.' Rhi laughed.

'Why, what happened?' Pia's gaze switched between her two friends.

'You must have heard? I had a party on Christmas Eve with Rhi and Luke, and Abbey and Sam, none of us realising that there would be a heavy snowstorm that night. Honestly, we'd never seen anything like it.'

'I remember,' said Pia. 'I was at home peering out of the window, watching the snow fall.' It had been magical, as though there was another land out there, somewhere her mum and dad might be waiting for her. 'It was really quite spectacular.'

'It was, but we quickly realised that nobody would be making it home that night. The taxis called to say they were cancelling all their pick-ups and there was no way anyone could walk anywhere in that weather so everyone had to stay put. In the meantime, Katy's husband, Brad, turned up totally unexpectedly, all the way from Australia – he only just managed to get back before the snow halted his journey – so you can imagine it was a real party atmosphere. I had to scrape around to find pillows and duvets and make up beds on the sofas downstairs.'

'A night I will never forget, that's for sure,' said Rhi. 'It really brought Luke and I closer together. We even sneaked off for a midnight snowball fight in the garden. It was the best Christmas ever.'

'Abbey should be here in a while,' said Pia, glancing at her watch. 'She's bringing Wendy along, my old next-door neighbour, as well as a couple of the other residents from the home.'

In fact, there was a constant stream of visitors; some of the traders from the Sunday craft fairs turned up and several of their customers too, locals who used the book exchange on a regular basis, the villagers who were regulars at the charity coffee mornings usually held at the village hall, and even the vicar made an appearance. Rex came too, although he was disappointed to find that Jackson wasn't around.

'He planned that well, didn't he?' said Pia ruefully, out of earshot of their guests. 'You know what he's like, Rex. He hates these things, having to make small talk and be sociable, so he strategically arranged a game of squash. He'll put in a fleeting appearance a bit later just as the proceedings are coming to an end, I bet.'

Pia left Rex in the safe hands of Ronnie, who was more than happy to entertain him and plied him with a mug of frothy coffee, gave him a plate and pointed him in the direction of the cakes and biscuits. Pia spotted Abbey arriving along with Wendy, Stella Darling and Reg Catling.

'Hollo,' she called, going over to greet them. 'Come along in, it's lovely to see you all. Thank you for coming.' Pia gave Wendy an especially big hug, so thrilled to see her old neighbour looking so much better than she had in months. Although she needed to use a stick, her mobility was much improved since her fall earlier in the year, but even better than that, as far as Pia was concerned, was that her friend's joie de vivre had returned with a vengeance.

'Where's my best boy, then?' she asked, her face lighting up to see Pia.

'I've had to put the dogs in the office this morning as they'd only get in the way and I'm not sure I trust them not to pinch all the cakes.'

'The dogs?' questioned Wendy, not missing a beat.

'Ah yes, Teddy. He turned up here one day, caught up in the fencing and he's been with us ever since. He's a real little character and Bertie loves him, which is the main thing. Have your coffee and cake, and then I'll take you through to see them.'

'Well, this is very la-di-da,' said Stella Darling, looking around, soaking up every detail.

'It really is,' said Reg. 'I'm surprised they've let us in.' He chuckled.

'You're very welcome, and although the hall may be la-di-da, I can assure you that we're not.' Pia put an arm around Stella's shoulder and gave her a squeeze. 'We're just grateful that you've all come to support this event.'

With the latest visitors settled on the window seat with their drinks and a selection of Christmas sweet treats, Pia took the opportunity to talk to Abbey.

'Look at you. You have officially reached the blooming stage of pregnancy. You look amazing. How are you feeling?'

'Great. Luckily the sickness didn't last too long, which was a relief. I could definitely get used to this state, though, because Sam and everyone at Rushgrove Lodge are treating me as though I have some rare illness and insist on running around after me.'

'Well, I would make the most of it while you can. And on that very point, take a seat and enjoy your tea,' said Pia, laughing as she went off to collect the book of raffle tickets. Everyone was generous, with most people buying at least a couple of strips, and Pia was pleased that everyone seemed to be enjoying themselves. The main objective was to raise as much money as possible for the local charities and already they were well on track to reach and possibly surpass the targets they'd set.

When the rush had died down, Pia went over to Wendy. 'Are you ready to go and see Bertie?'

'I thought you'd never ask,' said Wendy, grinning.

Pia took Wendy by the arm and they ambled slowly through the kitchen and along the corridor, past the main drawing room on the way to the office, their progress leisurely as Wendy stopped to admire all the Christmas touches.

'I simply cannot get over how beautiful this place is.'

There wasn't a day that went by without Pia appreciating how stunning the hall and the grounds were; she would never take them for granted, but seeing it through her friend's eyes made Pia appreciate it all the more. 'I'll tell you what, if you sit in the drawing room, I'll go and fetch Bertie.' Pia directed Wendy to one of the big squashy armchairs that gave a view of the Christmas tree, the fireplace and looked out over the grounds, bathed in winter sunshine today.

Moments later, Pia was back with Bertie, who came lolloping past her legs as soon as he spotted Wendy. He danced about on his paws, acting like a giddy goat, burrowing his snout in Wendy's lap, responding to her squeals of delight with good-natured sighs and moans.

'Look at you, Bertie. I'm sure you've got bigger since I last you.'

'That'll be all the treats he gets,' Pia said with an indulgent smile. 'We're trying to cut down, but you know what he's like. He only has to look up at you with those big brown eyes and he's almost impossible to resist.'

'You don't need to tell me, but look how happy he is, and that's the main thing. I'll always be grateful to you for taking him in.' Wendy stroked Bertie's head as she spoke and he revelled in all the attention. 'And who is this?' Teddy came padding in to join them, his head held to one side, as though wondering what the occasion was.

'I thought I'd locked you in the office, but I suppose you've been whining and someone's let you out. Honestly, he's only been with us a couple of weeks, but he certainly lets us know what he wants. Teddy absolutely hates being separated from Bertie. They're best buddies.'

'Hello, little fella. Do you want to come up for a cuddle?'

Pia duly obliged and scooped Bertie up in her arms, handing him over carefully to Wendy, who laughed at Bertie's antics as he jostled to get even closer.

'Don't worry, Bertie,' she told him. 'You'll always be my favourite, you know that.'

Pia adored Wendy; she'd been in her life for as long as she could remember. A good friend to her parents, Wendy had been a huge support to Pia when she was nursing first her dad and then her mum through their respective illnesses. Wendy would run errands, collect prescriptions and sit and chat with her parents, raising their spirits with her sunny personality, bringing a touch of normality into their world when everything else was so uncertain. Most of all, Pia appreciated a listening ear, someone who only had her best interests at heart, and who would reassure her that she was doing a good job when everything threatened to get on top of her. These days the tables might have turned and it was Pia who was providing the support to Wendy, but wasn't that what friendship was all about, seeing each other through the good and bad times?

'What would your mum and dad have to say if they could see you now, so happy and settled?'

'I often wonder. They'd be thrilled of course. I wish they could have been here to see it, to come and sit out in the grounds with me, they would have loved that, but you know I carry them in here.' Pia tapped her heart and Wendy nodded in understanding.

'They'd be so proud of you. As I am. Seeing you succeed in a way that we all knew you were capable of. And how about you and Jackson? How's that going?'

'Good.' Pia felt her cheeks ping with heat. 'We're very happy.'

'I can tell that. He seems like a thoroughly decent chap. Your mum would definitely have approved.'

'Thanks, Wendy.' A swell of emotion gathered at the back of Pia's throat. A sadness at the reminder that her mum would never get to meet Jackson properly, that she would never see her daughter so happy and settled.

Pia stood up. 'I suppose I should get back to the kitchen. Are you coming with me? Or would just like to stay here and enjoy the peace and quiet for a moment with the dogs?'

'That would be lovely, if I'm allowed?'

'Of course, just wander through when you're ready or I'll come and collect you when Abbey makes moves to leave.'

Pia heard the laughter and chatter radiating along the hall as she approached the kitchen, the best possible sound. She glanced at her watch. The morning had passed in a whirl and Pia was pleased to see that all the cakes and biscuits had proved to be very popular with their visitors. There were still a few remaining for anyone who might want to take a bag home, she would put together a selection for those residents of Rushgrove Lodge who hadn't been able to attend, and if there were any left after that, she knew that Jackson and Mateo would make short work of them.

'Look who's here,' Pia said to Rex as she heard Jackson's car pull up outside. Never one to make a quiet entrance, moments later he came bounding through the kitchen door, his arrival causing everyone's heads to turn.

'I hope you've saved some cakes for me?' he said to the assembled crowd, greeting them with a smile, and stopping to chat as he made his way across to the table, pausing a moment to eye up the selection before taking a mince pie and a slice of rocky road.

'Looks as though it's been a good morning,' said Jackson to Pia. 'Great turnout.'

'It has been. And you're just in time because I was about to call the raffle. I'll just go and fetch Wendy from the other room first, but would you do the honours?'

'Of course.'

To a great deal of heckling and good-natured banter, mainly from the Rushgrove Lodge residents, the raffle tickets were pulled with the first prize going to Stella, who won a bottle of whiskey, much to her dismay, telling the assembled crowd that she hated the stuff. It was fortunate then that Reg Catling won the biggest poinsettia Pia had ever seen, and the two quickly came to an agreement where they swapped prizes. Other prizes included gorgeous festive hampers, a pile of new and autographed books that came from the authors who had attended the literary festival, a dinner for two at the Three Feathers, bottles of wine and champagne, and sets of beauty products too. Nearly everyone went home with a gift, some extra cakes and a full tummy.

When Pia closed the door on the last of the visitors, Ivy made a fresh round of coffee for them all. Ronnie cleared away the empty plates and mugs and filled the dishwasher. Jackson and Rex returned the chairs to their rightful places and Pia went to collect the dogs, who had been itching to get inside the kitchen all morning long. They came bounding in, looking up and around them to see who was here, before following their noses beneath the table to hoover up any crumbs that may have gone astray.

'A great effort, team,' said Pia, sitting for the first time all morning. 'I think we can safely say that was a big success. Not too many cakes left and everyone seemed to have a good time, and most importantly I think we've raised a decent sum of money. I'll have a tot up later.'

'Well done, Pia, and team,' said Jackson, his hands cupped around his mug of coffee. 'Whatever we've raised, Primrose Hall will match the sum to go to the local charities.'

'That's really generous of you, Jackson.' Pia's heart swelled. If she could have loved Jackson any more, then she might have done in that moment. 'So, how was your morning?' she asked him.

'Yeah, great. Thrashed him,' said Jackson, with an undisguised swell of triumph.

'Jackson was playing squash this morning with Tom,' Pia said for the benefit of the others, shaking her head resignedly.

'And you beat him?' said Ronnie with an indulgent smile.

'Annihilated him.'

'Well, that doesn't sound very charitable,' said Rex, chuckling.

'All's fair in love and war,' said Jackson with a nonchalant shrug.

Pia wouldn't have expected anything less but she was pleased that the brothers were actually interacting. She counted it as a small step in the right direction.

33

It was the final craft Sunday of the year. As usual Pia was up early to see to the animals before she went across to the stables to give a last-minute check to each of the individual units, making sure they were clean and tidy and ready for the traders before they opened up.

Outside there was a frost on the ground so she'd wrapped up warm in her hooded anorak and thick gloves, the cold air giving a suitably festive feel to the December morning. The stable block, which had been completely renovated in recent years, always looked impressive set against the backdrop of Primrose Woods, but today with the surrounding trees and the roofs touched with white frosting, the Christmas tree lit up outside and the wreath covered in red berries hanging on the main stable doors, it looked especially inviting and magical.

Pia had been so intent on admiring the stable block in all its winter morning glory that she hadn't noticed that there was a person huddling outside, wearing a big black puffa jacket, their attention distracted by their phone, a bag and plastic boxes at their feet.

'Hello,' Pia called. 'Can I help you?'

The person looked up and Pia saw that it was a young woman with an anxious expression and large hazel eyes. Her chestnut coloured hair was just visible beneath the hood of her coat.

'Hi, I'm Sophie. I've booked one of the units for today. Are you Pia? I know I'm early but it's my first time so I wanted to get everything sorted properly. I've not done anything like this before.'

Pia remembered Sophie from their email correspondence. When one of their regular traders had pulled out because of ongoing health issues, Pia had consulted her waiting list and offered the spot to Sophie, mainly because she lived in the next village and Pia had liked the look of her handmade silver jewellery in the photos that she'd sent over.

'You'll be fine. I'm sure people will love your stuff and you've come at exactly the right time with Christmas only a few weeks away. I think we're going to be especially busy today.' Pia opened up the double doors and invited Sophie inside, showing her the unit where she would be setting up.

Sophie pushed her hood down. 'Life's been a bit mad recently so I wasn't really prepared for this, but I know how hard it is to get a pitch here so I didn't want to turn it down.'

'Nothing that isn't easily fixable, I hope? It's always such a hectic time of year, isn't it? Very stressful.'

Sophie sighed and ran her hands through her hair, the mini curls growing wider and wilder with every touch she made. 'No, none of it's fixable, I'm afraid,' she said sadly, taking a breath, and then surprising Pia by promptly bursting into tears.

'Oh my goodness, I'm so sorry,' said Pia, rummaging through her pockets to find a clean tissue. 'I didn't mean to upset you. Look, you don't have to participate today if it's come at a bad time. There will be other opportunities next year, I'm sure.'

'No, I want to be here, I really do. It's just my life is pretty shit at the moment and sometimes it hits me with a sledgehammer. I'm fine really.' She sniffed, making good use of Pia's tissues. 'I've recently split from my boyfriend. We lived and worked together in his family business so when I left, I lost everything in one fell swoop. I won't bore you with the details, but I had to get away so it's all for the good, but, you know, sometimes it can be hard. I'm renting a room in a house in the village until something more suitable comes up.'

Pia placed a hand on Sophie's shoulder feeling an affinity with the woman, who she suspected was of a similar age to her. She could feel her hurt and vulnerability and sadness, and had Pia known her better then she would definitely have hugged her tight and told her everything would be all right. Instead, she did the next best thing and offered her a cup of tea.

'Are you sure?' Sophie's face lit up. 'I don't want to put you to any trouble.'

'No, it's absolutely fine. I could do with one too.'

When Pia returned with the mugs of tea, Sophie had set up her display and Pia was impressed as she closely surveyed the items. Sophie had a selection of bohemian necklaces, bracelets and earrings in simple designs and more elaborate geometric motifs too.

'It looks great,' Pia said, her hand running over some of the chains. 'Do you make these all yourself?'

'Yeah, it started off as a hobby, just making stuff for myself, and then I branched out into making presents for friends. I turned the study at home into a little studio and would go there to escape. I find it relaxing working with my hands. It helps me unwind and takes my mind off everything else that might be going on, if only for an hour or two. I've sold a few items, but never on a huge scale so I'm hoping today I might be able to get a few more of my pieces out there.'

'Well, I'll definitely be buying something,' Pia said, not out of any sympathy for Sophie, but because she already had in mind some gift ideas.

'Aw, thanks. That's really kind. You don't have to.'

'I know I don't have to, but I want to,' said Pia, laughing, 'and I think you really need to improve your sales technique if you want to find some new customers.'

'You're right,' said Sophie, smiling. 'I've got so much to learn.' She glanced at her watch. 'Crikey, I was very early, wasn't I?'

'It doesn't matter,' Pia reassured her. There was still half an hour to go before the rest of the traders would arrive but Pia was more than happy to sit and chat with Sophie in the meantime.

'So do you live at the hall?' Sophie asked.

'I do.' Pia wasn't sure why she always felt slightly embarrassed admitting to that. 'I know, I'm very lucky. I get to do a job that I love in the most beautiful of settings. With my boyfriend too.'

'Jackson Moody?'

'Yeah.' Pia nodded.

'I've heard a lot about him,' said Sophie with a knowing smile. 'Well, you've really got this whole life shebang sorted out,' she said, with no hint of sarcasm or envy. 'Do you have any tips for me?'

It might seem that Pia led an idyllic life at Primrose Hall, but she could relate to Sophie in a way that the other woman probably wouldn't realise. Just a year ago, Pia had been in a similar situation, feeling rootless, not knowing where she would end up living or working, and the underlying fear that caused.

'Only that things will change. It sounds as though you're having a tough time of it at the moment, but it won't always be this way. You're taking control of your life, which is the most important thing. So much can change in the space of a few months.'

'I hope you're right.' Sophie nodded. 'Being here today is pushing me right out of my comfort zone, but I'm glad for the opportunity.'

'Honestly, you'll have the best day. All the other traders are really friendly so if you have any queries, just ask. I'll be around too, so drop me a message if there's anything I can help with.'

'Thanks, Pia. You've made me feel better already. It's been great putting a face to the name. Let's do this,' Sophie said, rubbing her hands together in a rallying call.

'Good luck. And I'll see you later.'

As Pia suspected, there was a big turnout of customers, all looking for those special Christmas gifts. The vintage refreshments van was outside selling tea, coffee and hot chocolate along with a selection of seasonal wraps and toasted sandwiches, and people were huddled on the benches, braced against the cold, still enjoying the festive atmosphere. As it was the last fair of the year, Pia made a point of going round to talk to each of the stallholders in turn, thanking them for their continued support.

'I've loved it,' said Katy, 'thank you for having me.' Lizzie's daughter had been a regular ever since the fairs had begun. She made distinctive stationery items with her own illustrated wildlife drawings, and on most occasions Pia wouldn't be able to resist buying some of her pretty notecards or greeting cards. Today she picked up a couple of notebooks, one for herself, as she used them all the time in the office, and one for Ronnie, as a little extra stocking filler. 'This place has been like a lifeline to me. I always enjoyed drawing and making the products, but I look forward to coming along to these Sundays. I've made so many friends and we've become a proper tight-knit group. I only wish we could do it every week.'

'Well, there might be some good news on that front. We're thinking of making it a fortnightly event when we come back in March. There seems to be a demand for it, but I'll keep you posted once we have some more details.'

'That would be great. I know all the traders here would jump at the opportunity.'

'By the way, we have a newbie today. Her name's Sophie and she's taken over Bobby's spot. She's lovely but very nervous. It's her first time doing anything like this.'

'I'll go and have a chat with her. I can remember feeling like that not so long ago. A few months and she'll be an old hand like the rest of us. Oh, I should warn you, Brad will be bringing Rosie and Pip along later. I think she's holding you to that promise that you would let her go and see Little Star and Twinkle, if that's okay?'

'Perfect. I could do with a couple of little helpers on the grooming and feeding front. We'll have some fun.'

Pia spent the whole day over at the stables, mainly chatting to people, reminding them about the upcoming Christmas carols event and pointing them in the direction of the book exchange, which currently had a good selection of festive reads. She also spent half an hour with Rosie, helping her to brush down the pony and the donkey, with Rosie chatting all the time.

'Where is Mr Jackson today?' she asked Pia as she patted Little Star's mane. 'Good pony, good pony,' she repeated.

'He's around somewhere. I expect you'll see him if you keep an eye out for him.'

'Are you going to marry Mr Jackson?'

Pia laughed, glancing across at Brad and Pip, who were watching Rosie from one of the benches. 'I don't know about that.'

'You don't know!' said Rosie incredulously, spluttering with laughter. 'That's silly. My nana thinks that Mr Jackson is a very nice man.'

'Well, he is. I'd have to agree with your nana on that one.' Pia couldn't help wondering what exactly Lizzie had been saying about Jackson. 'I hear you're going to your nana's on Christmas Day. You'll have the best time.' Pia was keen to move the topic of conversation off her marital status and on to something less personal.

'Yessss. Santa is coming to see us. Last year he brought me Daddy home. This year I want a big dinosaur.'

'Well, that sounds very reasonable,' said Pia, smiling.

'Look, there he is. There's Mr Jackson. He's coming this way.'

Pia could understand Rosie's excitement. She felt the same way every time she clapped eyes on Jackson. He came over to join them.

'I see we have a new member of the Primrose Hall team. You're doing a great job there, Rosie.'

'Can I ride the pony one day?' Rosie asked, looking up at Jackson, who must have seemed a long way up to the little girl.

'I don't see why not. We'll have to get a saddle for you and a hat, but I'm sure Little Star would enjoy that. It'll have to be after Christmas now, when the weather's a bit better, but we can definitely get something arranged.'

'Yay. I tell Mummy and Daddy.'

'Come on, then,' Pia said. 'Shall we get you back and you can tell them all your news?'

Rosie gave Little Star and Twinkle one final brush and told

them to be good ponies and donkeys and that she would come and see them again soon, before taking hold of Pia's hand.

'Mr Jack-son?' There was a plaintive tone to Rosie's voice.

'Yes?'

'Are you going to marry Pia?' She held up a hand in question. 'She just doesn't know.' She shook her head, giggling, as though it was a most ridiculous state of affairs.

'Good grief, no. Whatever gave you that idea?'

Poor little Rosie's face fell in disappointment, which gave Pia the perfect excuse to cover up her own dismay, not so much at what Jackson had said but the way he'd said it so resolutely and quickly. She had been in no doubt about Jackson's view on marriage, he had made that perfectly clear to her before, but she could have done without the reminder on what until that point had been a perfect day. How could she explain to a little girl that her boyfriend didn't believe in the institution of marriage, when she couldn't understand it herself? She supposed it was her traditional and conventional background coming into play again.

'Have you written your letter to Santa yet?' Pia asked brightly, giving a wave to Jackson as he walked off in the opposite direction, putting all thoughts of weddings and Jackson's view on such subjects out of her mind. Pia smiled as she half-listened to Rosie babble on about all her Christmas plans.

'Daddy!' Soon they caught up with Brad and Pip. 'Jackson will let me ride the pony soon with a hat.' She tapped her head by way of demonstration. 'But he doesn't want to marry Pia,' she said, sticking out her bottom lip.

'Right, well, I'm not sure that has anything to do with you,' Brad said, looking over his daughter's head at Pia.

'Yes, but Mummy said...'

Brad gave a sharp tug of Rosie's hand to stop her from

divulging the family secrets, which only caused Pia to smile to herself. Brad whispered an apology, but Pia batted it away.

'I'll leave you to it and we'll see you soon. Bye, Rosie, and thanks for all your help today.'

Over in the stables, the traders were beginning to pack up. Pia made a beeline for Sophie's unit, remembering that she wanted to buy some pieces of her jewellery. Luckily, Sophie was still serving a customer so hadn't yet started to pack away. When she was free, Pia asked, 'So, how's it been?'

'Brilliant.' Sophie beamed. 'Really busy. I must have sold about fifteen pieces, much more than I was expecting to, and everyone's been so friendly. There was a moment, when I was standing outside this morning, when I thought it might be better if I just turned round and went home. I'm so glad you came when you did or else I might not have stayed.'

'See, what did I tell you? I'm just going to have a quick look, if that's okay?' After a few minutes of deliberating over different pieces, all of which would make lovely presents, Pia picked up a hammered chunky silver bangle that she knew would be right up Ronnie's street, a tree of life silver necklace for Abbey and a pair of leaf hook earrings for Rhi. 'I'll take these please.'

'Sure,' said Sophie, beaming. 'I'll wrap them up for you. So, how do I go about booking a unit for next time?'

'You speak to the person in charge and that's me,' Pia said with a big grin. 'The craft Sundays won't start up again until March, but I've got your name on my list and I'll be in contact in the new year.'

'You think you'll have space for me?'

Pia nodded. 'Bobby won't be coming back and we'll also be opening fortnightly so it will mean there'll be extra slots available.'

'That's great,' said Sophie with a sigh of relief.

Pia helped as Sophie packed away her items into her bag and plastic boxes.

'Have you got any plans for Christmas?' Pia asked casually.

'Not sure yet. Probably making lots more jewellery now over the Christmas holidays. To be honest, I can't wait to get this year over and done with. Then I can look at finding a job – I'm working in the superstore in town at the moment – and finding a better place to live. Next year has to be better than this one.'

'I'm sure it will be.' Pia's heart went out to Sophie. She could imagine how she might be feeling: apprehensive, hopeful and impatient for the future. That's how Pia had been feeling this time last year, and her life had been transformed into something extraordinary in the meantime, something she could never even have imagined back then. 'Who knows what next year has in store for you!'

When Sophie was ready to leave, she stood up straight, looking Pia straight in the eye. 'Thanks for everything, Pia. You have no idea what today has meant to me.'

'It's been a real pleasure and great meeting you.' Pia hoped that she'd given Sophie a little positivity and encouragement to carry forward into the new year. 'I'll be in touch after Christmas, but if there's anything you need in the meantime, then just give me a call.'

The two women hugged and said their goodbyes. Pia really hoped that it wouldn't be the last time she saw Sophie.

34

The Primrose Hall team were seated around the kitchen table enjoying a celebratory brunch. Ivy had prepared a sumptuous full English breakfast of local sausages, bacon, hash browns, mushrooms, baked beans and fried eggs, and everyone was tucking in enthusiastically. There was brown and white toast, jams and marmalades, plus a wide selection of pastries including croissants, pains aux raisins and chocolate brioches. Jugs of orange and apple juice were in the centre of the table, and Ivy had made coffees and tea.

'Well, today is the day of the final event on the Primrose Hall calendar, and what a year it's been. I just wanted to say a huge thank you to each and every one of you for all the hard work you've put in at the hall and for making it such a huge success. It has been a real team effort and we couldn't have done this without you.' Jackson took hold of Pia's hand on the table. 'I am very proud of everything we've achieved and so should you all be. We've got great plans for next year, which promises to be bigger and better than ever.'

'It's been an honour to work alongside you, boss,' Frank said. 'I never look on this as a job. It's much more than that for me. I wake up every morning and I'm itching to get here. Playing a small part in the transformation of the hall and the grounds since the beginning has given me a huge sense of satisfaction.'

'I am happy to be here too,' said Mateo. 'You give me good job and home. You good boss, Mr Moody, and Pia.'

'We're very happy to have you here.'

'It wouldn't be the same without you,' said Ronnie, putting a hand on Mateo's arm.

'So for today,' Jackson went on, 'I think all the hard work has been done, so it's just a case of some last-minute checking, putting the bins out, making sure all the illuminations are working and that the units in the stables are ready for this evening, especially, of course, Santa's grotto.'

'Oh, what fun.' Ronnie clapped her hands together. 'Let's hope Santa's got some surprises in store for me,' she said with a gleeful expression.

'Abbey's going to bring Reg over later. We've tried him in his costume and he looks great. I think he's quite looking forward to it. And that reminds me, Ronnie, you and I need to wrap all of the presents for the grotto. That should take us the best part of the morning.'

It turned out to be the case, as the morning passed in a flurry of shiny wrapping paper, sticky tape and plenty of laughter, interrupted by lots of phone calls, texts and emails, with people toing and froing from the hall across to the stables, while the festive atmosphere and excitement for the evening ahead grew with each passing hour.

Late in the afternoon Frank went down to open the gates while Mateo opened the doors to the stables, and people started arriving at the house, including Rex and Tom. Ronnie was delighted to see them.

'Two of my favourite men,' she said gleefully. 'Should we have a drink to get the party started? We don't want to wander over too soon.'

'I'll have a beer, if there's one going,' said Tom.

'A lime and soda for me,' added Rex. 'Although I should probably get into the habit of making it for myself really, shouldn't I, in light of the new arrangements?' Rex flashed a smile at Jackson, who nodded his approval.

'Yep, just make yourself at home, guys. I'm going to head over to the stables, but I'll see you all over there a bit later.'

'What new arrangements?' Ronnie asked, her gaze switching between Rex and Jackson.

'Jackson's invited me to move into the guest suite.'

'What?' Ronnie looked aghast. 'Permanently?'

Rex nodded with a smile. 'I'm going to move my stuff in on Monday.'

'But you offered that place to me, Jackson!'

'I did, on several occasions, and you turned it down every time. It's a shame for it to be empty so I thought Rex might be able to make good use of it.'

'Well, that's charming, isn't it?' she huffed.

'Don't complain,' chided Jackson. 'You've had your opportunity. Besides, if you want to come and live at the hall then you can do. There are plenty of other rooms, as you well know.'

'Ha!' she said, bristling. 'Well, I'm not sure what to make of all this.' She looked around at Pia and Tom for some moral support, but they only shrugged and smiled, and Pia noticed that Ronnie was struggling to keep the smile off her own face, as her mouth twisted and chewed in contemplation over the news.

'Hmm, I suppose it might be nice to have you around.

Although you do realise there'll be no escaping me now. When I'm feeling cold, or lonely, or unable to sleep of a night, and I do suffer from insomnia from time to time, I'll be able to pad along to see you. You've always known how to cheer me up.'

Rex grimaced exaggeratedly. 'You did say there was a bolt on that door, didn't you, Jackson?' He laughed at his own joke. 'You know I'm only kidding. You're always welcome in my bed, Ronnie.'

'Oh please! On that delightful thought, I'm out of here.' Jackson left to the sound of much laughter from the others, joshing and larking about. After a celebratory drink, sparkling elderflower for Rex and Prosecco for the others, they all wrapped up in their winter coats and hats, and made the short walk across to the stables. Pia hung on to Tom's arm, who shared the same sense of wonderment as Pia.

'Wow. It looks amazing,' he gasped, catching sight of the light tunnel, the trees lit up against the starry sky and the magnificence of the hall pooled in floodlights. 'This is a sight to see in daylight, but of a night with the lights and the Christmas decorations it's taken to another level.'

There was a wonderful sense of festive goodwill as people walked up the driveway and meandered across the grounds, viewing the decorations, stopping to chat with their friends. When the carollers started singing beneath the lamplight, it sent goosebumps tingling along Pia's arms. She'd always loved Christmas carols, but hearing them sung in such harmony, with the assembled crowd joining in too, touched her deep down inside in a way that brought tears to her eyes.

'Pia! Lovely to see you.'

She turned round to find Rhi and Luke arm in arm, their hands clasped around mugs of mulled wine.

'Hey, you two. Are you having a good time?'

'Brilliant, but then we always knew we would. The Christmas market is so authentic. It feels as though you could be in a snowy European resort.'

'Only better, right?' said Pia with a smile. 'Look if I don't see you again, have a wonderful Christmas.'

She turned round and bumped straight into Lizzie and Bill.

'Oh, sweetheart, what an amazing show you've put on here. I've had goosebumps and not simply from the cold. Although it's taking us a long time to walk around the grounds because we keep bumping into everyone that we know. It's such a lovely way to bring all the community together. Send our regards to Jackson, won't you? We're off to find Katy and the kids. I think they've gone to see Father Christmas.'

Tom had slipped off with Ronnie and Rex to take a wander around the stalls, so Pia took the opportunity for a quiet moment. She sheltered beneath the walkway of the barn, watching everyone as they enjoyed the festivities, chatting and laughing with their friends, soaking up the celebratory atmosphere. Pia felt immensely proud of the Primrose Woods team and the effort they'd put in to making this evening happen. Everyone she spoke to complimented her on what they'd achieved and it gave her a huge sense of satisfaction to know that she'd played a small part in such a memorable evening.

Pia dug her hands into her jacket pocket and was just about to go off in search of Jackson when she bumped into Abbey and Sam.

'Hi!' The old friends fell into a hug, until Pia pulled away to look at Abbey, her gaze running the length of her body. 'How are you?'

'Great. We're really well, aren't we?' Abbey said, sharing a conspiratorial glance with Sam, clasping hold of his hand. 'Really happy to be here. Last year it was the first time we'd seen the hall properly since it had been renovated and we were all so impressed and now, another year has gone and, well, it's even better than before, which is hard to believe.' Her gaze took in the hall and the stable buildings. 'So much can change in the space of a year.'

'Well, it certainly has for you with a wedding and a baby now on the way.'

'And you. A new job, a new house and a new man. That's not too shabby either, I don't think,' said Abbey, laughing. 'I'm so pleased you've found your place here, Pia. You seem very happy.'

'I am.'

'Anyway, we've had some exciting news. We had our scan in the week and we found out we're having a little girl and we're going to call her Willow.'

Pia gasped. A swell of emotion rose in her chest and tears gathered in her eyes. 'That is amazing. Hello, Willow,' Pia said softly, holding out a hand to rest it on Abbey's tummy. 'Such a beautiful name and so apt.'

'We thought so. Sam chose it, of course. There was something else. Something we wanted to ask you.'

'Yes, sure?'

'Sam and I wondered if you would be up for being godmother to Willow? It would mean the world to us.'

Momentarily, Pia was lost for words as a warm shiver ran over the length of her body. 'Really?' she managed to splutter, wondering if she may have misheard.

'Really,' said Abbey, nodding. 'Who else was I going to ask other than one of my oldest best friends?'

The tears that had wetted Pia's eyes now ran freely down her cheeks, her heart filled with happiness and gratitude.

'Just when I thought this day couldn't get any better. It would be an absolute honour,' she said, wrapping her friends in a hug.

35

'What a night. Can we do it all over again tomorrow?'

The last of their visitors were leaving the grounds, jumping in their cars for the journey home or walking through the light tunnel and then down the long driveway towards the village, stopping to admire the illuminated deer, squirrels and foxes on the lawns.

Jackson laughed. 'Maybe not tomorrow, but definitely next year.'

'I couldn't stop looking up at the hall, lit up against the night sky and thinking how breathtaking it looked. I have to pinch myself sometimes to believe that I can actually call this place my home.'

'Well, you'd better believe it, Pia, because I don't want you going anywhere.'

She looked up at him and beamed.

'It was just what we needed, a bit of magic to take us into the Christmas holidays. Everyone seemed to have a great time, especially the kids. Drafting Father Christmas in was the best idea.'

Pia giggled. 'Yes, Reg did a grand job. I think he was in his element. He had that whole *ho-ho-ho* thing off to a tee.'

'I saw Rosie, bless her, and she said to me, "Thank you, Mr Jackson, for organising Santa." Honestly, it made my heart melt. Her little face was so excitable and happy.'

'Jackson! I don't know what's happened to you. You actually like children now?'

He turned to look at Pia, squeezing her hand tight. 'You're what's happened to me, so it's all your fault. Besides, I've always had a soft spot for that kid and her brother. I'm not a complete monster.'

'I'm pleased to hear it,' said Pia, giggling, 'because...' She paused dramatically. 'There might be more children appearing in our future.'

'What?' Jackson took a step backwards, his brow furrowed, his eyes scanning her features worriedly as he reached for her arms. 'Don't tell me...'

'No, nothing like that,' she said, amused by seeing the alarm on his face. 'Abbey and Sam have asked me to be godmother to their baby, Willow, so I can see a lot of babysitting coming up. Isn't that amazing?'

'Wow.' Jackson nodded slowly, a smile spreading across his face, and Pia was certain she could see the relief radiating from his body.

'I'm so chuffed. I didn't see it coming at all, and it feels like such a privilege to be asked to play such an important role in Willow's life.'

'That child will be very lucky to have you looking out for them. It's great to have a constant in your life, someone you can rely on, other than your parents.' Jackson was thoughtful for a moment, his gaze drifting skywards, and she knew he was thinking about his late aunt Marie.

With everyone departed from the grounds and the stables locked up, Jackson said, 'Come on. I think we're done here. Let's get back to the house. I've got a surprise for you.'

'Really?' she said, huddled into his side. 'That sounds exciting. What kind of a surprise?'

'A get-into-your-swimsuit-and-I'll-meet-you-in-the-garden kind of surprise.'

'The hot tub?' she asked excitedly.

'Well, I know how much you love that thing so I thought why not. Should be nicely warmed up by now. We probably need to rest our aching limbs after all the hard work we've done today. The champagne is on ice and it will be the perfect opportunity to completely unwind.'

Jackson *was* in a good mood. She'd managed to get him in the hot tub only once before, albeit reluctantly. Despite his protestations, he'd actually enjoyed it in the end, but she'd never quite persuaded him to try it for a second time. For him to arrange a night-time dip off his own bat was a delightful surprise for Pia. Minutes later, after quickly returning to the house and changing out of their clothes, they were outside again, and Pia hung on to Jackson's hand.

'Oh my goodness, it's so cold! Is this really a good idea?' Dressed only in her swimsuit and her towelling dressing gown, Pia squealed as they walked the short distance from the hall to the hot tub on the decking, which, like the rest of the structures in the grounds, had been bedecked with twinkling lights. Looking up, she saw mistletoe hanging on the wooden struts of the pergola and smiled.

She took a deep breath, bracing herself as she slipped off her gown, throwing it on the nearby table, her bare skin immediately reacting to the cold night air and erupting in goosebumps.

'Oh... Ah... Brr!' Pia hugged her arms tight around her body, giggling and shivering at the same time as she stepped carefully into the bubbling tub. As soon as her toes hit the water, she gasped in relief and delight. 'That. Is. Lovely.' She sat down on the seat of the tub, submerging her shoulders beneath the water, the warmth enveloping her, wrapping her in a hug as she gazed up at the night sky.

'Come on, get in,' she called impatiently. 'It's wonderful.'

'I'm coming.' He laughed. 'I'm just pouring the champagne.' Jackson slipped off his robe, her eyes alighting on his firm, toned physique. He wandered over with the two flutes of bubbles, handing one to her.

'Mmm, perfect. Thank you.'

'Here's to us, and our continued success and many more good times at Primrose Hall.' His eyes snagged on hers and she felt her toes curl with anticipation.

'Here's to us,' she said in return, clinking his glass as he sat down in the water beside her. 'What a day. What a year it's been. Who'd have thought it, eh?' She stretched out her legs, wiggling her toes in front of her. 'When I turned up for my interview in the café all those months ago, I was so shocked to see you I almost walked straight out again. It scares me to think what would have happened if I had. I might not be sitting here right now.'

'You don't think I would have let you walk away that easily. That I wouldn't have gone chasing right after you?'

'Would you? That's good to know,' she said, reaching out for his hand and sighing in satisfaction. 'This is so romantic. Look at the stars. It's as though we can reach out and touch them, as though their purpose is to reassure and comfort, to guide us in the right direction.'

'I like that idea,' said Jackson with a serene smile.

Pia sipped on her champagne, the bubbles on her tongue

tickling at her nose, matching the bubbles of the water. 'I like to think of my mum and dad as stars sparkling up in the dark night sky, looking out for me from a distance. I know it might sound daft, but I find it reassuring to think that there's a higher force out there, don't you?'

'I don't know about that. I'm more pragmatic, I guess. It's served me well up until now, but there's no denying tonight there's a mystery and magic in the air.'

They fell into a silence as they both contemplated the beauty of the night sky above them, and the stillness and peace of their surroundings, until Pia turned to look at Jackson.

'You are all right, aren't you?'

'Absolutely. Why do you ask?'

'I don't know. The whole hot tub thing. It's so unlike you. You seem… Oh, I don't know. Tired maybe? Distracted?'

'All of the above, probably,' he said, laughing. 'It's great to take a moment to contemplate and appreciate everything we've achieved after such a busy year.' He tilted his head backwards, drinking in the sky. 'I'm looking forward to our first Christmas together.'

'Me too. I can't wait.'

'Actually, there was something I needed to ask you.' It was clearly the night for questions.

'Really?' She turned to face him, puzzled by the change in tone to his voice. 'What is it?'

'Hang on. There's something I need first.'

He reached for his gown, delving into the pocket, and she suspected he was looking for his phone to show her something. He turned back to face her and it was only then that she realised it wasn't a phone he was holding in his hand, but a small black box, which he presented to her as a gift.

She looked at it, not comprehending. What was it? A present

for the work she'd been doing? How sweet of him, but she was only doing her job. *Please don't drop it in the water*, was her main thought. She gave an imperceptible shake of her head. Her mind was playing a narrative that was making absolutely no sense, while her body was reacting to the way he was looking at her, his deep, dark gaze unwavering.

'What is it?'

He didn't answer; he simply pushed open the lid of the box to reveal a ring. She gasped in surprise. Not just any ring, but a platinum diamond solitaire that sparkled as brightly as the stars in the sky overhead.

'Will you marry me, Pia?'

'What?' Her hand flew to her mouth and she actually laughed. 'You're kidding me, right?' It would be one of those joke rings that you could buy from the party shop. Her gaze took in the ring again. It was a very good imitation.

'This is no joking matter, Pia. I'm deadly serious.' Judging by his expression, the intent in his features, she had to believe that he was telling the truth. And now staring into his gaze, she realised that he was actually kneeling on the step of the hot tub, which must have been terribly uncomfortable.

'But you don't agree with marriage. It's an outdated institution, according to you.'

'Everyone's allowed to change their mind,' he said softly, reaching out to stroke her face, wobbling slightly precariously as he grimaced and shifted his position on the ledge.

'But what made you change your mind?' she asked, her brow furrowing in confusion as she narrowed her eyes to look at him closer in the shadows of the night. Part of her wanted to grab hold of him and hug him tightly, to scream excitedly her response, but the part of her that doubted what was happening had a dozen questions rattling around her head that needed answering.

'Ow, hang on, I wasn't expecting this to take quite so long. I thought it would be a simple yes or no answer. I'm going to have to shift or else I think my whole body is liable to seize up on me.'

He manoeuvred his body, wincing as he did, so that he was sitting on the ledge, the relief from the change in position evident on his face. His body was still turned in her direction, his mouth set in a smile.

'Look, Pia. I want to marry you, it's as simple as that. I love you and want to spend the rest of my life with you.'

Every nerve cell in her body tingled to hear those soft, sweet words fall from his tongue, something she'd never expected to hear from him.

'I've known that since you came back into my life, there was never any doubt in my head, but it took me a while to realise I was only looking at the situation from my perspective.'

Pia nodded, hanging on to his every word.

'I couldn't understand why you were looking at properties when you had a home here, what I naturally assumed you would consider to be your forever home. It hurt me to think that you were even considering what your escape route would be.'

'I didn't want to.' Pia was quick to reassure him. 'I suppose it was just my own self-preservation kicking in.'

'Yes, I get that now, but I hated that you felt that way. All I've ever wanted is to make you feel loved and secure.'

'Oh, but I do. There's nowhere else in this world I'd rather be. And that's not because of Primrose Hall and the luxury of living in a stately home, or even your peculiar family, who I absolutely love as my own, but it's about you, Jackson. I just want to be with you, wherever that may be.'

'Well, that's good to know, just in case we should ever fall on hard times and end up living in a tent in a field somewhere, but we won't worry about that now,' he said with a crooked smile. 'You've changed me, and I couldn't be any happier about that fact. For the first time in my life I want to get married, maybe have some kids of our own one day, to have that happy family life that for a long time I didn't think even existed, with you and my very dysfunctional family and those pesky dogs too.'

Pia looked into Jackson's eyes, which were heavy with intent, believing she might burst with excitement at any moment.

'So...?' He glanced down at the ring in his hand that he'd been clutching on to all this time, then back into Pia's eyes again.

'So...? Oh, yes. Definitely. Absolutely, but can we do that bit again, please?' she said, laughing. 'Now I'm ready and prepared.'

'Good idea.' Jackson got down on one knee again, or at least an approximation of that position, as it wasn't easy to achieve in a hot tub. He held up the black velvet box in one hand, prising the lid off to display the beautiful ring and Pia gasped again at the sight. With his other hand, he took hold of Pia's. 'Pia Temple. I love you. With all my heart. Will you marry me?'

'Yes!' This time there was no hesitation, no confusion and no misunderstanding, just a heartfelt and joyous declaration of acceptance. She shouted the word out loud into the night sky, hoping her mum and dad would be shining their light and love from up above, sharing in Pia's magical moment. 'Jackson Moody, I love you too. With all my heart. It would make me the happiest woman on this planet to be your wife.'

Jackson beamed, slipping the ring onto Pia's finger, while deftly placing the box out of harm's way. Now, there was no doubting where he wanted to be. He lifted her over so that she was sitting on top of him. He held her face in his hands, his fingers running through her hair and kissed her passionately, his mouth on hers sending delicious sensations to every part of her body. She gasped, and slid further beneath the water, her hands and legs wrapped tight around his body, safe and perfectly secure in his hold, just where she'd always wanted to be. Exactly where she intended to stay.

36

Christmas Day dawned and Pia was woken by Jackson's arrival at the side of the bed with the perfect Christmas morning offering: a warm mug of tea.

'Merry Christmas, darling,' he said, kissing her on the lips.

'Merry Christmas!' She pushed herself up, resting against the pillows, excited for the day ahead. At that point the dogs came bounding up the stairs and launched themselves on the bed, or at least Bertie did and Teddy looked up at Jackson with a pleading expression.

'Hello, Bertie,' Pia said, laughing, submerged under a flurry of Dalmatian kisses. 'Oh, Jackson, don't be cruel. Help him up, bless him.'

'What happened to the no-dogs-in-the-bedroom rule?'

'Not sure we were aware of that one, were we, lads?' she said, giggling as the dogs fought for her attention.

'Presents!' Jackson said, whipping out a bag from behind his back, sitting down on the edge of the bed.

'Oh, exciting. Are we doing them here?' said Pia, her face lighting up.

'Not for you,' Jackson gently rebuked her. 'These are for the boys.'

'Really? You did get them gifts after all. You big softie.' She kissed him on the cheek. 'Why didn't you say? I might have also bought them a few treats.'

'The most spoilt dogs in the county, I reckon,' said Jackson with a wry smile.

Pia was probably more excited for unwrapping the dogs' packages than she might have been if they were her own. She undid the sticky tape on each of the parcels and them gave them each to the dogs on the bed, their paws scrabbling excitedly at the paper, shredding it into pieces, making her laugh.

'Look, matching collars. How sweet! Won't you be the best-dressed dogs in town?' Pia turned over the brown leather collars in her hands, noticing the shiny new tags with their names engraved. 'Does this mean we are officially adopting Teddy? That he's found his forever home with us?'

'Was that ever in doubt? It was a done deal from the first day he arrived at the hall.'

Pia grinned. She couldn't deny that. She took off the dogs' old collars and replaced them with the new ones, giving both of them a kiss as she did so.

'I'm just so happy for him, and for Bertie. And most of all for me, for us. I still can hardly believe that this is my forever home too.' She laughed, holding up her left hand, waggling her finger in the air.

Jackson had collected the resized ring yesterday and Pia still hadn't got used to the sight of the big sparkly diamond on her finger. Today she would wear it properly for the first time.

'Well, you'd better believe it because after today everyone in the neighbourhood is going to know.'

It had been difficult to keep the news to herself. There'd

been several times when she'd been bursting with excitement and wanted to spill the news to Abbey, or Lizzie, or Ronnie, although knowing if she'd dropped a hint to Ronnie, everyone in the vicinity would have known by now.

'I can't wait to tell them all. It's so exciting. I'm not sure I could love you any more than I already do, Jackson.'

'Well, as long as you keep trying, that's all I can ask,' he said with a delicious flicker of mischief in his eye and a smile on his lips. 'Look, I'm going to get started on the veg, but there's no hurry. Just come down when you're ready.'

'I'll be ten minutes. I just want to send a few texts before I have a quick shower, then I'll be there.' The dogs jumped off the bed, with a bit of help for Teddy, following Jackson down the stairs, and Pia took the opportunity to send a few quick Christmas messages to her friends: Abbey, Rhi and Lizzie. She would call Wendy later before she went off to celebrate Christmas with her son, Simon, at his new house. She messaged Connor, wishing him a happy Christmas, and saying how much she was looking forward to seeing them later. She put down her phone and swung her legs round onto the floor, about to jump into the shower, when a thought stopped her. *Sophie!* What might she be up to? She hadn't been sure of her plans when Pia had asked her the other week. She fired off one further text.

Merry Christmas, Sophie! Hope you have a fabulous day whatever you're doing! Have a great time. Much love, Pia. See you in the new year!

By the time Pia had showered and changed into a wide-legged olive-green jumpsuit, applied a light covering of make-up and curled her hair, there were five replies to her messages, including one from Sophie, which immediately caught Pia's attention. She tapped on her name.

Thanks, Pia, and a very merry Christmas to you too! I'm celebrating with a mac n cheese and some soppy films. Should be the best Christmas yet. Xx

Sophie's message stopped Pia in her tracks. It was cheery enough but reading between the lines it sounded as though she might be spending it alone. Surely not?

You're not on your own, are you?

Yep, just the way I like it. Enjoy your day!

Pia didn't stop to think as her fingers flew across the keyboard.

Aw, please don't spend it on your own. Come down and be with us. There'll be a crowd of us here. And there's plenty of food and booze. Xx

Thanks, Pia, that's really kind of you to invite me, but I'm honestly happy doing my own thing xx

If you're sure??? Should you change your mind, then pop down. We'd love to see you! Xx

At least she'd tried. Pia had spent last Christmas alone and while it had probably been the most miserable Christmas she'd ever had, it had been exactly what she'd wanted to do, not wishing to inflict her low mood on anyone else. Perhaps that was exactly how Sophie felt.

***

'Merry Christmas!'

Downstairs, Rex and Ronnie were already in the kitchen, in high spirits, and they both greeted Pia with a hug. Jackson, with his usual efficiency, had already prepared the potatoes, parsnips, Brussel sprouts and carrots, which were sitting in saucepans of cold water on the hob. Pia was in charge of the Yorkshire puddings, the pigs in blankets and stuffing, which could wait until a little later, at least until she'd had her glass of Buck's Fizz, and the turkey was on the worktop, covered with bacon and butter, ready to go in the oven.

'What are you two doing exactly?' she asked as they stood in the middle of the kitchen floor, with Rex's arm thrown casually around Ronnie's waist. 'You look furtive.'

'Well, we were just going to practise our dance moves, actually. Rex and I were talking about when we used to go to the clubs, and we would jive the night away.'

'I never knew you two were dancers.'

'You'd better believe it. We even won a couple of competitions.'

'Well, come on, then. Don't let us stop you. We want to see you in action.' Pia went to stand at Jackson's side, slipping her hand into his.

Ronnie instructed the smart speaker to play some fifties rock and roll and when the music erupted in the kitchen, the pair of them were off, surprisingly light on their feet, spinning and kicking their way around the floor. Pia clapped her hands and tapped her toes in time to the music, enjoying every moment of Rex and Ronnie's energetic movements.

'They're brilliant,' she gushed to Jackson. 'Wouldn't you love to be able to do that? Perhaps we should take up dance lessons – what do you reckon?'

'Absolutely not, I don't dance, Pia.'

'Oh, but there's a lot of things you've told me you don't like or you're not interested in doing, and look how you've changed your mind about those,' she teased him.

'Bravo!' Pia called when the music ended.

Rex staggered across to a chair and plonked himself down, gathering his breath. 'It's been a long time since I've done that. I'm out of practice.'

'Well, we should start up classes again in the new year. What do you think?'

'That might be fun,' said Rex, 'although I probably need to get a bit fitter before then.'

'We could join you too,' said Pia.

'Count me out,' said Jackson with a firm shake of his head.

Jackson poured the drinks and they wandered through to the drawing room to open some presents under the twinkling Christmas tree. Ronnie loved the silver bangle from Pia and put it on immediately, admiring it on her arm. Rex perched the country gent's cap he received on his head, and Jackson was genuinely delighted with the designer slippers that Pia had bought him to replace the ones destroyed by Teddy. She suspected he would love them all the more once he'd worn them in and they were a bit tattier and more comfortable. The only issue would be keeping them out of the way of Teddy.

Mateo was pleased with his pile of presents, but insisted he wouldn't open them until after his Christmas dinner. Pia opened one of her many presents from Jackson, a wax jacket that she'd had her eye on for several weeks now. It was exactly the one she wanted, and when she slipped it over her shoulders, it fitted her perfectly.

When the doorbell rang a little later, they all traipsed back through into the kitchen to greet Connor and Ruby, and Tom, who had arrived at the same time. Ronnie put the music back on, although this time Rex was a bit more reluctant to engage in any energetic dancing, and instead he changed the channel to some smooth background music, which was much more befitting of the occasion.

Pia felt a swell of gratitude at being here with her new family. Christmas at Primrose Hall was unlike any of the Christmases she'd had at Meadow Cottages, but it was the differences and the new traditions that made it all the more special.

The smells emanating from the Aga had been enticing them all morning and when the turkey was finally ready, they transported the serving dishes and meat platter through to the dining room. Jackson carved the meat, while it was all hands on deck to get the vegetables and accompaniments onto the table. The long table was big enough to get everyone around it comfortably, Jackson, Pia, Ronnie, Rex, Connor, Ruby, Mateo and Tom, and it had been decorated beautifully by Ronnie, with a crisp white cloth, a gold runner, gold charger plates, flickering candles and crackers. They had all taken their places when there was a knock at the door and everyone looked at each other, wondering who it could possibly be.

'Let me go,' said Pia, dashing out to answer it. She pulled open the door and let out a gasp of surprise. 'You came! Welcome, welcome, welcome.'

'Are you sure it's okay? I was sitting there contemplating

putting my macaroni cheese in the microwave when I thought it was far too sad for words. I'm not intruding, am I?'

'Not at all,' called Jackson, who hadn't actually seen who it was at the door, but had appeared at Pia's shoulder. 'Come on in.'

'Everyone, let me introduce you to Sophie,' Pia said, leading her through into the dining room. 'A friend of mine and a trader at our craft fairs. Come and sit down. It's great timing as we were just about to eat. I'll put you next to Tom.'

With the introductions made, the glasses topped up by Tom and the food served by Jackson and Pia, Christmas dinner was under way, and it was a long, leisurely celebration that was savoured by them all, with everyone going back for seconds of the delicious food. There was chatter, laughter and an impromptu but surprisingly funny game of charades.

'This is the best Christmas I've had in years,' said Rex. 'Having all my family underneath the same roof, well, that's pretty special I think.'

'I'm very grateful that you invited me along,' said Tom.

'Me too,' said Sophie. 'I wasn't expecting any of this so it's been a lovely surprise.' Her gaze travelled around the grand drawing room. 'Much better than being stuck at home in my poky little room. Thank you.'

'Well, we're very grateful that you've come here today to join us,' said Jackson, raising his glass to the others.

'I couldn't have spent it with a better bunch of people,' said Ronnie, 'although the day is still young and there's still plenty of time for more games and dancing.' That was met with groans and cheers in equal measure.

'Actually, we've got something to tell you,' Ruby piped up and all heads turned in her direction. She took hold of Connor's hand on the table. 'We're expecting a baby!'

'What?' Pia leapt out of her chair and immediately went round to hug Connor and Ruby. 'Congratulations, that's brilliant news. I'm so happy for you both. I'm going to be an auntie; that's the best Christmas present ever.'

Everyone stood up to offer their congratulations to Connor and Ruby.

'You know what this means, don't you?' said Ronnie.

'No, what?'

'Well, Abbey's expecting a baby, and now Ruby is too. There's bound to be a third. Things always happen in threes.'

'Actually, funny you should say that – we have some news of our own too,' Jackson ventured.

'Oh my goodness. You're not pregnant are you, Pia? You're not going to make me a grandmother at last, Jackson?'

Jackson chuckled. 'Don't get carried away, Ronnie. We're not expecting a baby, but we are happily engaged.' Jackson held up Pia's hand to show off the ring. There was a big whoop of delight from everyone around the table and another round of kisses and hugs.

'Wow. Not sure I've ever seen a ring as big as that before,' swooned Sophie. 'I shall have to come round here more often, if it's always like this.'

'Ah, don't worry. We're not all over-achievers. I'm the poorer, less successful, not quite as good-looking brother. Someone has to lower the tone round here,' said Tom to Sophie, out of earshot of the others.

'Aw, don't say that. I think you're very lovely company, if that makes you feel any better.'

Tom grinned, as though it just might.

Jackson topped up the glasses and made a toast to all the good news, hugging Pia into his side. She had tears in her eyes as she thought about the new family member about to enter their lives, remembering her mum and dad and imagining how happy they would be at Connor's news. She might be daft, but she could definitely feel their presence here today. The year had ended on a high note, but she was confident that this was only the beginning and she looked forward with hope and love in her heart to more good times to come at Primrose Hall.

ACKNOWLEDGMENTS

It's always such a thrill to get to this point in the writing process, knowing that the book is complete and ready to be sent out in the world and soon to be in the hands of readers. Exciting and nerve-wracking in equal parts.

As always, I have to thank my amazing publishers, Boldwood Books for giving me the opportunity to share these stories with you. Boldwood's success goes from strength to strength and I am delighted to be a part of such an amazing team. Thank you Amanda, Nia, Claire, Jenna, Marcella, Ben and the entire Boldwood crew for everything that you do.

Special thanks to my editor, Sarah Ritherdon, who is always so supportive and encouraging – and such a calming and reassuring presence in the storm of deadline day and structural edits. As before, I couldn't do it without you.

To all the bloggers who have signed up for the blog tours – a huge thank you for championing my books and spreading the word. Your support means so much and I am very grateful to you all. Thank you Rachel at Rachel's Random Resources for organising the tours.

To my family and friends, thank you for being there. Nick, Tom, Ellie and Amber – I love you and couldn't do it without you. Ellie, thank you for being such a supportive listening ear, for all your helpful advice and suggestions, and for making me laugh when I need it the most. You're a star!

Finally, to every single reader who has picked up one of my

books to read – thank you. I really hope you're enjoying reading the Primrose Wood series as much as I'm enjoying writing them. A writer's life can be a solitary one so it's always a delight to hear from you, knowing that my stories have provided an escape, for a short while at least. Your messages of support mean the world and really are the icing on the cake. Thank you again.

Love Jill xx

ABOUT THE AUTHOR

Jill Steeples is the author of many successful women's fiction titles – most recently the Dog and Duck series - all set in the close communities of picturesque English villages. She lives in Bedfordshire.

Sign up to Jill Steeples' mailing list here for news, competitions and updates on future books.

Visit Jill Steeples' website: www.jillsteeples.co.uk

Follow Jill on social media here:

facebook.com/jillsteepleswriter
twitter.com/jillesteeples
instagram.com/jill.steeples

ALSO BY JILL STEEPLES

When We Meet Again

Maybe This Christmas?

Primrose Woods Series

Starting Over at Primrose Woods

Snowflakes Over Primrose Woods

Dreams Come True at Primrose Hall

Starry Skies Over Primrose Hall

Dog & Duck Series

Winter at the Dog & Duck

Summer at the Dog & Duck

Boldwood

Boldwood Books is an award-winning fiction publishing company seeking out the best stories from around the world.

Find out more at www.boldwoodbooks.com

Join our reader community for brilliant books, competitions and offers!

Follow us
@BoldwoodBooks
@TheBoldBookClub

Sign up to our weekly deals newsletter

https://bit.ly/BoldwoodBNewsletter

Printed in Great Britain
by Amazon